*The*
# Cartographers Guild
### and the
# Search for the Jade Mask

The
# Cartographers Guild
### and the
# Search for the Jade Mask

## Aaron Cummins

**Palo Pinto Books**
Weatherford, Texas
2022

First Edition 2022

Published by:
Palo Pinto Books
1286 Tidwell Road
Weatherford, TX
www.aacummins.com


ISBN: 979-8-9858573-1-3 (paperback)
979-8-9858573-0-6 (eBook)

Design by Matthew Young

Jade mask image courtesy of Gary Holstrom, Curator, Esoteric Stuff
Global Art and Artifacts (www. EsotericStuff.com).
De Havilland Dragonfly biplane image courtesy of Andrew Oxley.

∞ Printed in the United States of America on acid-free paper meeting
the requirements of ANSI/NISO Z39.48-1992 (Permanence of Paper)

Library of Congress Cataloging-in-Publication data available from the publisher.
LCCN 2022905268

## Dedication

To all of the librarians in the Canyon Independent
School District and the Canyon Public Library
who helped me find worlds of adventure.
This book wouldn't be here without you.

# Acknowledgments

There are a few people whose support has been instrumental in pulling this together.

First, my I want to thank my beautiful wife, Laura, for putting up with me.

Second, my three sons, who inspired me to write something exciting.

Finally, my sister April, who believed in me before I believed in myself.

Heartfelt thanks go out to all of you.

# Contents

# Chapter one

"I'm telling you, there are flat-out lies in the history books. You'll see soon enough, Mickey. We'll follow this river to a hidden valley and find a secret lost to history." Doctor Leonidas Zsezsnky—Doc Z to friends—stooped in the dirt. He peered at a few round stones laid in a gentle curve. "This formation isn't natural—we're looking at the remains of a Roman fort—a castrum, they called it. The secret histories tell of a legion sent to find some sort of mask thought to possess magical abilities."

Doc Z was a tall, lanky man with a shock of wild white hair that stood out like he'd been electrified. He moved like a marionette, all elbows and knees and jerky twitches. Unlike a puppet, his eyes were bright and piercing. Zsezsnky was an anthropologist, archaeologist, and historian by training. He had come to document local peoples and customs as part of a Cartographers Guild survey of the Pamir Range in central Asia.

Mickey Charles rolled his eyes and sighed. "I've told you a thousand times, Doc. There are natural formations all over the world that look artificial. Volcanic action, glaciers, floods—there are a hundred ways for nature to place rocks in a line. The Romans never sent an army within a thousand miles of here, and never built anything within fifteen hundred or more. And your mask?" He chuckled. "Pure fancy. Some old Roman probably trying to sell books, or something."

Mickey paused to survey his surroundings. The pair stood atop a small hill next to a fast-flowing river. They were at the bottom of a long, narrow valley; towering peaks hemmed them in on both sides. The valley floor was brilliant green, covered in meadow grass; the mountains were covered in pines, so dark they looked black. Here and there, clumps of trees dotted the valley floor. Snow-capped peaks loomed in the distance.

Doc turned over a stone with his foot. "Oh really? Then what do you make of this? Come see—there's a Latin inscription on this stone."

Mickey didn't respond; Doc turned to gloat. The geologist lay sprawled on the ground, face down. He didn't move. Mickey was a short, thick man, made shorter by his constant bending down to examine rocks and soil.

1

Mickey always wore coveralls, and they were always dirty from stooping and digging.

"What are you doing, Mickey?" Even for a man interested in rocks, this lying around came as a surprise. "Is this some new examination technique you're developing? Breathing on the soil or some such?"

A clatter of falling stones caused the anthropologist to look up. Three men stood there in the wool robes and the flat, circular hats all the locals wore. One held a rifle, one an ax, and one a long staff—almost a club.

Doc Z frowned at the strangers. He spoke in the most common language of the region—Uzbek. "What is the meaning of this? We are duly delegated representatives of the Cartographers Guild, approved by the government and sent here to map and describe—"

The rifleman cut him off. "Quiet. Come with us."

The anthropologist sputtered. For once, he found himself at a loss for words. While the rifleman covered him, the other two toughs approached. The ax holder dropped his weapon and freed a coil of rope slung over one shoulder.

The rope cleared things up for Doc Z—these men were going to tie him up and take him somewhere. If they wanted him, the rifleman wouldn't shoot. Probably. He took the chance, spun on his heel, and sprinted. He shouted at the top of his lungs.

"Help–help–fire–bandits–help!" One foot caught on something, then the other. Doc Z toppled forward; his feet were tangled up with a stick. No, not a stick—a club. The man had thrown the club and tripped him.

He pushed up on his hands and knees, got his feet under him. Before he could stand, he felt a sharp pain at the back of his head. Everything went black.

Robert "Ace" Barrett stood on a small hill and surveyed the river valley. The nameless river ran between banks of steep hills. It was not much more than a creek—thirty to fifty yards wide, flowing fast and shallow over a rocky bottom. It ran straight but for a single sharp curve; the expedition's tents were pitched inside the narrow tongue of land. Patchy vegetation covered the hills—thick stands of dark pine mixed with open meadows. Grass covered the near bank; pines clothed the far side. Black mountains capped with white-topped the hills to the south. They were the Pamir Range, the Roof of the World. There were a dozen or more peaks in the range higher than anything back in America.

Ace had a pleasant face, now covered with a week's beard. He was of moderate height with a slim build. His dark eyes were active, taking in everything around him. Ace had flown planes in the Great War; now, he served as the pilot for the expedition. Since the aircraft came equipped for aerial photography, he was also the team's photographer. He wore the leather jacket and silk scarf that had become the standard pilot's uniform. He also wore a ten-gallon Stetson—not a pilot's hat, but the style he'd grown up with back in Texas.

He turned to his companion. "Hell of a view, ain't it, Davis?" Davis was the team's fixer—the only permanent member of the expedition who hadn't come from the U.S. Davis was American, probably, but he lived in Tashkent—the largest city between the Hindu Kush and the Caspian Sea. His background was foggy; Davis said nothing to clear it up. He had military experience of some kind; he knew how to fight with a rifle or fists. He also spoke half a dozen languages and knew who to bribe, threaten, flatter, or cajole in every town and village from Tehran to the Taklamakan Desert.

"Nice view, alright. You want to take the plane further tomorrow? Margaret says we'll be ready to move upriver again once Doc and Mickey finish arguing about their rock pile."

Ace snorted. "Doesn't matter when we leave. Those two will argue about them rocks until they see something new to argue about."

Davis smiled. "True enough. Mickey's a scientist, Doc's a mystic. I'm surprised they agree about the color of the sky."

A shout drifted up the valley. Both men turned to face the source of the shouting—a large mound of black basalt across the river and five hundred yards up the valley.

The sound continued for a bit, then cut off abruptly. Ace cocked an ear; Davis closed his eyes to concentrate.

Ace spoke first. "Did that sound like someone calling for help? You reckon those two finally decided to duke it out?"

Davis shrugged. "Maybe. We'd better go see—".

A small rock ten yards away exploded into powder, followed by the crack of a rifle. Ace and Davis dropped instinctively.

A second shot cracked, but the bullet flew wide of the hilltop.

Davis pulled out a pair of binoculars. He spoke without looking at Ace. "The shots are coming from the dark timber across the river, but I don't see anything."

Ace looked at the tree line, then the stone formation where Doc and

Mickey had gone. Nothing caught his eye. "Our guys are in trouble out there. I'm going to help."

He rose to his feet; another shot rang out. Whoever was out there couldn't shoot worth a damn. Or maybe they just wanted to keep this pair down.

Davis still scanned with the binoculars. "Something's off here. Bandits should either attack the camp in force and take what they want, or show up as a mob to threaten us into paying. The shooter in the trees is just keeping us pinned down. Why? What's the game here?"

"I can't say, Davis. I do know somebody yelled for help from the rock pile. I'm going over to check. You got a rifle—cover me. I'm going down the back of the hill and around, then I'll run like hell for the rock pile."

Davis slithered back, letting the hill's crown conceal him from the rifleman. He sat up to address Ace—too late. The pilot was already jogging down the reverse slope, getting ready to run. Davis swore, then unslung his rifle and returned his attention to the dark trees across the river.

Ace's legs ached. His lungs burned. This run was crazy—he had to cross the river and cover a half-mile of the valley to reach the outcrop. The shots kept coming from the trees. Not a lot, but it only takes one bullet. At least the bad guys couldn't aim. He heard a couple of rounds impact behind him; a few more whined overhead. Ace kept his head down and his legs churning.

He reached the edge of the river near a deep, calm pool. It was thirty, maybe forty yards across. Not a long swim, but the river flowed fast and deep. His boots splashed a few steps into the water; he jumped and dove.

The cold cut him like a knife. He gasped; the water stabbed at him, made his muscles ache. The icy chill shocked him—the Rio Grande where he'd learned to swim as a boy was always warm and sluggish. This frigid current buffeted him around and around.

He forced his head up and gulped in a breath, then surged forward again. The current crashed him into a submerged rock. Damn, but it hurt. He surfaced, took another breath. Keep swimming. Move forward. Mickey needs you. Doc Z needs you. Move, move, move.

His hand hit gravel—the far bank. Ace struggled to his feet; the water was hip-deep. He wiped droplets out of his eyes, then looked around to get his bearings. He had drifted a fair distance down the river, past the rock pile. The crack of a shot focused his attention. He ran again, trying to keep the hillock between him and the riflemen.

He moved around one boulder, jumped over another. Mickey sat against a rock. His mouth hung open, and his eyes stared without focus. The geologist rubbed his head with one hand.

"Mickey—where's Doc Z? What happened?"

Mickey looked around, unable to locate Ace for a moment. "Oh, Ace. Um. When did you get here? Did Doc find you?"

Ace snapped his fingers under Mickey's nose. "Focus, Mickey. Get your head in the game. We've been attacked. Where's Doc? What happened?"

Mickey shook his head to clear it. "We were examining the formation. Doc was talking—you know how he is—and then. Wow, I don't remember. I must've hit my head or something. Where's Doc?"

Ace knelt and examined the ground. He could make out the prints of boots with heels like those the expedition members wore. He saw a drag mark leading away from the rocks, away from the river and camp. Another print—flat-soled, like what the locals wore. Doc had been kidnapped.

~

Margaret Atherton squinted at a set of field notes. "Mr. Charles may be a fine geologist, but his handwriting is a disgrace." She tilted the notebook toward the expedition's research assistant, Verity Hester. "Please, Miss Hester, could you fetch me the magnifying glass?"

Margaret was the only female expedition leader in the history of the Cartographers Guild. She was also the only third-generation member. She had been raised in expedition camps around the globe, like her father before her. Margaret could pack a horse, run a survey crew, speak a dozen languages, and quote chapter and verse from the Guild's handbook. Tall and statuesque, she always kept her dark hair perfectly coiffed; she wore proper attire for every occasion.

Verity Hester was her opposite in most ways. Short and slightly built, Verity wore her hair in a short flapper bob. The research assistant was unfamiliar with camp life; Margaret sometimes wondered if the woman had lied on her expedition application. Such a thing seemed unlikely, though. Why would someone lie for a chance to spend six months in the remote mountains of Turkestan?

Today was an easy day—the two women sat at a folding table in the expedition's large headquarters tent. Verity transcribed field notes while Margaret prepared a dispatch to send back to the Guild in Baltimore. A compact wood stove kept the tent at a comfortable temperature; a tea kettle hissed gently on the stove.

Most days saw both women tramping around the mountains, carrying measuring or sampling equipment, helping Doc Z and Mickey record observations. It was backbreaking work lasting from dawn to dusk. The cartographers spent evenings in this large tent, talking over the day's work and planning for the next.

A crash brought Margaret back to the present. It sounded like a camp chair being knocked over. "Mind the chairs, Miss Hester." She squinted again at the paper, struggling to read Mickey's writing. A sharp metallic click broke her chain of thought—the sound made by a gun's safety catch.

Margaret looked up from the page to see two men in the headquarters tent. Both wore native dress—the furs and leathers of the steppe nomads, she noted, not the the wool robes of the hill shepherds.

One of the newcomers pointed a rifle at Margaret. The other held Verity, one arm around her neck, the other hand clamped over her mouth. Their struggle had knocked over the chair. Verity froze now. Her eyes narrowed—she watched, thinking.

Margaret drew herself up to her full height—half a head taller than the bandits in the tent. She made a guess about the invaders, then spoke in Mongolian. "What is the meaning of this?"

The rifleman glared. "You will come with us. That is all you need to know."

A slow movement caught her eye. Verity toyed with the stone and leather bracelet she always wore; Margaret decided to play for time. "I will not. I will stay here." Her Mongolian was weak, but this conversation was simple enough.

The rifleman shouted at her. "You will come or get shot. We need you in the hills. No arguing—you will come along."

As he spoke, Verity slipped the bracelet off her wrist. She untied it, leaving the stone dangling on a length of leather cord. She flicked her wrist, snapped the weight up and over her shoulder. It crashed into the head of the man holding her. He grunted and fell to his knees, clapping his hands over the lump on his head. The rifleman spun. He fired a wild shot. Now freed, Verity surged sideways—toward the small stove in the corner. She grabbed the teakettle, flung it at the rifleman. The kettle did not hit hard, but the scalding water splashed over him. The man dropped his rifle and put his hands over his face. Verity dove for the gun, rolled across the tent, and rose in one smooth motion. She leveled the rifle at the intruders.

The former rifleman realized the danger he now faced. His partner moved slower, still dazed from the blow to the head. The rifleman yanked him to his feet and put an arm around him. The pair fled from the tent.

Another gunshot sounded, this one from up the valley. Margaret and Verity left the tent. They saw the would-be kidnappers disappear into the small grove of trees next to the camp. More shots rang out in the distance.

Emergency procedures came as second nature to Margaret. "Verity—go to the medical tent. Alert Dr. Carambo. She needs to prepare to treat gunshot wounds or other injuries. Have her come to the headquarters tent when she's ready. Help the doctor if she needs it; otherwise, come see me. I'll grab rifles for us, then ring the alarm bell to summon everyone back to camp." With that, Margaret dashed to the equipment stores to break out rifles.

Verity ran the short distance to the hospital tent. The white canvas displayed a large red cross. She opened the flap and cast around for the doctor. The medical tent stood ten feet by twelve, smaller than the headquarters or kitchen tents but bigger than the single-person sleeping tents. A curtain divided the tent into infirmary space in the front and the doctor's quarters in the rear. The front portion included a large cabinet that served as tool storage, pharmacy, and desk for the doctor; a folding chair; and a folding examination table. The chair and table lay on the ground, knocked over in a struggle. Verity didn't see the doctor.

She walked to the back of the tent and called out. "Dr. Carambo? Alicia? Are you here?"

Verity pulled the curtain aside. A long slice in the rear wall of the tent opened toward the river; Dr. Alicia Carambo was nowhere to be seen. A clanging noise erupted behind her—Margaret, ringing the emergency bell.

Verity crossed to the back of the tent and looked through the gap—nobody. The tree line stood only fifty yards from the tent. Easy enough for kidnappers to grab the doctor, silence her somehow, and carry her to the cover of the trees. She glanced at the ground—grassy. No tracks. At least, none she could see. Other team members possessed experience with wild animals; perhaps they could tell more.

She returned to the front of the tent, cast an experienced eye over the medical tools and supplies there. Nothing stolen, as far as Verity could tell. Low-rent kidnappers would have taken the morphine, maybe a few other drugs. The valuable stuff stood untouched.

She scanned the camp before leaving the medical tent. No motion.

Verity entered the headquarters tent. "Margaret, we have trouble. Alicia has been kidnapped."

Footsteps clattered outside. Margaret drew a pistol from the gun belt she now wore. She said something in Uzbek, then repeated it in English. "You there, outside the tent—identify yourself, or I'll shoot."

A male voice muttered swear words in two languages. Davis called out, "It's Davis. Don't shoot—I'm coming into the tent. We need to talk; there's trouble brewing."

Margaret lowered the pistol but kept it in her hand. "Is it just you, Mr. Davis? What's happened to the others?"

Davis pulled back the flap and entered the dark tent. After the bright daylight, the tent was dim. He blinked a few times to acclimate his eyes. "Just me for now. Bandits took a few potshots at us and probably at Doc and Mickey. Ace ran out to the rock pile to check on them. I haven't seen or heard anything yet. How are things here?"

Verity inhaled, then exhaled sharply. She started to speak before Margaret could say anything. "Not good here, I'm afraid. Alicia's gone, probably kidnapped. Somebody sliced the back of her tent open. She's missing, but her gear is still there. No blood, either. I'd bet someone came in the back way, hit her with a blackjack, and dragged her into the trees behind the tent."

Now Margaret chimed in. "We were almost taken, as well. Men came in here while Miss Hester and I sat transcribing notes. One pointed a rifle at us while the other grabbed Miss Hester. Fortunately for us, Miss Hester was able to...." Here Margaret hesitated, unsure how to describe Verity's unorthodox fighting methods. "She used her bracelet and the teakettle to free herself and disarm the rifleman. Once she took the rifle, they fled. I rang the emergency bell to summon aid here, but it appears we have been outfoxed."

Davis frowned. "Where's the gun? We might be able to figure out a little more about the attack if we know what they were shooting."

Margaret indicated the rifle laid out on the worktable. "Here, Mr. Davis. Is this a familiar model?"

Davis rolled his eyes. "Just 'Davis,' if you please, Margaret. No need to be formal." He stepped over to the table and picked up the rifle. It was a bolt-action with a short magazine extending below the stock just before the trigger guard. A golden-brown wood stock stretched the entire length of the barrel. The rifle had a blocky look, despite being nearly four feet long. He worked the action repeatedly; seven rounds flew clear before the magazine was empty.

"Yeah, I know this rifle. We called 'em smellies during the great war. The proper name is Short Magazine, Lee-Enfield—SMLE, or smelly. It's British, and this one looks brand new. What a shiny new Brit army rifle is doing in the hands of bandits is beyond me, though."

Shouts from outside interrupted the conversation. "Alicia—Alicia, come quick! We need a doctor. Come on out, Alicia." It was Ace, returned from the rock pile. He wrapped one arm around Mickey, half carrying the geologist. Mickey's shoulders slumped and his head sagged, but he could move his feet.

Davis rushed to the pair and got Mickey's other arm over his shoulders. The fixer and the pilot hustled Mickey to the medical tent and laid him on a cot. Ace stood and stretched. "Where's Doctor Carambo? Somebody socked Mickey upside the head. He needs help."

Davis shook his head. "Verity says she's been kidnapped. A couple of goons tried to grab Margaret and her, but it seems our research assistant is more fierce than she looks. She hit one on the head and threw a teakettle at the other. They dropped a gun and ran off. Say—where's Doc Z? Shouldn't he be helping lug Mickey around?"

Ace shrugged. "Dunno. He was gone when I got to the rock pile. I saw some tracks and drag marks there. Probably a couple of the hillmen dragged him off."

Margaret examined the knot on Mickey's head. She spoke without turning her head. "Not hillmen, Mr. Barrett. Mongols. I got a good look at the kidnappers here, and one of them spoke to us. Our attackers were steppe nomads, not hill folk."

Mickey groaned. "No, I saw the guys right before they whacked my head. Hillmen all the way. Wool clothes trimmed with yak fur—not all the leather that the nomads wear."

Ace agreed. "The bootprints are different, too. Hill folk wear flat-soled shoes, like moccasins. Better traction on rocks. Nomads are horsemen—they have heeled boots to catch on a stirrup. The prints I saw were flat, not heeled."

Margaret raised one eyebrow. "I know what I saw and heard, Mr. Barrett. Nomads. Steppe horsemen, no doubt looking to kidnap members of the expedition for ransom."

Ace set his jaw. His temples flexed as he gritted his teeth. "And I know what I saw. Flat boots, no heels. Hillmen can ask for ransom, too."

Margaret and Ace stared at each other. Defiance showed on Ace's face; quiet confidence on Margaret's.

Verity broke the silence. "It is also possible that two groups of people are in league with one another. I've seen it before. Get a score big enough, even the Martinos and the—" She cut herself off. "I mean, when the stakes are high enough, people who don't get along can find a way to cooperate. At least until one side can get the upper hand on the other."

Margaret composed herself. "At any rate, we must find out what happened to Doctor Carambo and Doctor Zsesznky. Mr. Davis, Mr. Barrett, please arm yourselves with rifles and pistols. Examine the ground around camp for footprints, then examine the rock pile together. Miss Hester, please arm yourself as well. I will see to Mr. Charles. Miss Hester, you will need to guard the camp while we work."

—

Alicia Carambo struggled against the ropes holding her in place. She hung beneath a pole, tied hand and foot to the rod. A pair of men carried the stick, treating her like the trophy from a hunt. She chewed at the rag in her mouth, desperate to remove it. Alicia swayed gently as her bearers traversed the dark pine forest. They arrived at a clearing, perhaps a mile from camp. The bearers placed her on the ground with care; she felt thankful they hadn't dropped her. She moved her shoulders in small circles, testing her bonds. Her joints ached from the time spent hanging upside down.

A shadow loomed over her. The silhouette of a man, backlit by the sun. He was thin, probably tall; she couldn't be sure. He said something. She couldn't understand, shook her head.

He spoke again. "You most certainly do understand me, Dr. Carambo. I know you do." French—he spoke French, not a local language.

She responded in the same tongue. "Who are you? What do you want with me?"

The shape shook its head. "More will be revealed to you as you have need. For now, I require an answer to my first question: do you wish to ride a horse like a civilized person, or must we bear you like a piece of luggage? Nod if you wish to ride; remain silent, and we will treat you as a parcel."

She nodded; anything was better than being trussed up like a chicken to roast. The black shape turned, shouted something in a local language. Her bearers returned; they untied her hands, helped her sit up. They re-tied her hands in front of her, but looser, with more play between her wrists. Once her hands were secure, they untied her feet. One of the men bent and wagged a finger in her face. His speech was clipped and forceful; he was giving orders. Alicia couldn't understand a word he said. His expression made his meaning clear: don't move a muscle.

Her eyes roamed over the glade. Six or seven men. Half wore the leather and furs of steppe bandits; the other half, the wool robes common to the mountains. She counted a dozen shaggy little mountain ponies, plus three yaks with packsaddles.

One of the yaks had a pair of brown canvas pants hanging off one side. No, not pants—legs. Someone lay draped over the yak, unconscious. Alicia tried to stand; a hand gripped her shoulder, pushed her back down hard.

"Let me up. I'm a doctor; he needs my help. Let me up, for God's sake."

The hand pushed down again. One of her captors approached, said something. He shook a finger in her face again. She got the meaning: stay down. Don't interfere.

Two more men entered the clearing, arms around each other. One leaned hard on his companion. His head rolled, his feet dragged. The second man was red-faced. Had he worked so hard to bring in his companion? No—not red from exertion; it was patchy—a severe burn.

The thin man approached them; he spoke in Mongolian. The burned man answered, gestured at his companion, then his own face. The thin man responded. His voice came out harsh, his words clipped. The thin one shook his head, then placed a hand on the head of the semi-conscious man.

The thin man muttered something in what sounded like Latin. His voice was low, barely more than a whisper. He drew a pistol, extended his arm. A shot rang out.

The semi-conscious man collapsed face-down on the ground; his limbs twitched. His movement stopped and he lay on the dirt, still as the grave.

The burned man turned to run. The thin one barked an order. Others grabbed the fleeing man and dragged him back to the thin man. He struggled. Comrades held his arms; they outnumbered and overpowered him. Step by step, he was forced back to face the thin man.

The thin man said something in Mongolian, then repeated it in a Turkic language. His voice carried; he spoke to the others, not the captured man. He held up the pistol; another shot rang out. His victim collapsed.

Alicia screamed. Someone struck her; she turned to face her attacker—a Mongol. He said something, then pointed at his captive. He clapped a hand

11

over his mouth, then drew back a fist: shut up, or I'll hit you again. Alicia drew a breath.

The thin man turned to face her. "We will depart now. Obey your captors and stay on your horse. I do not wish to harm you, but do not think that I will not. Cooperate, and you will be safe. Look on these men and know what happens to those who defy my will."

The men led Alicia to a horse; she mounted and followed the column out of the clearing. She glanced at the victims as the group rode away. Two corpses lay on the ground.

—

"Something here doesn't add up." Verity frowned as she stared into the campfire. "Bandits should either kill us all and loot the camp, or threaten us and take what tribute they can. Kidnapping seems too complicated."

Verity, Margaret, and Mickey sat in the orange glow of the fire. The pine logs popped and crackled; pine smoke scented the air. Davis had taken a post somewhere in the darkness nearby, formally on guard duty. Ace also sat with his back to the fire; he claimed it was an old trick his grandfather had used in his Indian-fighter days.

Margaret pursed her lips. "No, Miss Hester. It is not complicated. The bandits have taken two team members hostage. No doubt we will be receiving a ransom message soon."

"The percentages don't work," said Verity. "They took Doc Z and Alicia. They tried to take you and me. They sapped Mickey, but left him. They didn't try anything with Davis and Ace. What's the game? Why leave Mickey? Why attack camp instead of the outlying groups?"

"No doubt the kidnappers simply grabbed who they could grab, Miss Hester. They want easy money, and it seems they believe kidnapping cartographers is the way to get it."

Ace chimed in. "We need to figure out where they went and take our people back. Motives don't matter; rescue is the important thing."

Margaret sighed. "No, Mr. Barrett, we do not need to pursue them. The Guild has standard procedures for events like this. We are to retreat, safely, to the nearest secure town. I will speak to the magistrate and involve the local authorities. Once we have the ransom demand, we can either pay and get our people back, or assist the local constabulary in eliminating the scourge."

Ace snorted. "Authorities and constables, nothing. The local chief is probably part of the scam. He gets a cut of the ransom, has his guys shoot up some old shacks or something, then sets up the next kidnap. We've got to hit these guys hard, with all we've got. Soon. I can fly us ahead of them—we can be waiting for these creeps when they get back to their hideout. Easy as pie."

Davis called from the darkness. "I don't even know where to start with that mess, Ace. First, you don't know who took our people or where they are going. Second, you don't know any good places to land the plane in the mountains. Third, even if you did know where to go and where to land, you have the only airplane for a thousand miles. They'll hear and see you coming. You'll be lucky if you even get to land—the hillmen will just shoot you out of the sky. And you have a two-seat plane. You'll be outnumbered and outgunned as soon as the plane touches down."

Ace pounded the ground in frustration. "We'll head them off, then, stop the kidnappers before they get home."

"How will you do that?" Davis asked. "We've already seen they were smart enough to use tree cover to approach and withdraw. They probably used rock formations and maybe streams to cover their tracks. The hillmen know this valley better than you know your living room. You put the plane up, they take cover. You won't ever see a thing."

Ace swore. "Maldito sea. We've got to do something. I'll be damned if I just sit around town and wait for ransom demands to come in."

Margaret's voice was sharp. "That is exactly what you will do Mr. Barrett, if you wish to remain with this expedition. We will follow Guild procedures."

# Chapter two

A ce dipped his biplane low, following the course of the Vakhsh River and the road that tracked its windings. The engine droned like a giant wasp; sunlight glinted off the river's curve and the rice paddies on the terraces beyond the town of Dushanbe. God, but he loved flying.

He saw movement on the road—a small group of shepherds rode alongside a flock of sheep and goats. He dove the plane lower, buzzed over their heads at tree-top height. Ace pulled up and looked over his shoulder; the herd scattered in panic. Half the herders were fleeing, the other half flat on the ground. He laughed and climbed the plane higher, scouting the road below.

He spotted the landing field and base camp a few miles outside the growing town of Dushanbe but kept flying. Ace could see more action on the road half a mile outside the city. This was a bigger group, hiking away from the town.

Ace dived low again and circled the mob. He looked them over with care. Wool robes over baggy cotton pants, green arm sashes. All men, mostly young. A few carried rifles. Some of the men threw rocks toward the plane. Ace laughed at the feeble efforts and pulled the plane higher. No goat herders here; the sashes proclaimed them as Basmachi. They were ultra-nationalists dedicated to expelling all foreigners from central Asia. The power of the Basmachi waxed and waned as foreign influence weakened or grew over the rugged mountains and remote valleys. Right now, the Basmachi were strong and active. Ace would have to warn the team when everyone reached base camp.

He dove the plane again and roared over the mob at tree-top height. Now they scattered. He laughed, pulled the plane up, and flew back up the river.

The road stood empty now. Ace saw no one until he overflew the other cartographers hiking back toward base camp. Damn, but it felt good to be in a plane. He looked over the road: narrow, rutted, and twisty. No place to land a plane. Ace pulled out a hand mirror and circled the team. He flashed the mirror at them—three quick flashes, three slow, three quick again. SOS—the international symbol for danger. One raised a stick with a red flag tied to the end. Brown jacket, black skirt—Maggie. She waved the flag—their symbol for message received.

Ace waggled the wings now, another prearranged signal: danger past camp. Beware, but don't stop. Maggie waved her flag—message received. He turned the plane back toward Dushanbe. He glanced at his gauges—low on fuel. Time to head back to camp.

Ace landed on the grass runway in the camp. Everything was in order—tents still squared away, supply crates neatly stacked and nailed shut. He didn't see any of the guards they hired to watch things, but they were clearly still on duty. He taxied the plane to the end of the runway and shut off the engine. He climbed down from the biplane's cockpit and scanned the camp. Still no guards—strange. Ace walked toward the large mess tent at the heart of the base.

A shout rang out behind him. Ace spun, looked for the source of the sound. He scanned the meadow next to the camp, then the line of trees beyond it. There—movement under the trees. A man emerged, then another, and another. Damn—fifteen or twenty men, at least. All waving sticks and clubs, all wearing the green arm sash of the Basmachi.

Ace sprinted back to the plane. The mob gave chase. Their shouts faded in his ears—he heard nothing but the pounding of his heart. He leaped onto the wing, dove for the cockpit. The fuel gauge sat near empty; no chance for a getaway. Time to face the mob down. Ace reached behind the seat and pulled out his submachine gun. The pilot rounded to face the crowd. A hail of stones rattled against the plane; Ace flinched, but none hit him.

He faced his attackers and pulled the trigger on the submachine gun. The gun coughed, four rough barks in quick succession. He shot wild; the shots went over the mob. Still, it halted their charge.

The men shouted and threw stones at the plane. Ace fired one more time, again deliberately high.

"Oye! You lot clear out, hear?" He aimed the gun at a Basmachi brother who seemed to be a leader. "You there, scram. Vete! Get outta here before I fill you with lead."

The man shouted in Tajik and gesticulated. Ace didn't know the words, but the body language was clear: get out of our country.

Ace shook his head. He made a slight gesture with the gun barrel: get back. He took care not to let it deviate too far from the leader. He kept his eyes—and the submachine gun—focused on the crowd.

He estimated the size of the group—twenty, maybe twenty-five men. He started with twenty rounds in the magazine; he had already fired six or seven. Not enough left to win this fight. Time to bluff.

Ace squatted on the wing, lowered himself to a sitting position. He put his feet on the ground and stood.

Someone at the edge of the crowd moved forward; Ace swung the gun to point at him. The man hurled something at the plane, then retreated. He returned the muzzle to point at the leader, then pointed at the man with his lead hand.

"You—you there. I swear I will kill you, no matter what else happens here. Get this bunch outta my sight, or I will shoot you first."

Ace began to advance on the leader with deliberate steps. The gun's muzzle never wavered from his heart. The man shouted again, then stepped back. Ace took another step forward.

The world froze; the shouting stopped. Ace breathed hard. His heart pounded in his chest. Here it was—the moment. Like facing down an angry bull on a cow pony. Like braving machine gun fire when flying over enemy trenches. He could lose everything here.

The Basmachi leader stared at him, then spit on the ground. He shouted something at the mob behind him.

They started to turn, to walk back toward the trees. Ace remained on the spot, gun raised, until the last of the nationalists faded into the trees.

Only then did he lower the gun and sink to his knees.

—

The other cartographers arrived at noon the next day. Ace slumped against the biplane's crimson fuselage, eyes half-closed. His head nodded lower and lower, then jerked up. He slapped his face.

Davis hailed him. "Ace! Everything good here?"

The pilot started, then reached for his submachine gun. He recognized the others; a broad smile spread over his face. He laid the weapon back on the plane's lower wing.

"Boy, are you a sight for sore eyes. Been a long night here."

Margaret frowned. "What happened here, Mr. Barrett? Are you all right? Are the samples and field reports safe?"

Ace rubbed a hand over his face. "I'm okay, and the samples and stuff are fine. Some Basmachi wanted to dispute my landing site; I stood guard all night to keep an eye on things."

Margaret frowned. "Was anyone hurt, Mr. Barrett? Guild rules specify that firearms are only to be used as a last resort—"

Ace laughed and shook his head. "No casualties, Maggie. I fired into the air; everybody here left just fine. I know better than to start a gunfight I can't win."

Margaret clenched her teeth. "Mister Barrett. My name is Margaret. Ms Atherton, if you would prefer to be polite. Not 'Maggie.' Never Maggie. And I really must object to you firing a weapon, even in warning. That is most certainly against the rules of the Cartographer's Guild."

Ace rolled his eyes. "All's well that ends well. I was outnumbered by an angry mob. A couple of 'em threw rocks. If that got out of hand, they could have ruined the plane—or me. Warning shots were enough to cool things down. No harm done. It was like a rough landing in a plane. Any time you set her down and walk away, that's a good landing. I walked away, so it's all good."

Margaret shook her head. "We will discuss protocols later. Have you delivered the samples and notes to the bank?"

"Couldn't do it," Ace said. "Things were too hot to leave the plane behind. I've been here since I landed yesterday. I didn't want to leave her to the mob, even for a second."

"At least you did one sensible thing. Very well. Mr. Davis, call in the porters. They will protect the base camp here. The five of us will proceed to Dushanbe proper with the samples and notes. We will lodge in town while I meet with the magistrate."

Davis nodded. "Yes, ma'am." He started the porters setting up camp and guarding the plane.

Ace caught Margaret's eye. "Bad news, Margaret. I got away from the mob just fine. Rosie, there—" he gestured toward the plane. "Rosie took some damage from rocks before I could run off the varmints. I need three or four days to work on her before I can take her up again."

Margaret nodded slowly. "I see, Mr. Barrett. Do we have the necessary supplies for you to repair the craft?"

"I think so. It's mostly stitching canvas patches over the holes, then laying varnish over them for waterproofing. I've done it before, during the war. We've got everything we need for the fix."

"Very well, Mr. Davis. Given the current situation, I believe that all of the visitors to this land should stick together for the time being. I would like you to accompany the rest of us to Dushanbe tomorrow, then repair the airplane once we have returned."

Ace shrugged. "I'd rather get Rosie up and flying again, but I'll stick with the rest of you. At least I might find a fight in Dushanbe." He grinned at that thought.

The five remaining members of the expedition—Margaret, Verity, Mickey, Ace, and Davis—approached the west gate of Dushanbe around mid-afternoon. The town was too small to be significant but big enough to fend off bandit attacks. It served as the administrative and commercial center for the hills and valleys that fed the Vakhsh river basin.

A crowd loitered at the gate, mostly men with grim expressions. There were a few kids around the edges of the group, watching. The men at the front of the mob began jeering the expedition as they approached the gate.

Ace spoke under his breath. "What are they saying, Davis?"

The fixer answered without showing any interest in the mob. "The usual. Foreigners go home, the mountains are ours, leave our wealth alone. They just want to live their lives, like anybody else."

Ace tried not to stare. "I still don't like it. We ain't done nothing to them. We're here to help, to make trade easier. They need to lay off us." He turned and shouted at the mob. "You hear that? Leave us alone!"

A pair of toughs detached themselves from the mob and approached Ace. Young men, probably late teens. Neither stood as tall as the pilot, but they were heavily built. One pointed at Ace and shouted. Davis put a hand on Ace's upper arm. "Stay calm, Ace. These guys are looking for an excuse. One wrong move, and we could all be toast. Don't give them the satisfaction—just pass by."

Ace stopped and stared at the two but said nothing. The rest of the cartographers passed him and entered the city proper. One of the protesters stood nose-to-nose with the pilot. He ranted and raved, waved his arms wildly, but never touched the pilot. Ace took a deep breath and stood still. The man extended an index finger and poked Ace in the chest.

The pilot exploded. He grabbed the offending finger with his left hand and bent it back as far as it would go. As he did, he threw a series of short jabs with his right hand, hitting his would-be tormentor in the ribs half a dozen times. The man fell to his knees, dazed.

The second protester grabbed Ace in a headlock and twisted him around. Ace reached up with both hands to struggle against the grip. Five or six more protesters joined the fray, burying the pilot under a pile of bodies. Fists and feet thudded into flesh, again and again.

Davis hardly had time to react before a whistle blew. Guardsmen from the city gate waded into the throng, flailing about with short staffs. The crowd turned and scattered like quail; Ace remained on the ground, battered and bruised. The guards grabbed him under the armpits and hoisted him upright. They trotted into the city, dragging the pilot along with them. The expedition was down another member.

~

Margaret and Davis arrived at the mansion of the district magistrate bright and early the following morning; the petty bureaucrats forced them to wait until nearly noon. Locals came and went from his office. Some were admitted upon arrival; others waited for a few minutes. Much of the time, the magistrate sat alone in his office. Despite the deliberate provocation, both cartographers kept calm.

When they were admitted at last, Margaret addressed him in Russian— the official language—rather than the Tajik tongue spoken by the locals. "Thank you so much for seeing us today, your excellency. We know you are a very busy man. We appreciate your time." Margaret bowed her head low as she spoke.

The magistrate stared in silence after she finished. He was portly, with a soft face and round body. That was unusual; food could be in short supply in the hill country. The people he ruled tended to stony faces and lean bodies. His hands were restless; his fingers, short and pudgy. Here sat a man used to a life of ease, even in the small market town.

His office was large, with a high ceiling. Floor-to-ceiling windows made up one wall; delicate shades covered them, giving the room a diffuse golden light. A secretary sat at a small desk in one corner, ready to record the conversation on a small notepad.

Eventually, he gave a slight nod. "I am most pleased to meet with a member of the esteemed expedition into the back country. How may I help you on this auspicious day?"

Margaret held up two fingers. "I have two problems—one difficult, one easy. First, the difficult problem." She summarized the attack and kidnapping. The magistrate rested his elbows on his desk and steepled his fingers.

After she finished, the magistrate remained motionless, staring at the pair. Margaret opened her mouth to speak again; the official held up a hand to silence her.

At last, he spoke. "Members of your group have been taken. What do you wish of me?"

The secretary interrupted. "Sir?" He extended pen and paper toward the magistrate.

Without looking, the magistrate waved him off. "Not yet. First I will discuss a course of action. Once the discussions are complete, you may record our conversation." He extended a hand to Margaret. "What do you wish of me? Please, proceed."

"We must recover our team members alive, as quickly as possible. If you have contacts with Basmachi—"

The magistrate slapped a palm against his desk. "Preposterous! I have no dealings with Basmachi or others outside the law."

Margaret continued. "Otherwise, we must ask you to dispatch troops at once to search for our people."

Again the magistrate interrupted. "Sadly, I cannot dispatch troops right away. All the forces at my disposal are deployed. To withdraw them will require time. Some cannot be spared at all; the work they perform is too vital. When troops are available, they will be assigned to assist you."

Margaret glared. "Our expedition has been officially sanctioned." She let those words hang for a moment. "If we fail, if we must withdraw, if our personnel come to harm, that will reflect badly on you in Moscow."

The bureaucrat leaned forward, extending one finger toward Margaret's face. "I am the magistrate of this district. My power here is supreme. You will do nothing to interfere with my duties, do you understand? You will not interfere."

Margaret drew herself up a little taller in her chair. "I can send negative reports to our contact in Moscow, to our ambassador, to merchants seeking trade with your country. If you refuse to support us, I will see to it that you never command anything again."

The magistrate leaned back in his chair and made a steeple with his fingers. He sat up, squared himself toward Margaret, made a writing gesture toward the secretary, and began to speak.

"I must advise you against this course of action. The high mountains are a hotbed of anti-foreign sentiments." Margaret frowned; his statement made no sense. The magistrate continued. "You will pass from the benevolent and generous protection of this oblast, and there is no certainty that the governor of the next oblast will be able to protect you." The secretary's pen scratched on paper.

Margaret interrupted. "What are you talking about? We need help with bandits, here, close to Dushanbe. No one has proposed moving—"

The magistrate held up a hand, cutting her off. "If I may continue, your safety cannot be guaranteed should you leave Dushanbe Oblast and enter another. Should you encounter difficulties there, it will be your own fault, and in no way involve this office." He turned to face the secretary. "Did you get that?"

The secretary bowed his head. "Yes, sir."

The magistrate turned to face Margaret and Davis again. Davis spoke first. "I've seen this before. You are setting us up—if we wind up dead, you can show that we left your protection. Yes?"

The magistrate beamed. "Close. Often your people do not comprehend the ways of the bureaucracy. Yes, I must protect myself in the event that your expedition comes to harm. Should you wish to blacken my name, I will see to it that the rest of your expedition disappears as well. As to your problem, this kidnapping, there is very little I can do. The provincial security forces are stretched thin at the moment. We have other crises, serious issues that require much manpower. I will instruct my inspectors to assist you as they can."

Margaret folded her hands in her lap and gave a small, polite smile. "A thousand thanks, oh wise magistrate. If I may inquire, what are the other crises that you face? Surely the kidnapping of two members of an official expedition are of the utmost importance."

The magistrate sat, impassive. "Everything is a crisis at the moment. There is an unknown epidemic in the hills; people there grow angry. They demand medicines, doctors, help from the capital. A shipment of guns has gone missing. Good rifles in the hands of bandits are a serious problem. Even worse if the Basmachi get them. The central government and the British diplomats who sent the shipment are restless, demanding answers. There are a thousand other things happening, as always. I will devote as much time to your missing members as I can. Instructions will be sent to constables and police inspectors. Field teams will search as they can. This is everything that I can do. You must understand, Miss—um—" He waved a hand, dismissing the importance of her name. "This is the way of central Asia. We on the front lines of service do what we can."

Davis smiled, but his eyes stayed cold. His expression rang as false as the magistrate's promises. "I am sure your men will perform with great distinction. I anticipate with pleasure reporting their success in the capital city." He left out the qualifier: if we get out of this place alive.

The magistrate sat stone-faced. He stilled his hands, palms down, on his desk. At last, he inclined his head a fraction of an inch. "I thank you. I am certain your recommendation will carry great weight. Now, if you would be so kind, I must resume my labors." His hands searched among the papers on the desk.

"A moment more, please, sir." Margaret responded. "There is a second matter—one that I am certain will be easier for you to accomplish."

The magistrate arched a single eyebrow. "Yes? And what is that?"

"One of my people has been taken into official custody. I do hope you can find it in your heart to release him."

He stared again, breathed heavily. "When was this man arrested?"

The secretary shuffled through a stack of papers. "Yesterday, around the middle of the afternoon. Security forces took the American into custody near the west gate."

"For what crime? Why did my guards seize a foreigner?"

"He was—" Now Margaret paused. "A mob set upon him. Men attacked him; he merely sought to defend himself. Nevertheless, the constables arrested him when he did so."

The magistrate beckoned his assistant to come close. The man bent over his supervisor; they spoke with lips almost touching earlobes. Margaret could not make out the discussion. At last, the assistant left through a side door, backing out of the room and bowing as he went. When he opened the door, a clatter of dishes could be heard; the aroma of food wafted through.

The bureaucrat turned back to face Margaret. "Just a misunderstanding, I believe. Your man was not arrested. The guards took him into protective custody to keep him from harm. The nationalist mobs are quite dangerous, you see. Your team should be careful, lest the Basmachi put you in peril."

Davis nodded. "Thank you, exalted one. Your…concern…for our safety has been noted. Can you release our associate from custody?"

"My secretary is seeing to it now. Just be careful. The security forces cannot be everywhere. And now, I really must resume my duties." He rang a bell on his desk; the side door opened, and a servant entered, bearing a tray of food. The cartographers were forgotten before they left the room.

After they left the building, Margaret turned to Davis. "What was the business about us leaving the province?"

"Plausible deniability." Davis shrugged. "He can't, or won't, do much to help us. He probably thinks we'll do something dumb and get ourselves killed. If we do, he's got the record of a conversation where we decided to leave his protection, against his advice. It keeps him out of trouble with the capital."

"That's despicable," said Margaret. "Is there any way we can expose him?"

Davis shook his head. "No. He won't produce the record unless he needs it. If we stay safe, if we succeed, he gets credit. If we die, he's got proof we acted against his advice. We are on our own."

Hands clapped down on their shoulders. A too-loud voice said, in English, "Great—I love being on my own. Where we going?"

Ace was back. He sported two black eyes, one swollen shut. His lower lip was split, and dried blood crusted his face.

Davis faced him. "Jeez, Ace. You look like hell. Did they work you over in the cells last night?"

Ace laughed. "Nope. This is all from our friends outside the gate. Those boys work fast."

Margaret eyed Ace. "Mr. Barrett, are you all right? Are you able to work, to fly?"

Ace laughed again. "It's gonna take more that a few punches to keep me down, Maggie. Lemme clean up and get a hot meal in my belly, and I could whip my weight in wildcats."

Margaret paced in the sitting room of their dingy hotel. Ace napped, recovering from his beating and night in jail. Davis, Verity, and Mickey sat in the hard chairs that came with the room.

"I cannot stand this waiting. After that, that…." Here Margaret paused; her polite vocabulary wouldn't let her fully vent her anger. "That petty, self-interested…."

"Weasel," suggested Mickey.

Davis offered, "idiot."

"Jackass," said Verity. "Definitely a jackass."

Margaret nodded. "At any rate, we must do something. Simply waiting around a hotel isn't good enough for Alicia and Doctor Zsezsnky."

Mickey shrugged. "What do you want us to do? We don't know who took Alicia and Doc, where they went, anything. All we can do is wait."

Verity opened her mouth, then hesitated. She started again. "Maybe there is a place in town where we could get information. A bar of some kind, or a cafe. Wiseguys need places, too. I'm sure there's a joint around here somewhere where we can find out."

Mickey scoffed. "A joint? Wiseguys? What are you, some kind of gangster? Don't be ridiculous."

"That's not a bad idea," said Davis. "Whoever took Doc and Alicia needs food, ammunition, supplies. They've got to have contacts around here somewhere. Maybe somebody knows something." He started to formulate a plan.

Margaret shook her head. "We have no way of finding this place, no way to make the right contacts. It's all highly irregular. We would be thoroughly off the books in such an establishment."

"No, we can find it. We just have to think." Verity smiled, eyes bright. She had found her groove. "The big money here is in river trade. Boats come this far, then have to stop to unload. Shipments come up river at all hours. Now, let me think. The river comes up from the west, so the big warehouses are all down there. It would look strange for boats to go past the warehouses without stopping. It can't be east. The warehouses are all fenced and guarded. That's probably where the big deals go down, but we can't get in there." She paused, concentrating.

"Davis, is there a neighborhood downriver from the warehouses? Maybe a bad one, one where marks—I mean, respectable people—don't go?"

The fixer shook his head, uncertain. "No, there's not much along the river west of the docks. It's pretty open until you get to Hisor Fort. It's about five miles or so downriver. We can't get in the fort, but outside the walls it's a hellhole. Full of out-of-work sailors, opium dens, brothels. It's nowhere we should visit."

Verity smiled. "That sounds perfect. The place we need will be in the neighborhood outside Hisor. When can we go?"

Margaret whipped around to face Verity. "We will not be visiting Hisor. It is far too dangerous."

Davis held up a hand. "Wait a minute, Margaret. That's not a bad idea. It's too dangerous for you or Verity, but the three men could go. I think we would be safe enough."

Verity made a noise in the back of her throat, halfway between a sigh and a growl. "No, no, no. I have to go. None of you will know how to spot the place. You don't know the signs, know what to look for—"

Margaret cut her off. "And you know the signs of one of these dens of iniquity? You are a research assistant, for god's sake, not some sort of crime fighter."

Verity rolled her eyes. "That's right. I'm just a research assistant, and I only know how to copy notes and file artifacts. And Ace is just a pilot, not a two-bit boxer. Davis is just a liaison, whatever the hell that is, not a briber and scout and shooter. People can have many skill sets, Margaret. I can find us the right bar in any town in the world."

"And how did you come to acquire that particular skill?" Margaret's voice was icy.

Verity crossed her arms and looked away. "I haven't always been a research assistant. I know a few other things."

Mickey cocked an eyebrow. "Such as? From what Davis says, you're talking about walking into a snakepit. I want proof that you're a snake charmer before anyone goes in."

Before Verity could respond, Davis cut in. "No. Maybe you can spot a crook bar, maybe you can't. You don't speak the language, and you're no fighter. You stay behind."

Verity laughed. "No fighter? I cold-cocked one of the bastards—"

Margaret interrupted. "Language, please. This is a proper expedition."

"I cold-cocked one of the unsavory fellows that invaded the camp, and scalded another. Mickey got sapped and you hid on a hilltop the whole time."

Davis leaped to his feet. "I did not hide. I took cover while making a tactical assessment—"

Margaret cut in again. "You performed admirably when circumstances required, Miss Hester. We are all very proud of you. As the expedition leader, I am not sending you into the lion's den if it can be helped. We will send the men—Mr. Davis, Mr. Barrett, and Mr. Charles. They should be able to make contact with the villains and start negotiations for ransom."

Verity laughed again. "Ace? Negotiate? Please—he can't go a day without getting himself arrested for fighting."

Davis shook his head. "The team isn't up for discussion, Verity. The three men go in; you and Margaret wait here where it's safe."

Verity plopped back into her chair, arms crossed. "Fine. At least let me tell you how to spot the place."

Davis, Ace, and Mickey walked down the main street outside the fort in a tight triangle. None of the buildings was more than a shack; most were built from whatever materials the owner could scavenge or steal from someone else. Tin, canvas, and bamboo comprised the main ingredients of the buildings. Unfriendly faces glared at the trio from every porch and window.

Mickey gave a furtive glance at one watcher. "I think I see one of the lookouts Verity mentioned. Whittler, five o'clock."

Ace feigned a neck roll and looked at the man. He was short, middle-aged. He gripped a stick in one hand and a knife in the other. "He's no watcher. That's just some idler making sawdust to pass the time."

Mickey shook his head but didn't look back. "No. He's not. There is no sawdust—he's not whittling. He's standing around with a billy club and a knife, watching for trouble."

Davis kept walking. "Which door is he watching?"

Ace made another stretch to check the watcher. "Ahead, on the left. Maybe that dump with the blue door."

Davis nodded, scanned the street ahead. "There's another watcher across the street, on the balcony. Don't look—he's spotted us."

A pair of dull thumps sounded from the balcony. Ace saw the man on the balcony tap a beer bottle against the rail from the corner of his eye. A subtle alarm. They would be expected.

The trio opened the blue door and walked into a dim space about fifteen feet wide and twice as deep. Smoke hung in the air; a curtain shielded the room's rear from inspection. Hard drinkers sat at the few tables. No social club, this joint. It was a place for hard men to get drunk on hard liquor.

Heads turned to watch the three foreigners as they approached the bar. Davis caught the barman's eye, said something in Tajik, held up three fingers. The barman began drawing three mugs of beer. One of the drinkers stood and slipped out the back. The front door opened. The whittler entered, knife in one hand and a short club in the other. A second man followed him; brass glinted at his knuckles.

Conversation stopped; all eyes turned to the Cartographers. After a pause, the patrons turned their attention back to their drinks. Unease infused the atmosphere. Two men emerged from the back—a small man in European clothing and a giant. The big one was bald except for a topknot. He wore a filthy sheepskin vest and leather trousers—the garb of a bandit. The big man rolled his head left and right; the cracks sounded like gunshots in the silent bar.

He took up a position next to Ace, glaring at the pilot. The small man approached Davis. He said something in Russian; Davis answered, then translated.

"He wants to know why three foreigners are here. I'm going to try to negotiate. Ace, don't do anything stupid. Just be quiet and drink your beer so we can get out of here."

Davis turned back to the small man. They conversed in low tones.

Mickey watched with fascination as the giant picked up a metal plate from the bar. He grabbed both sides of the platter; his knuckles showed white as he gripped it and rolled it up. He dropped the tube in front of Ace—a challenge.

The pilot looked at the cylinder and nodded. He pushed his sleeves up and made a show of stretching his wrists and fingers, then reached out his arms and extended the thumb and index finger on each hand. He took a deep breath. At last, Ace picked up a peanut with both hands. He cracked the shell delicately, ate the nuts, and dropped the empty husk in front of the giant.

The giant reached in front of Ace and took his mug of beer. He lifted it, drained it in a single gulp, slammed it in front of the pilot. Ace smiled and waved to the bartender. He held up two fingers.

As the bartender drew two mugs of beer, Ace smiled and spoke in a light, conversational tone. "This gorilla here is about to rip my head off. Get ready to run when I give the signal."

Mickey frowned. "What's the signal, Ace?"

The pilot kept smiling as the bartender pushed two more mugs toward him. Ace lifted one and turned to the giant, smiling. He offered the drink; the giant reached out a massive hand.

Ace drove the mug forward, smashing the giant in the nose. He grabbed the second mug from the bar and broke it over the giant's bald head.

"Go, go, go!" Ace scooped up a chair and flung it at the knife wielder. It missed but forced his opponent to dodge. Ace kicked him in the knee as he went by.

The pilot pulled up short with a whoof of air—the man with brass knuckles slugged him in the gut. He doubled over in pain. Before the thug could follow up, a body crashed into him—Davis threw the small man into Knuckles. Davis grabbed Ace by the collar and started dragging the pilot to the door.

Davis shouted as he ran. "Mickey, come on—let's go! You missed Ace's signal."

The geologist shook his head like a man awakening from a dream and sprinted. They emerged from the bar and raced down the street toward the docks. Shouts echoed behind them.

"Run, dammit, run. Move or die!" Davis still dragged Ace by the collar; the pilot stumbled along, gasping for breath. Bystanders started to turn and point at them. The pursuers were attracting the wrong kind of attention.

Davis saw a ship pulling out from the pier. "There—make for that boat!" Mickey sped past them down the dock. He leaped like a deer, landing lightly on the deck. Davis followed though the gap was wider; his belly hit hard on the rail. He clung for a moment, swung a leg over, and stood on the deck panting.

Ace's luck ran out. He jumped last, still slowed by the gut-punch he'd taken. His leap fell short, landing him in the muddy river. He disappeared into the brown water. Davis stripped off his jacket, ready to leap in and rescue the pilot.

Ace's head broke the surface before Davis moved. Mickey took a mooring line from a dumbfounded sailor and tossed it to the pilot. "Ace—catch!" As they reeled in the pilot, half a dozen toughs reached the end of the dock. They brandished weapons and shouted; Davis laughed and shouted back.

Someone approached the three, shouting. Davis turned and faced the man—the captain. Smooth as always, Davis smiled and bowed. The captain shouted again, gestured at the boat, then the dock. Davis smiled and spoke; he extracted a wad of cash from a pocket. The captain glared and said something in a guttural voice. Davis added a few more bills; the captain was mollified. Half an hour later, they stepped off the dock in Dushanbe.

⁓

The following morning, the mood was still sour. The cartographers gathered in the hotel's sitting room, but no one spoke. Margaret transcribed field notes; Mickey examined rock samples. Verity fidgeted with a coin, making it roll down her fingers, disappear from one hand and appear in another. Ace laid on the floor, legs crossed and eyes closed. Davis stared out the window, brooding.

They went out that afternoon. They had no goal in mind; everyone needed a break from the tedium of the sitting room. They strolled the busy streets of Dushanbe, watching commerce roll by. They dined al fresco, buying tidbits from street vendors.

An hour into their exploration, Verity turned to look at her reflection in a store window. She fussed with her hair a bit, then took Ace by the arm. She spoke loud enough for all to hear, but faced into the street. "I think we've got a tail. Ace and I will to into this store to look around a bit; you three move on. Don't worry; we'll catch up in a sec. Ace, step in here with me."

Margaret, Davis, and Mickey continued down the street. Verity pulled Ace into what turned out to be a hardware store. She smiled, then looked out the picture window. "Ace, be a dear and buy some rope for us. At least six feet, maybe ten. Quarter-inch or so—strong enough not to break, but slim enough that we can tie someone up."

The proprietor approached them, speaking Tajik. Ace pointed at the rope, pantomimed measuring out a double arm's length. The man smiled, nodded, measured the cord. He rubbed thumb and fingers together in a money gesture, held up three fingers. Ace handed over three coins. The shopkeeper smiled, nodded, cut the rope. Ace coiled the cord and approached Verity. The shopkeeper followed him, pointing out other delights from his store. Ace shrugged, pointed at Verity.

When the shopkeeper approached Verity, she waved him off without looking. Her eyes stayed glued to the window. He said something else, less politely; Verity waved him away again. At last, she darted out the door.

A boy, maybe twelve years old, lurked outside the store. He wore dirty clothes; his pants were a couple of sizes too small, while his robe had been made for someone much taller. Verity tackled him and threw his arm into a hammerlock.

"Ace, now! Bring the rope—tie this kid up!"

The pilot followed, then the shopkeeper. Ace sat on the struggling boy and forced his wrists together behind his back. The merchant stared, puzzled. He asked a question in Tajik, then followed it with a bit of Russian. Ace made out the word for thief. "Da," said the pilot, nodding. "Da, yeah. He'a thief."

Verity nodded. She reached a hand into his pocket and extracted a silver fountain pen. "My pen. Mine."

The commotion drew the others back. Margaret frowned at the scene. "What is the meaning of this, Miss Hester? What are you doing to this child?"

Verity scowled. "He's been following us since we got here. I saw him with the crowd the first day, and I've seen him outside our hotel. He's been tracking us through the streets today. Please tell these people that he's a thief, that he stole my pen from me, and that we're taking him to the coppers."

Margaret's mouth worked, silent. She didn't know what to make of the situation.

Davis handled things better. He stood and addressed the crowd in Tajik. "This boy picked her pockets. He's a thief; we are taking him along to the magistrate for punishment. Nothing to see here, just a thief being caught. Please go."

The American's explanation, along with the boy's ragged clothing, mollified the crowd. They dispersed, leaving the team alone with their new captive.

Davis addressed Verity. "What now? We can't take him too far without attracting attention."

Ace scowled. "When did the kid get your pen? And how? I thought you said he was following us, not picking our pockets."

Verity laughed. "He was following us. I just needed the crowd to think he was a pickpocket so they would leave us alone. The pen was just a distraction."

"But how—you pulled the pen out of his pocket. I saw you. He did have it."

Verity shook her head. "The pen doesn't matter. Forget it." She scanned the area. "There—that alley. We can get him in there and talk without too much trouble. Margaret, if you please, buy this boy some food. Anything will likely do—he probably doesn't get much. Ace, Mickey, please help me get him off the street." The men grabbed him by the arms and hustled him into the alley mouth, ready to help Verity interrogate her prisoner.

Their captive squirmed and struggled, cursing in Tajik the entire time. Davis grabbed him by the shirt front and pinned him against a wall, slapping a hand over the boy's mouth as he did so. "We mean you no harm. We just want to ask a few questions, that's all. Can you be still and talk?" The boy glared, then tried to bite the hand over his mouth. Davis snatched his hand back but kept the boy pinned.

Margaret arrived with a fistful of grilled beef skewers and a bag filled with other treats. "Please, let him down. Mr. Charles, Mr. Davis, please hold his arms. Mr. Barrett, free his wrists but tie the rope around his chest like a leash. We will let him have his hands free, but keep him reined in." She addressed the boy then, in Tajik. "You be still. I'll let you eat as soon as your hands are free. Are you hungry?"

The boy glared, sullen and silent, but he stopped struggling. Ace soon looped the rope around his chest. As soon as he did, Margaret handed the boy a skewer. He looked at her, suspicion in his eyes. Margaret smiled and made a little 'go ahead' motion to him. He took a small bite, then another. Soon the boy was wolfing down the food, skewers, dumplings, and meat buns alike. Margaret waited as he ate; as soon as he finished one item, she handed him another.

At last, he slowed his eating and looked around. "What do you want? What are you going to do with me?"

Margaret translated for the group. Verity said, "ask him why he was following us."

When asked, the boy shrugged. "What makes you think I followed you?"

Verity explained that she had seen him often since their arrival—in the mob at the gate, at the hotel, around town.

He shook his head. "No, I'm not following you. It's a small town. Maybe you just see me around, that's all."

Verity laughed. "I know when I've got a tail. Someone wants you to watch us. Who? Maybe we'll follow you back to him."

The boy shrugged. "Won't work. Someone paid me to watch you and keep track of what you are doing. He's gone now, but he'll pay for a report when he gets back. I won't go to him; he'll find me when the time comes."

Davis frowned. "Who? Do you have a name, or an address or something?"

The boy shook his head. "No, I don't know who he is. Some foreigner like you. I thought you brought some argument from wherever you come from."

"Why? What did the foreigner want?"

The boy shrugged again. "I don't know. He got to town and picked me out of a crowd. He paid me to show him around, help him find some things here and there. Then he tells me that some other foreigners might follow him. He said I should watch them, find out what they do and where they go. He says he'll pay me for information. That's all."

Margaret tilted her head and looked him over. "Where did he go? What did he do? Can you show us?"

Another shrug. "Maybe, most of it. Not much out of the ordinary. The foreigner bought food, hired porters, that kind of thing. He planned on taking a trip up to the hills somewhere. Foreigners do that sometimes—go looking for traces of old empires. It seemed like that. Oh, except for one thing. There's a kind of holy man he wanted to see. Old Yando. He's a monk of some kind, but he's also crazy. The foreigner wanted to see Yando."

"Did he say why? What did he want from this Yando?" Davis frowned, perplexed.

The boy reached for a sweet on a stick, bit into it, savored it. He swallowed and answered, "I'm not sure. He never said why he wanted Yando. He knew the name, knew Yando is here in Dushanbe. He wanted directions, so I took him. That's all."

Davis nodded. "Could you take us to see this Yando?"

"I don't see why not, but it will cost you. My time isn't free, you know."

Davis snorted. "Your time's not free? How much have you eaten the last few minutes? You don't think we've earned some directions?"

The boy laughed. "You bought answers, and you've got them. You want more, you pay more."

Davis rolled his eyes. "How much, kid?"

The boy thought for a moment, the quoted a number.

Margaret scowled at him. "You're just a child. We won't entrust you with that kind of money. Be reasonable."

The boy smiled again. "That's enough for me to eat for two weeks. You'll spend longer than that looking for Yando. Pay me and you find him tomorrow."

Davis sighed, then shrugged. "He's got a point, Margaret. Pay the man."

~

Dushanbe real estate displayed wealth in two different ways: proximity to the deep river for commercial properties and warehouses; or distance from floodwaters for residences, offices, and government buildings. The cartographers roomed in the wealthiest district in town, atop a high bluff overlooking the river. Yando lived in the mudflat district—the poorest neighborhood in Dushanbe.

The mudflat district sat inside a hairpin bend in the river. The surface was usually mud, though floods brought water into the neighborhood a few times per year. The buildings and even the sidewalks were built in bamboo pilings sunk into the mire. The stilts elevated everything about five feet above ground level—tall enough to avoid all but the worst floods.

Their guide, Shuhab, had been right about finding Yando. The mudflat district was a warren of elevated walks, private and public courtyards, and homes. He led Margaret and Davis through a bewildering array of gangways, passages, open-air courts, and even what felt like a few homes. Though compact, navigating the mudflat district was a nightmare.

Shuhab took them to the far end of the mudflat district, as far from the rest of Dushanbe as could be. He indicated a hovel—little more than a pile of tarps and poles leaning over the river. Davis scoffed. "This? This shack is the home of a great priest and wise man?"

Shuhab shrugged. "This is where Yando lives. The other foreigner wanted to see him; don't ask me why."

Margaret looked around to get her bearings. "You will, of course, wait for us until we are ready to return." A statement, not a question.

The boy shrugged. "How much?"

Davis shook his head. "No. We paid you enough to eat for two weeks. You will at least show us back to land."

Margaret put on a stern impression. "Supper tonight—all you can eat. And we say nothing about you to the police. Do not bargain, young man. You'll accept this offer, or get nothing else."

The boy nodded. "Well then, if that's the way you want to be. A guide home for supper tonight."

A canvas curtain hung in place of a front door. Margaret knocked on the wall next to the opening and called out in Russian. "Hello! Hello the house!" She added the same in Tajik a moment later.

A rough voice croaked an answer. "Who goes there? Who visits?"

"We are foreigners, venerable Yando. We come looking for information."

The voice croaked again. "Please, enter. What would you learn from Yando?"

The interior of the hut was a single, spartan room. Coals smoked on a small brazier, boiling a small pot of soup; a pair of blankets laid out on the wooden floor made a bed. Floor-to-ceiling bookcases lined every wall. Each shelf groaned under the weight of books, scrolls, and bundles of paper. Yando himself was tiny—barely taller than Shuhab—and as wrinkled as an old apple. A wispy fringe of white hair floated around his head. He wore only a mustard-yellow robe.

"Please, come in, sit down. What can Yando tell my visitors this day?"

Margaret and Davis sat cross-legged on the floor; Yando squatted, facing them. Davis started. "A thousand thanks, oh wise one. This is Margaret Atherton of the Cartographers Guild. I am called Davis. We are cartographers mapping the Vakhsh River valley and the surrounding mountains.

"We come to you seeking knowledge. Some of our members have been kidnapped. Might you know anything about that, or about basmachi in that area?"

The old man frowned, puzzled. "Why would I know about basmachi? I keep myself here in Dushanbe, where it's safe. Also, I'm a scholar and not a constable—or a bandit." He chuckled at his last remark.

Margaret tried a different tack. "The young man who brought us here—Shuhab—was set to watch us by another foreigner. Shuhab says the foreigner came to see you. Perhaps you could tell us about him."

Yando closed his eyes and thought; he breathed deeply once, twice, three times. Margaret and Davis exchanged nervous glances. Finally, Yando nodded and opened his eyes.

"Yes. I remember the foreigner. He wished to know about Emal Mora, the city in the hills."

Davis frowned. "Emal Mora? I've never heard that name. And there's nothing bigger than a village between here and, hell, probably Kashgar on the other side of the mountains."

Yando chuckled. "No, nothing now. Emal Mora is—was—an outpost of the old Roman Empire. It's been vacant for the better part of a thousand years. I believe it lies somewhere up the Alay valley; I've never found it myself."

"Who came to you, and what did he want to know?" Margaret grew impatient; finding lost cities was not part of the mission of the Cartographers Guild. Her chief concern was finding the lost team members. Once reunited, their goal was to map the middle reaches of the Vakhsh River valley for possible rail development.

"He gave me no name, nor did he tell me where he came from. He was most eager to learn about ruins in the upper reaches of the Vakhsh, but said no more."

Davis leaned forward. "What did you tell him?"

Yando told them what he knew about the Vakhsh, about the lost city of Emal Mora, and what the Romans might have done there. He told the story of a strange mask, far more ancient than Rome, lost in the mountains. The mask was said to have great powers, though the nature of the powers was never specified. At last, he rose and hobbled to one of the shelves.

"There is one more thing I showed him, one important thing." He pulled down a sheaf of papers tied with a purple silk ribbon. He sat down, the bundle in his lap. He thumbed through them and pulled out a smaller set of documents. No, not a set—a single large paper, folded into quarters. He unfolded it and laid it on the floor before Margaret and Davis. He rose then and went to another shelf, talking to them over his shoulder.

"That is said to be a map to Emal Mora, copied from the imperial library of the Forbidden City in the east. I have never made sense of it nor understood what it was supposed to depict. Perhaps you will have better fortune."

The 'map' was a series of wavy lines. They were arranged in rows; the lines zig-zagged without any pattern. Each row bore a single cross-hatch somewhere on the row. Yando returned to them with pen, paper, and ink. He pointed to a block of ideograms on one corner of the page. "These are not part of the original. They were added later, in China. The text describes how the map was found carved into a stone in a city called Bereem, located in a chain of islands southeast of China.

"Here, you may copy the map if you wish." Davis turned the map as they examined it; Yando turned it back so that the rows were horizontal. "This is how it appears on the stone. The double mark goes at the top." He pointed to the row at the top of the page. Davis noticed the top line displayed two cross hatches instead of the singles on the rest of the page.

He looked at Margaret. "You're the cartographer. This make any sense to you?"

She shook her head. "No. This is strange. I don't see how it could be Roman, but also from an island in the South China Sea; that makes no sense. How I wish we had Doctor Zsezsnky here! He is deeply familiar with the legends of this part of the world; he might be able to shed some light on it." She took the offered pen and paper and copied the map with quick, sure strokes. Even if Margaret didn't understand the map, she possessed enough experience drafting maps to make good work of the copy. Once she copied it, she double-checked her document against the original. Manuscript in hand, the pair thanked the scholar and returned to their hotel.

~

Driving rain cooped the team up the next day. Margaret sat at a desk, tracing copies of the document from Yando. Mickey and Ace poured over one copy, trying to find meaning in the lines.

Ace traced a line with his finger. "Rivers, maybe? These lines could be rivers."

"No. Doesn't match any rivers in this part of the world, for sure. I would guess it doesn't match rivers anywhere else, either. The bends are too sharp; a river this wavy would have rounded bends, not these hard elbows." Mickey scratched his head. "I can't think of any landforms that look like this."

Davis shrugged. "Does it matter? There's no connection. Some old man owned the paper; some other European looked at it. Doesn't connect to us, or to Doc and Alicia, or to anything, really."

Verity crossed her arms and looked out the window at the rain. "We're missing something. Whoever took Alicia and Doc took them for a reason. It's not ransom. So what is it? What else could they want? There's an angle here we're not seeing."

A knock at the door cut the conversation short. The magistrate's secretary stood at the door; he bore a sealed letter marked with the magistrate's official seal. The man bowed low, handed the letter to Verity, and left without a word.

Verity passed the letter to Margaret. She opened it and scanned the neat rows of text; she went pale as she read. She murmured softly, then put a hand to her mouth. Her face went pale.

Everyone remained silent as she read; Ace spoke first. "What is it? Bad news? Did they find something? Some—remains?"

Margaret shook her head. "No news on Doctor Carambo and Doctor Zsezsnky. It's the nationalists—the basmachi. A strong force has been rioting in the next city down the river. The magistrate fears that we will be in danger if we remain in Dushanbe much longer. We must evacuate soon."

The room fell silent. No one spoke or even moved; the only sound came from rain driving against the window. Lightning flashed outside; a peal of thunder rattled the window. The spell of silence broke.

Ace punched his fist into his palm. "We can't go. We can't leave Doc and Alicia—we have to find them, and damn the basmachi."

Margaret pressed her lips together into a tight line before speaking. "Language, Mr. Barret. This is a proper expedition. And I'm afraid we cannot search for the missing doctors. The goal of the Cartographers Guild is to unite the world with maps, not to fight insurgents. If this province is too dangerous for us to work, I fear we will have to find a boat back to Turkmenabat. Perhaps we must even withdraw to Sochi and on to Istanbul. I cannot risk lives in a revolution."

Ace stood now, pointing wildly upriver. "No. No! I will not leave anyone behind. We've got to go back upriver to find Doc and Alicia. We've got to!" He shouted, his face red.

Mickey stood and put a hand on Ace's arm. "Please, Ace. Calm down. You've got to see this is the only way. There are only five of us. Margaret and

Verity can't fight, and I've never done any kind of military service. You're a pilot, not an infantryman. Davis was a marine; he's had the training, but I don't think he wants to charge into this. We don't even know where to go—what would we do, just blunder around waiting to get shot at? No, home is the only option here."

Verity shook her head. "I can't go back—it's too soon. I mean, we should at least stay in country for a while. Maybe we can find a way to help them. We can't do anything from Istanbul. Hell, we can't do it from here—we've got to stay close."

Margaret looked at Davis. "It's two for staying, two for leaving. What is your thought, Mr. Davis?"

Davis sat for a moment, thinking. He inhaled deeply, released the breath slowly. "I'm staying in country, if not in Dushanbe. Turkestan is my home now. And there are always basmachi around—just up river, around the bend, in the next city over. We could probably manage to get around them, if we need to. The question is where we go in the meantime. Mickey's right—we don't know where to start looking for Doc Z and Alicia. Until we have some kind of a lead, heading upcountry is dumb. Beyond that, I don't know."

Ace clenched his jaw and growled. "Not good enough. If it's dangerous for us, it's dangerous for Alicia and Doc. We've got to find them, no matter what. I'm not leaving them behind. I won't!"

"Please, Mr. Barrett." Margaret tried to smooth the waters. "We are not agreed on a course of action yet. Perhaps some time apart would give us better perspective on the situation. Why don't we all retire to our own rooms this afternoon and reconvene here tomorrow?" With that, she stowed her drawing tools away and left the room.

Mickey turned toward the door. "Not a bad idea. I could use a nap, anyway. Think on it this afternoon, Ace. Maybe you'll see some sense." He left before Ace could answer.

The pilot slammed a fist against the table in frustration. "I need a beer. I'll be in the bar if anybody wants me." He stomped out, leaving the door open.

～

Verity and Davis sat in the room alone. The research assistant left her perch by the window, closed the door, and locked it. She recrossed the room and knelt by the side of Davis's chair, placed one of her hands over his. She gazed up into his face, her eyes wide.

"Davis, you have spent so long here in Turkestan. Surely you have some exciting stories to tell."

He looked at her for a moment, head cocked and one eyebrow raised. "You want to hear my stories? Or maybe you just want to get me talking, bragging. Maybe you want to make me feel important."

She smiled, rubbed his hand softly. "Maybe I just want to make you feel. The life of an American on the silk road must be so exciting. I'd like to get closer to you, learn about life over here."

Davis chuckled. "We've shared hotels, train cars, boats and tent camps for the better part of two months. This is the first time you've showed any interest in me. I wonder if it's because I'm the swing vote on leaving the country? Maybe you are trying to persuade me."

"Oh, you silly man," Verity said. "I've found you attractive since we met. I just hadn't found the right opportunity to let you know."

"And the right opportunity comes now, when you need me to support staying. Very convenient. Maybe I should be asking what your angle is."

She rubbed her hand up and down his forearm. "Why would you think I have an angle? You're a handsome man. We should spend some quality time together while we have a chance. Companionship would be nice, don't you think?"

"It might be nice. It might also obligate me to support you if there's a vote about where we go next." He removed her hand from his and stood up. "I need some time to think. Good afternoon, Miss Hester."

She leaped to her feet. "Wait—don't go, Davis. I do have an angle. Think about what's out there—a lost city. Maybe one that hasn't been plundered. You are a businessman, Davis. Think about the wealth—artifacts, artworks. Maybe even some special items Doc thinks there's some kind of mask out there with magic powers.."

He smiled. "That's more like it. You're a greedy little thing, aren't you? You want to stay to grab some treasure, not rescue Doc and Alicia."

"Oh, Davis. Does it matter why I want to stay? The important thing is that we don't need to be in a hurry to get home."

Davis inclined his head toward her, once. "You are an interesting woman, Verity. Now if you will excuse me, I really do want to think about what comes next." With that, he exited, leaving Verity alone in the sitting room.

The rain broke over night; the cartographers reconvened in the morning. Dawn brought no news of the missing cartographers or the rebels.

Margaret surveyed the group. "Well? Has anyone had a change of heart? Or are we still at an impasse?"

Before anyone could answer, someone knocked at the door. It was the magistrate's secretary, again delivering a message. Once more, he left without saying anything.

Margaret opened the note, read it, and went white.

"It says that an army of Basmachi is coming—they are expected to arrive this afternoon. We are ordered to evacuate at once."

Ace glared. "No. We. Are. Not. Leaving. Them." He pounded his fist into his palm, emphasizing each word.

Mickey rolled his eyes. "We'd like to help, Ace, but we don't have a lead. We don't know where to go. We can't just blunder around the hills, hoping to find something. It's too dangerous."

Verity held up a hand. "Wait. I think I've got it. We just need to find the angle, right, Davis?" She started pacing, thinking out loud.

"First—Doc and Alicia are kidnapped. Doc only, and not Mickey. Alicia grabbed from the medical tent.

"Second—the rifle they dropped. An Enfield—British. We know a shipment of British rifles was stolen a couple of weeks ago at Daroot-Korgon.

"Third—the epidemic, in the Alay Valley—upriver from Daroot-Korgon. They are begging the magistrate for medical personnel.

"Fourth—the lost city. It's upriver from Daroot-Korgon, probably. Our mystery searcher went there with a stupid map no one understands.

"Doc and Alicia weren't taken for ransom; they were taken for knowledge. Whoever is looking for the lost city grabbed Doc to help decipher the map. He must be in the area where the epidemic is spreading. Whoever helped him—whatever locals he hired—decided to grab a doctor, too. Doc and Alicia must be upriver from Daroot-Korgon. That's where the trail leads."

"Yes!" Ace pumped a fist in the air. "Daroot-Korgon—I'm in. Who's with me?"

Davis nodded. "Your line of reasoning makes sense. We might be able to track them down from there. Margaret, Mickey, what do you think?"

The expedition leader shook her head. "Proper procedure is to alert the authorities and let them oversee the investigation. I'm sure the magistrate would appreciate this information."

Ace snorted. "As if he didn't know it already. He already knows about the epidemic and the rifles. I doubt adding a kidnapping to the list will move him. If we don't act, no one will."

"I'm with Margaret." Mickey looked grim as he spoke. "We're not fighters. We shouldn't try to tackle this on our own until we have exhausted all other options. Verity? What are your thoughts?"

The research assistant stared out the window, intent on something happening in the street.

Mickey called her again. "Verity—Verity! In or out? Should we head back to the mountains, or downriver to safety?"

Davis shushed him. "No rush, Verity. We have a day or two to pack. We can keep talking and make a decision when we leave."

A brick crashed through the window; shouting could be heard from the street below. Verity turned to face the room.

"The Basmachi are outside and shouting for blood. We have to run—right now."

# Chapter three

*Ten days earlier…*

D octor Zsezsnky awoke with a splitting headache; the ground passed by above his head. Not above—below. He hung upside down, mostly, draped over something shaggy. His head dangled on one side, his feet on the other. The hairy thing moved.

Yak—the shaggy thing was a yak, and someone had slung him over its back. His head pounded; he groaned.

"Oh good—you're awake. You worried me. These men wouldn't let me examine you." A female voice with an odd accent—partly urban, partly southern. Doctor Carambo—Alicia.

He groaned again, tried to move. No luck—ropes bound him to the yak. His heart raced; Doc Z started to struggle against the ropes holding him in place.

Alicia spoke again. "Calm, Doc. Calm. Don't fight—they might crack your skull again."

The yak took issue with his struggles as well; it snorted and danced around on the lead. He heard other voices, footsteps. The yak calmed; a man talked to it, soothing it.

He heard Alicia speaking Tajik. "He's awake—help him! Someone help this man. He's hurt and needs attention." She switched back to her accented English. "Sorry, Doc. I don't know what language these guys speak. They don't seem to understand Tajik at all."

Doc paused to listen to the speech around him. He heard two distinct languages—Pashto? No—Pamir, the language of the remotest valleys. The other sounded like Mongolian—nomads from across the Pamir Mountains and Taklamakan Desert. What an odd pairing. He called out in his rough Pamir. "Someone, please untie me. Help me, please."

A man's voice addressed him now. "You are awake? Can you ride a horse, or should we leave you strapped in?"

"I can ride, I think. Please, just untie me, let me sit up." Doc hoped getting upright would help the headache.

Hands untied him, hoisted him upright. They stood him upright on his feet. The world spun; his legs collapsed. The ground rushed up to meet his face.

Laughter, followed by hands. One of the hillmen spoke.

"His legs are asleep and he's still dizzy from being hit. Let him sit and recover for a moment."

"No. We don't have time—they will be pursuing soon." This voice spoke Pamiri, but with an accent. Maybe one of the nomads.

"They can't follow us," the hillman said. "It would take our best trackers a day to figure out the trail we left, and I doubt his people can track half so well. We have time for him to recover. Your chief ordered us to bring this one in unhurt. Let him rest, so he feels better."

"Fine." Back to the nomad. He was shouting now, calling orders to the troop. "Dismount and refresh. Take ten minutes, then we ride again."

The bandits pushed Doc into a sitting position on a rock; someone passed him flatbread, dried meat, and a cup of water. They permitted Alicia to sit on a rock near him.

He spoke to her in a low voice. "Alicia—are you all right? What's going on?"

She looked him over. "I'm more concerned about you. Did they hit you over the head? You could have a concussion, or worse."

He laughed. "My old skull is thick enough to handle a bump or two." He fingered the egg-sized knot on the back of his head. "It hurts, but there's no blood. I think I'm all right."

She stood and approached; voices shouted at her.

Doc translated. "They want you to stop." One of the kidnappers—a hillman by his clothing—leveled a rifle at her and said something.

"He wants to know what you are doing."

"Tell him I want to examine you, that I'm concerned you got injured when they took you."

The man spoke again. "He wants to know if you really are a doctor, trained in Europe."

She shook her head. "You know perfectly well I'm a doctor and that I was trained in New Orleans, not Europe."

Doc translated again; the man shrugged, said something brief. He lowered his rifle and wandered off.

"He's disappointed you aren't from London or the like. He says you can check me, as long as you're quick about it."

She stood behind Doc and took his head between her hands. She turned it this way and that, occasionally touching the knot gently. She faced him and looked into each eye, lifting his eyelids as she did so.

"How do you feel, Doc? I assume you have a headache, but how about any dizziness, nausea, seeing stars, anything else? Your collapse worries me."

He shook his head. "I feel terrible, but I'm stable. No other symptoms. I think the spill came from standing up after being strapped across a yak for…." He paused. "How long was I out, anyway?"

She shrugged. "I'm not sure when they hit you. It was about half an hour from when the shooting started until they brought you to the yaks. We rode for another two while you were out."

Doc furrowed his brow, trying to piece the incident together. "I don't remember any shooting. They must have hit me before it started. So I was out for at least two and a half hours, probably more like three. Do you know where they are taking us, or why?"

Alicia shook her head. "No. I speak Russian and a little Tajik, but I haven't heard either here. I've tried to count. I think there are six nomads and eight or nine hillmen. I'm not sure—the hillmen have scouts who are staying out of the main group. I can't get a good count on them."

"Do you think we could escape? Dash into the trees and follow the trail back?"

"No. I'm not certain where we are." Alicia frowned as she spoke. "They kept a blindfold on me for a while after they grabbed me. We went up and down, so I'm sure we left the valley, but I don't know which direction we went. There won't be much of a back trail to follow, either. They have picked rocky paths for us, probably to avoid leaving a heavy track. I'm afraid running would put us into more trouble. At least these people are inclined to feed us."

Doc looked around. "I don't know. We can't have gotten far. Maybe we could make a break for it and try to find our way back. The mountains can't be that dangerous."

A sound ripped through the air then. The deep roar sliced through the air and silenced all conversation; chills traveled down Doc's spine. His basest instincts—the core of his most primitive soul—recognized the call of a predator.

A tiger stalked the hills.

Alicia looked around, eyes wide. "Still think we can survive out there on our own?"

Doc sighed. "Our new friends will take us somewhere sheltered, at least. Margaret is probably already working on rescue or ransom. These men want us for some reason; let's wait and see what it is."

~

The kidnappers placed Alicia and Doc on stout hill ponies and tied them in place. They spent the remainder of the day and most of the next traveling through one valley after another. Their route tracked either up or down—steep mountainsides bordering the narrowest valleys. They saw no signs of people there in the eastern fringes of the highest mountain range in the world. Alicia couldn't tell if the region was uninhabited or the leader chose desolate areas to avoid detection.

They emerged from the mountains at one end of a long, narrow valley. Mountains loomed on every side; the valley floor stretched perhaps ten miles wide in the center but extended three times as long. Open terrain covered with grass made up the valley floor.

The kidnappers took them to a hamlet in the hills perched on a rock shelf above a river. Sun-baked mud bricks composed the buildings; gaily-colored pennants fluttered from roofs and across streets. Low stone fences surrounded some of the buildings, apparently more to keep out wandering livestock than two-legged invaders.

People—mostly women and children—emerged from houses to greet the party. Alicia noticed the locals greeting the hillmen with affection, hugging, kissing, playing—but ignored the nomads. Curious—why would these groups be working together to kidnap cartographers?

When they arrived at the muddy main street, the groups diverged. The nomads continued through the village with Doc Z, but the kidnappers stopped Alicia's horse in the center of town. They dismounted and started to untie her.

Alicia panicked. She shouted and kicked her heels into the horse's flanks. The horse tried to run, but one of the hillmen clung to the reins. The horse reared and kicked. Alicia tried to leap off, but ropes held her tight to the saddle. She began to slip sideways.

More hillmen rushed to grab the horse. Soon, they surrounded the beast. Two men held the reins; others leaned over the saddle. Someone threw a blanket over its head, and the animal stilled. The men shouted at her, angry. She couldn't understand a word.

The men pulled her off the horse. Not rough, but brooking no dissent.

Hands grabbed her, gripping her arms and legs tight. Another hand clapped over her mouth, muffling her cries. She struggled to break free, but too many foes held her. They carried her into a windowless hut. The door slammed closed behind her; she heard something clunk across it. They locked her in the hovel, all alone. She tried the door; it did not even rattle in the frame. She paused, gathered her thoughts.

Little light entered the room; it took her eyes some time to adjust after the bright daylight. She had visited the huts of the hill people before; they usually suffused with a warm orange glow from a fire they never let die down. No fire here, and the room lacked the small touches that made the huts feel like homes. No decorations, no personal items or tools, no preserved food or cooking utensils. Two sleeping platforms with sheepskin rugs and wool blankets took up most of the floor; otherwise, the hut stood empty. Alicia noticed recent repairs to the roof and walls; she also saw the old window holes covered by boards. It looked like someone fixed up a derelict building to make a jail cell.

A man entered, breaking her concentration. He displayed the short, stocky build typical of the Pamiri people. He wore the quilted wool robe standard in the hills but with more color and decoration than most—a sign of wealth. Gray hair showed at his temples; a few wrinkles around his eyes showed his age. Despite the signs of age, the man stood tall and moved with grace. Older, then, but not elderly.

She glared at him. "What do you want with us? Why are we here? Where is Doc—what have you done with my companion?"

The man shook his head, then bowed and addressed her in the language of the hill people. Pamir, Doc called it.

Alicia shook her head. "I don't understand—I can't speak your language." She realized she was speaking English; of course, no one here would speak that. She said the same thing in Russian.

He frowned, said something else. Alicia shrugged, said nyet—no. The man mumbled something under his breath and left.

A few minutes later, a different man arrived, tall and thin with a high forehead. Short ginger hair lay plastered on his head, combed forward like a bust of an ancient Roman. He wore a short, pointed beard in the latest style of the capitals of Europe. He dressed like a Pamiri, but with more expensive fabric, with some European touches. It looked like he had paid a fine tailor to copy the hill clothing.

He gave a slight bow. "Greetings, Dr. Carambo. Welcome to the Pamir

Mountains." He spoke English accented with another European language, perhaps French; Alicia couldn't place it.

She glared at him. "Why have you brought us here? What's your game?"

The man smiled faintly. "I have not brought you here. I needed to consult with your colleague, Dr. Zsezsnky." He emphasized the 'I' in both sentences and pronounced 'Zsezsnky' smoothly. "However, my gracious host wished to add a doctor trained in Europe to my shopping list when he learned I would obtain an expert. I believe he is somewhat disappointed to learn that you received training in the United States rather than Europe. I did not provide him with all of your credentials, but I believe you will prove satisfactory for his purposes."

Alicia stared, mouth open. "First of all, my credentials? Really? What do you even know about me? Second…"

He cut her off. "Your credentials are thus: Alicia Carambo, born to a family of wealthy but disfavored merchants in New Orleans. First of her sex and race to graduate from both Tulane University and the Tulane medical school. Top of your class both times. Not content to serve as a simple country doctor, you signed on with a mapping expedition to the mountains called 'The Roof of the World.' Now your services have been requisitioned here, to assist the people of this…place. You don't need to know the name; too much information is never good for a captive. Tell me, please, do you speak any of the local languages? Your inability to converse in Pamiri disappointed our host."

Alicia's mouth hung open. "How did you know—where did you find out…."

Again he interrupted. "Languages, please." His voice grated now, tinged with anger. "I am a busy man Dr. Carambo, and I will not stand around this hut all day discoursing with you."

She stammered. "I can't—that is I can, I know Russian and a little bit of Tajik. I never heard of Pamiri before yesterday."

He nodded. "Excellent. I'm sure we can find a translator. I bid you farewell, Dr. Carambo." He turned toward the door.

Alicia followed, grasping at his hand. "Wait—don't leave me! Where is Doc Z? What do these people want? Who are you?"

He pushed her away with a snarl. "You will remain here. I have business to which I must attend."

Alicia clung to his hand; the man backhanded her across the face. "Release me, or I shall do worse."

She stepped back; her head spun. She worked her mouth, but no words came out. Before she could collect her thoughts, the man stepped out and slammed the door behind him. A dull clunk sounded after he slammed the door—a bar on the outside.

Alicia sat on one of the beds to think. She felt despair—kidnapped, locked up, hit in the face. She faced a terrible situation: alone, God only knew where. A bar on the outside held the door closed. The kidnappers had taken steps to prevent their trail from being followed—the remainder of the expedition wouldn't know where to start looking.

She took a deep breath and gathered her thoughts.

First, these people want a doctor for something. They likely won't harm me, at least while I'm useful. Second, this vile man wants Doc Z for something. He knows my history—he probably knows Doc's as well. Probably something to do with the old silk road.

Why would bandits need a doctor? Can I treat a criminal in good conscience? When I became a doctor, I affirmed my dedication to healing those in need. When I became a Christian, I accepted my duty to bring peace to the world, sheltering the vulnerable. Where does healing a bandit fit? He is in need, yet he harms the weak. What about compulsion? These people have wronged me; they have taken me by force to make me heal. Yet I would gladly heal those who ask.

Alicia brooded in the gloom; she didn't notice the sound of someone removing the bar or opening the door until brighter light streamed into the room. She turned, surprised by the change in light. Her body tensed; she readied herself for another attack, for wicked men to grab her.

An old woman stood in the door, wearing the wool and fleece garb of the hills. Short but stout with wispy white hair surrounding a face as wrinkled as a dried apple.

The old woman bowed and smiled. "Greetings, honored physician. Welcome to Daroot-Korgon. I wish you health and prosperity. My name is Omarah." She spoke Russian; Alicia recognized a traditional greeting.

Alicia returned the bow and offered a polite response. "Thank you, honored host. My heart is gladdened to join you in your honored home." She relaxed; nothing to fear from a grandmother.

The woman sat on one of the beds without invitation. "Forgive my rudeness; my body is not what it used to be." She patted the bed beside her. "Please, join me. I know your mind must be spinning with a thousand thoughts. My thoughts ran wild when I first came here as well. Sit and let us talk."

Alicia sat. She knitted her eyebrows. "When you first came here? Are you not native to this place—this Daroot-Korgon?"

The woman laughed. "No, I'm an outsider, even though I have been here longer than almost anyone else. I grew up on the shore of the Caspian Sea; we are speaking my mother tongue now. Not long after I reached marriage-able age, my family came up the Amu Darya to Dushanbe to trade. I saw a boy there among the hill people—oh, he was the handsomest boy I ever saw. I ran away with him, back to his home in Daroot-Korgon. He made a wonderful husband, my Farzad. He's been gone for years now, but our grandchildren still take care of me."

She paused for a moment and chuckled. "Listen to me going on. I'm not here to reminisce; Bahman—he's the headman here—Bahman wants me to prepare you for work. There is a sickness in Daroot-Korgon. Some think it's spirits, or a curse; others think it's the sort of thing one of your European wise men—wise women, I suppose—can fix."

"Sickness—many people sick, with the symptoms the same, or many different sicknesses?" Alicia had prepared herself to treat bandits wounded in fighting—stabbed or shot. The notion of treating ordinary people with ordinary illnesses came as a shock.

"Mostly the same," Omarah said. "There are some differences; not every person has every symptom. It's all the same illness, though. It's the rice-wa-ter sickness, I am certain."

~

The shape of the valley fascinated Doc Z. It had been terraced for growing crops; a road wound through it, smooth and level. Terraces were common in the hills of China, far to the east. The Romans also built them, fifteen hundred miles to the west. The residents of the Pamirs lived by herding sheep, goats, and cattle. Livestock did not need perfectly flat spaces. The Pamiris possessed neither the inclination nor the skill to build terraces.

Doc realized master engineers once reshaped this valley—perhaps the Romans? This could not be. Records existed of individual Romans visiting China. Few scholars believed an entire legion could have come this far east, but it was possible. Ptolemy wrote about a stone tower along the silk road somewhere; Doc thought the structure to be a Roman fort, a castrum.

This, though—the possibility of a Roman settlement, one with the size and longevity to reshape this valley—not even the most radical scholars accepted such a thing. If he could find hard facts to support it, Doc could become a world-famous archaeologist. His celebrity might even exceed the crackpot at Marshall College who claimed to have found—then lost—the Ark of the Covenant.

When they reached the village, Doc heard some commotion with Alicia's horse. He turned to see several men catching the beast, restraining it. One of his guards pulled the reins of Doc's mount; he lost sight of Alicia. He assumed the horse bucked her off, and she would follow soon.

His guards—Mongols from the steppes, by their dress and speech—took him along a wide, smooth path—likely an ancient road. After half an hour, they stopped and untied him. They were in a broad flat area, with large rocks poking up here and there through the grass. Doc noticed signs of digging around some of the stones; he approached one.

One of the guards followed him, rifle in hand. The others gathered into a small group, eating and joking.

The stone was big —six feet across and perhaps two feet thick. Three feet extended above the soil; another six or eight feet had been uncovered below ground. Markings covered the face of the stone. Letters? He squinted at them for a moment, then looked around. A ladder protruded from one side of the hole. He climbed down into the hole, then looked again at the stone.

The markings on the top were faint, eroded by wind and rain and time. The lower markings, covered by soil, held up better. Doc traced them with his finger—Latin. Forgotten notes from the depths of time.

He studied them for a time, awed to discover secrets hidden for nearly twenty centuries. He learned the valley's Latin name, its history, the legates who once commanded the legion here. He could only make out part of the legion's name: LEGIO IX HIS…; soil covered the rest. The information on this single stone could change history—how many had there been? What else could he learn?

He looked up at his guard. The man squatted on the edge of the hole, looking bored. "I say, my good man, have you any tracing supplies? Sheets of paper and a charcoal pencil would be best, though I could work with pen and paper if need be. Maybe even a notebook?"

The guard shrugged, puzzled. He responded in Mongolian. "Make sense, crazy man. I don't speak your nonsense language."

Doc Z raised his eyebrows, then shook his head; he looked like a dog trying to clear a bee from its ears. He responded in the same language. "Of course, my friend, of course. Have you writing equipment? Paper and pencil?" He pantomimed writing with one hand on the palm of the other.

Before the guard answered, another voice responded from somewhere outside the hole—in English. "Ah, my good Doctor Zsezsnky, I see you have discovered my monuments. I can provide you with whatever materials you need to analyze them."

Doc Z craned his neck to see a tall, thin man with red hair and a pointed red goatee standing at the edge of the hole. He dressed like a Pamiri but spoke English.

"Um, hello," said Doc. "Who might you be?"

The man bowed slightly. "You may call me Maes Titianus. I am a scholar of the old empire. Welcome to my great discovery. Please, come up from the hole and join me for a meal. We have much to discuss here."

Doc made his way up the ladder. He surveyed the ruins again. He could identify the pattern now— a small castrum, just a waypoint—a camp built to shelter traveling troops and support scouts.

"How did you find this place? I'm not aware of any Roman roadways in this region."

Titianus smiled and raised one eyebrow. "The makers of these roads did not publicize them. I believe there are…resources…in this region that the Roman Empire wanted to keep secret."

Doc gasped. He spoke more to himself than to Titianus. "Uncatalogued roads. A clear official castrum. Could this be? No…it can't. But what else?"

Titianus chuckled. "You've figured it out, then?"

Doc nodded. "Legio IX Hispana—the Spanish Ninth, the famous lost legion. Last recorded in Britain—everyone assumes it was destroyed somewhere in Scotland, but they are wrong. There are indications—not many, but clear—signs of the Ninth marching off east somewhere."

Titianus beamed. "Very good, Doctor Zsezsnky. The Spanish Ninth Legion came here, to this valley. What do you make of the carvings?"

Doc shrugged. "I didn't have enough time to study the markings. I do notice part of the stone includes a map."

"Yes. Can you read it?"

Doc shook his head. "No. We call them maps, but the Latin word means something closer to 'way-list'. No one now understands how to read them, or what they are supposed to convey. Much has been lost in the last two thousand years."

"Well, perhaps you will be the one to decipher them. I heard you ask for paper and charcoal to make rubbings. What other equipment do you require now?"

Doc thought for a moment, then looked around. "Paper and drawing charcoal, a journal and pen, a magnifying glass. It looks like you have enough shovels, but I need trowels, brushes—tools for fine digging. Those things should do for a start."

He thought for a moment. "Say, if you just wanted me to look at the waystones, why did you kidnap me? I would've been glad to come up here if you asked."

Titianus frowned. "Surely you cannot be so foolish, Doctor. Think a moment."

Doc ran a hand over his face. "Judging by who you hired for your diggers, you probably aren't licensed to dig. Which means you're not with a university. You're a thief yourself, aren't you?

Titianus laughed. "I do sell artifacts from time to time, but such is not my real business."

Doc tilted his head to one side, thought for a moment. "You're neither a scholar, nor a looter. Then what are you?"

Titianus gave a wry smile. "Look at the world today, my good doctor. Just a few years ago, it burned in the mud and trenches of the Great War. And for what? A family squabble—the cousins that wear the crowns fighting for precedence. Now, the world becomes decadent, savage, or both. A strong hand is needed to unite the world, to pacify and civilize. To restore the rule of the Caesars."

"No—you can't do such a thing! The empire was monstrous. It survived on slavery, cruelty, oppression. A return to the empire would mean a loss of freedom for, for...."

"For everyone, Doctor. My allies will become the rulers of all mankind. Wars will cease. Savages will be elevated; civilized men will end their decadence and serve as examples. Now you see why I didn't simply invite you to come visit my site, yes?"

Doc nodded, at a loss for words.

"I now go to retrieve your supplies. I suggest you try to make yourself as useful as possible while I am gone."

With that, Titianus departed, barking orders at the guards as he did so.

———

The stench assaulted Alicia's nose as soon as she entered the infirmary. Her eyes burned; even breathing through her mouth gave little relief. She looked around, counted patients. Ten figures on the floor, either reclining against the wall or laying down. Two lay unmoving; five were listless. The other three tracked her movement with their eyes—alert, at least. Clouds of flies buzzed around the sick.

She turned to Omarah. "What are the symptoms? What is wrong with these people?"

"The worst is the loosening of the bowels. The afflicted have uncontrollable…." Here she used a word Alicia did not know. Alicia frowned. Omarah tried again. "They pass water from behind. There is no normal stool—it is watery and pale. It looks like rice water."

One of the patients groaned—a boy, maybe ten years old. He held one arm at an odd angle, then said something to Omarah through clenched teeth. The old woman went to him, forced his arm to unclench. She massaged the bicep. "Their muscles…" Omarah said another word Alicia did not know. "The spirits grab the muscle, make it tight. We must pull the tension out and rub the spirit away."

Not a spirit, thought Alicia. Cramps. Why? Loose stool, cramps.

The old woman began tending a small fire in the middle of the hut, adding bundles of something to produce aromatic white smoke. "Sometimes the smoke drives the spirits away, but it has no effect here. These demons are worse, much worse, than most."

Something prodded Alicia's memory. The peculiar stench, loose stool, cramps—dehydration. She understood; a water-borne epidemic gripped Daroot-Korgon. Here, there could be no choice for her—she must help, kidnapping be damned. She couldn't recall the word in Russian, only English.

"Cholera. These people have cholera."

Omarah cocked her head. She tried to repeat the strange word.

Alicia looked grave. These children might be too far gone to save. "They need water, lots of water. Boil it first. Add salt and sugar—"

Omarah shook her head. "We all boil our water before we drink. Everyone knows that."

"What? If everyone boils their water… What could it be?" She was thinking aloud, trying to understand her situation. Contaminated water carried cholera; every doctor knew that. Boiling killed the pathogen—also settled.

She turned to Omarah again. "Show me. Boil water for me and let me see."

The old woman clucked her tongue and made a small hand gesture. Alicia understood right away—she had seen enough variations on 'crazy lady' through her life to recognize the sign.

Omarah added some dried wood to the fire and poured water into a pot. She placed it over the fire and waited. A few wisps of steam came off the pan; she waved to Alicia.

"See? The water boils." A few tiny bubbles trickled up from the bottom of the pot.

Something seemed wrong to Alicia. The boil seemed weak, the steam barely visible. She held a hand over the water: warm rather than hot, nowhere near scalding. Carefully, she lowered her hand, then dipped a single finger into the water. Too hot for comfort, but not hot enough to burn.

It's the altitude. How high are we? Mickey would know. At any rate, water boils at a lower temperature here. They need to add time to the boil. How to explain that?

"The water isn't getting hot enough to kill the sickness right away; you need to boil the water for longer, maybe fifteen minutes. That's the best way to be sure."

Omarah looked puzzled. "Boiling is boiling, yes?"

"No—we sit at the bottom of a great sea of air. But here, in Daroot-Korgon, we are higher than other places. We are not so deep in the ocean of air...."

"We are not so deep, so the air weighs less? It's like diving into deep waters—put just your face in, it's only wet. Dive deep for pearls and the water crushes you, pushes your eardrums. The air also is like this?"

Alicia smiled; this was easier than she had hoped. "Yes, like diving. Less air sits on the top of the pot, so the steam escapes faster. You need to boil longer to make up for it."

"I never thought of that. Food takes longer to cook here, too. It seemed crazy when first I came to Daroot-Korgon—everything took so long to cook. I was right all along. Do you really believe boiling the water longer will drive away the spirits?"

So much for science. "Yes, boiling the water longer will keep anyone else from getting sick. There will probably be a few cases the next few days—people who are infected, but don't show it yet. We still need to take care of them."

"I must think of a way to explain it to everyone else; they won't understand about the water. No one here swims, or even plays in the water. I may tell them it takes a long time to drive the spirits from the water. They will play along, at any rate." She turned and gestured at the sick within the hut. "What can we do for these? Will boiling water be enough?"

Alicia shook her head. "It may be too late, especially for those who are so weak. They need water, lots of water, to replace what has been lost. They need salt and sugar as well. Show me the cups they drink from."

Omarah stood, went to a shelf. She pulled down some battered tin coffee cups and held them out to Alicia.

The doctor examined the cups; they would hold about half a pint. "For this much water, put—" Another difficulty; these people wouldn't recognize the measurements Alicia did.

She looked around for a reference. She noticed Omarah wore a necklace threaded with coins. "Please, let me see your necklace. I can show you how much salt and sugar to put in with coins."

She sorted through them until she found one the size of a nickel. "For salt, use a pile big enough to cover this coin. For sugar…" Another coin, the size of a silver dollar. Perhaps more than necessary, but what child wouldn't like extra sugar? "This much for sugar. Get these children drinking lots of water—more than they are putting out. Make sure everyone else in the village knows to give the salt and sugar water to anyone who might be sick; it will help them stay strong and survive."

Omarah smiled and nodded. "At once, learned one." She departed the hut to spread the news.

Alicia stepped outside into the fresh air. She could see for miles down the valley. The weight of her actions hit her—she was saving kidnappers.

No, not kidnappers. Sick children. The sick children of kidnappers.

She leaned against the hut; her knees began to tremble. The weight of the last few days weighed her down—kidnapping, cholera, God only knew what would come next. She slid down the side of the hut to sit on the ground. Tears rolled down her cheeks.

~

Doc examined the standing stones until the daylight ran out. He emerged from the pit around the stone. The hour surprised him; time really did fly when he studied lost history.

His guards took him to a nondescript hut with a bar outside the door. One guard removed it, opened the door, waved him inside. Doc entered; the door slammed, and the bar clattered home.

Alicia sat inside, watching a pot of something bubble on the stove.

She looked up at him. Her face was lined with worry; tension radiated from her pose. She recognized him; Doc saw her expression soften and her shoulders lower when he entered.

"Oh, Doc—it's good to see you. No one here could—or maybe would—tell me where you went, or what they wanted with you."

He smiled. "It's good to see you, as well. They had me hard at work examining some Roman waystones a little way up the valley. Fascinating work—they reveal some things even I never dreamed about the Roman empire, and about the lost legion. There is enough material there to upend the field, to confirm some of my wildest speculations—"

He cut off abruptly, realizing he had ignored his fellow kidnap victim all day. "What about you? Are you all right? Have they harmed you in any way?"

She shook her head. "No. They put me to work—there's a cholera epidemic here. By the way—don't drink any unboiled water, not even a sip. I can't have you sick too. But these poor people—I've got to help, kidnapped or not. I'm tending the sick and giving advice on how to stop the spread. Plus all the usual ailments of a remote farm village—cuts, broken bones, other sicknesses. It's been overwhelming—I've had to do everything without any medical equipment whatsoever. It's like holding back the sea with your arms."

He sat. The events of the last few days caught up with him—the blow to the head, kidnapping, the rough ride through the mountains, and the hours he'd spent stooped over the stones. "What do we do, Alicia? These people have kidnapped us. We are prisoners here, against our will. They have wronged us, yet they need us. The stones out there—the waystones, the maps—this site may hold the key to finding out what really happened to the lost legion! This could lead to the greatest discovery in two thousand years! It's all so strange."

He paused, stared into the fire. "I don't know what to do. Part of me thinks we should escape, get to the expedition, come back here with digging tools, cameras, survey equipment. Part of me wants to drink it all in—it's so amazing!"

Alicia took a deep breath. "I can't leave yet. These people need me. I've got to get the epidemic under control, to help those who are suffering...."

Doc nodded. "I suppose I could use a few more days of work myself, to really gather the information."

"What do they want from you," asked Alicia. "Why kidnap a scholar to look at a lost Roman site?"

Doc shrugged. "I'm not sure. Titianus—the man in charge calls himself that, after a Roman who traveled the silk road—didn't say. He knows a great deal about the empire. He seems like a first-rate scholar, though I've never heard of him. He claims to want to restore the rule of the Caesars over the world."

Alicia tilted her head to the side, puzzled. "Restoring Caesar? I've never heard of that."

"People study the Romans for different reasons. Most want to under-stand the past, unravel puzzles, tell the story of what happened. A few, like me, believe the ancients possessed secrets that could benefit the world today. We are politely called unorthodox, or more often crackpots. This Titianus would restore the old empire with all its cruelty and oppression. I've never met his like."

"Why would anyone want to restore the old empire? Some of the sto-ries—torture, mass execution. The Roman Empire was awful."

"I have no idea," said Doc. "Power, I suppose. There are always people looking to take advantage of others."

Alicia went pale. "Doc, if this Titianus really wants to restore the Roman Empire, do you suppose he would hesitate to harm those who might im-pede him?"

Doc thought for a moment. "Maybe. It's possible, I suppose. He did kid-nap us; that's not the behavior of a law-abiding man. Why?"

"You really don't see it? I think, once he's done with us, Titianus will kill us."

Doc frowned. "Why would he do such a thing? You are a doctor—you help people. He brought you here to cure an epidemic—not the act of a monster. I'm a scholar. What risk would I pose?"

"He brought me here because Bahman—the headman is named Bah-man—made him. I'm the price Titianus is paying to use the village as a base for his explorations. Titianus doesn't care about this village at all. You are a tool he's using to advance his agenda. I think, once he's done here, he'll dispose of us both to keep his secrets."

"So what, then? What do we do, Alicia? How do we get out of this?"

"Delay, to start with. You string him along, give him enough informa-tion to keep him interested, but make him think something bigger is just around the corner. And we plan—figure out where we are, where we need to go, gather supplies, that sort of thing."

"I—I think I could do that. Maybe follow some false trails, ask for equip-ment he'll have difficulty getting. I'll buy us some time."

Blood drained from Alicia's face; her mouth pulled into a tight line. "Thank you. The risk you are running, the delay—it will save lives. You're doing the right thing."

Just then, a strange sound echoed through the night. It started as a rumbling growl, then rose to an ear-splitting screech. A second call answered from the opposite side of the valley, then a third farther up in the hills.

The sound made the hair on the backs of their necks stand up. It was unearthly, a sound made by neither man nor beast.

Alicia's eyes opened wide. "Doc, what made that sound?"

His countenance reflected her fear. "I've never heard anything like it before. It's not a bear, or tiger, or wolf. I've heard stories, seen anecdotes in old manuscripts, but—no, no, it can't be. They are just stories. Not real; they can't be real."

"What is it, Doc? What have you seen?"

He closed his eyes and took a deep breath. He opened them, looked Alicia directly in the face. "There tales of a bloodthirsty monster in these hills, a beast said to prey on humans and tigers and everything else.

"A creature called the yeti."

# Chapter four

*Dushanbe*

The brick fell on the sitting room floor with a heavy thud. Shouts rose through the window now, not ordinary street sounds but the roar of an angry mob. Verity announced, "the basmachi are outside and shouting for blood. We have to run—right now."

Davis looked at the brick, then up at the group. "Everyone, to your room. Grab as much as you can, then meet in the lobby—no, not the lobby, it's too visible—meet in the bar on the first floor. We might have as long as five minutes before they break in. Don't waste time."

The group broke up in silence, each to their own room.

They gathered in the bar, packs strapped on. Davis, Ace, and Mickey wore pistols on their belts; Davis and Ace also bore rifles slung over their shoulders.

Margaret frowned. "Are the weapons truly necessary? The Cartographers Guild frowns on violence."

Ace glared. "Them basmachi love violence, and they'll dish it out whether we like it or not. At least a couple of rifles give us a chance—"

Davis pushed a palm toward Ace. "Hush. Now's not the time. We have to choose how we leave the hotel, right now. I don't think we can change course much once we're outside—we have to commit to a path and run it as fast as we can. Which way? Out the front, to the river and down to a safer city? Or out the back and into the hills?"

Ace was grim. "I'm for the hills. We have a place to start now—Daroot-Korgon. I'm not tucking my tail and leaving Alicia or Doc behind. The rest of you can do whatever you want."

Verity winced. "It's dangerous, but I'm with Ace. We need to stick together and all that. I'm for the hills."

Mickey looked around. "It's going to be rough, whichever way we go. At least D-K means we are doing something, not just hiding. I'll go to the hills."

Margaret closed her eyes and tilted her chin back. She exhaled slow-ly. "I don't like this. It's not regulation," she said. Margaret tilted her head down and looked Ace in the eyes, "but I think the hills are the best route. If Miss Hester is correct, if the kidnappers don't want a ransom, then we must break the rules to get our people back." She turned to face Davis. "Mr. Davis, if you please, take us out of the city to Daroot-Korgon."

Davis raised the bar's entry flap and made an 'after you' motion to the team. They filed behind the bar and into the hotel's kitchen.

The kitchen stood deserted. The staff recognized the danger. Either ev-eryone fled before the mob arrived, or they never left home. The five car-tographers stalked through cook stations to the pantry, then out the back of the hotel into an alley.

~

The clamor of the mob outside grew louder. The narrow alley connected two broad, parallel streets. They could see motion out one end of the pas-sage, men wearing the wool robes of Turkmenistan. Almost everyone there wore green sashes tied around their arms, the symbol of the Basmachi. The other end of the alley was quiet; no one moved on the second street.

Davis made his way toward the quiet street; the rest followed. Running footsteps echoed down the alley—someone from the mob broke away to examine the group. The rioter called out to them in the local dialect; Davis answered. The man peered at them, then walked closer. He said something else.

Davis spoke in a low whisper. "Ace, Mickey—we've got to get rid of him, quietly. Any noise and the mob comes howling down on our heads."

Ace took his hand off his holstered pistol. "Nuts. I'm not much good at quiet, but the three of us should be able to do something." He reached a hand behind his back and pulled something from a sheath; twelve inches of bowie knife gleamed in his hand.

Mickey gulped and nodded. He squared himself up in a parody of a boxer's stance, back straight and fists facing palm-in in front of his face.

The rebel stopped a few yards away. A quick glance took in the three explorers; he smiled and chuckled. Davis noticed the man holding a stick as tall as himself. The rebel grasped the staff with both hands in the center, then whirled it around his head.

Mickey looked at Davis. "Um, guys? I think this will be a problem. We can't beat this guy fast without shooting him." He yelped and jumped back just in time to dodge a straight thrust from the pole.

"Spread out." Davis started moving to the left. "Ace, you go right. He'll probably follow you since you've got a pig-sticker."

Ace crab-walked to the side. "Maggie, Verity, get back. We don't want you to get hurt."

Davis lunged forward, grabbing at the man's arm. The rebel spun, swinging his staff. Davis backpedaled. He grunted as the stick hit his ribs with a dull thud.

Ace took that opportunity to lunge, blade extended. The Basmachi whirled his weapon back in a quick parry; it struck the knife. Ace held on to his weapon but retreated.

The three cartographers began to circle; the rebel kept his staff spinning. The noise outside the alley diminished; the only sounds were the hum of the spinning staff and the footsteps of the fighters.

The explorers moved with care, wary of the danger from the staff. The rebel showed equal caution; he kept his strikes short to preserve his ability to pivot and protect his back.

Ace lunged again; Davis charged at the same time. The rebel parried the knife blade with his staff, then launched a sweeping blow at Davis. The two cartographers dodged the swings, then hesitated.

The fighter stepped forward, intent on finishing the fight. Margaret used the opportunity to duck low and swing a broom handle at the rebel's knee. It connected with a sharp crack; the fighter grunted and fell to one knee. He thrust his staff into the ground to keep his balance.

Verity struck like a snake. Her weighted bracelet whistled, thumped into the back of his skull. The fighter collapsed like a bag of flour.

Ace laughed, a low chuckle. "Nice work, ladies. Maybe next time we should let y'all take point in a fight."

Margaret patted her hair and smoothed her dress with her palms. "Sometimes the unexpected is the best way to win a fight. Now, let us continue toward the gate. We've taken long enough in this alley."

Davis nodded. "Check our friend there, make sure he's not going to cause more trouble."

Verity tossed the staff away. Ace knelt beside the Basmachi, knife held ready; he pulled back the prostrate man's head and examined his eyes.

"He's out, cold as a wedge. Probably have a hell of a headache when he comes around. No need to do more; we can be out of sight before he's awake. Let's move."

Mickey was already at the alley's mouth; he looked both ways along the street. He waved the team forward. "It's clear—come on." The cartographers left the alley and hiked up the boulevard toward the north gate of Dushanbe.

～

They reached the north gate with no trouble. Davis guided them along smaller streets, through residential areas where foreigners were rare. The rioters concentrated on the commercial quarter and wealthy neighborhoods where the hated outsiders stayed. Still, they proceeded with caution. Mickey scouted every intersection before they exposed themselves; Ace brought up the rear, ready to fight if trouble came from behind.

Mickey stopped them short at the final intersection before the northern gate of Dushanbe. Everyone clustered behind him.

Margaret spoke in a low whisper. "What do you see, Mr. Charles?"

"Guys watching the gate—ten or a dozen. Too many to rush. We could shoot them, but the noise would draw attention."

Davis frowned. "Maybe we can wait them out." He peered around the corner. "They don't look too interested in guarding the gate. I'll bet they wander off when they get hungry or tired."

Ace shook his head. "I don't like waiting. I'm afraid something will bust loose before they get tired. We need a diversion or something."

Verity held out a hand to silence them. "Stop—listen." Everyone froze; they hardly dared breathe. They saw no one else on the street. They could hear the noise of a crowd in the distance—the riots, spurred on by the Basmachi.

Margaret spoke first. "Are they getting closer?"

Verity nodded. "I think so. I didn't hear the riots at all when we arrived. They're coming this way."

"We've got to move, then," said Mickey. "We can't afford to get caught out here by a mob."

Davis took a deep breath. "What's the play? Force our way out the gate, divert them, or hide?"

Ace unslung his rifle. "I'd rather die fighting than running. At least that way, we've got a chance to make it out."

Mickey shook his head. "Dying is no good. Besides the fact we'd end up dead, it means abandoning Alicia and Doc. We're trying to save them, remember?"

Davis nodded. "Mickey's right. Shooting would draw the mob like ants to a picnic—we'd never make it out of the gate alive. We need a hole, or a diversion."

Verity whistled, then made a 'come here' wave. A small figure darted up the street—Shuhab still followed them. Verity smiled and held up a silver coin. "Margaret, would you ask our friend here to help us hide from the mob?"

Margaret started a conversation with the boy in his native tongue. Ace scowled. "Are you crazy? He'll probably just sell us out the the mob! We can't go with some stray kid—you're nuts."

Verity laughed. "He's not some stray, as you put it. He's been following us ever since we got to Dushanbe. He's the one who took us to Yando, and the one who gave us the information to puzzle out where Doc and Alicia are. Right now, he's the only one who can keep us alive long enough to get out of town. It's trust or die—I prefer trust."

Ace shook his head. "I prefer to see what's coming—not a knife in the back. Out here, at least we can use what we've got. Who knows where he will take us?"

Margaret interrupted her negotiations. "He says he knows a place—one he's used to hide from the police, many times. He says we'll be safe there."

"See? He'll help us, at least for the right price." Verity looked smug.

"No, I don't see. We're not safe yet—the mob is getting closer." Ace held his rifle in hand. The bolt was halfway open; a brass cartridge gleamed in the breech. He closed it with a solid click. "Let's find a sheltered position—I bet some thirty-aught-six will calm them down a little."

Margaret turned to him. "You may put your rifle away now, Mr. Barrett. Shuhab has agreed on a price to lead us to safety. And as a precaution, I have told him you will shoot him if he betrays us." She turned back to Shuhab, made an 'after you' gesture.

Ace stared at her, open-mouthed.

Verity laughed. "Cat got your tongue, Barrett? It seems like we've finally found someone you don't want to shoot."

―◡

They followed Shuhab down a side alley. Ace glared at every shadow, nook, and cranny. He muttered the entire time. "This is a death trap. Even if we can trust him—that's a big if—there's no way we can escape the mob in here. We'll get lost, or cornered or…."

Margaret silenced him with a glare. "We are in a difficult situation, Mr.

Barrett. Shuhab has offered us aid. Maybe he is honest, maybe he isn't. He most certainly is greedy, a trait which we can use. If we are captured, or killed by the mob, he gets nothing. Perhaps he will be hurt, as well. I trust his desire for silver outweighs whatever nationalist sentiment he may harbor. He will keep us safe for no other reason than simple greed."

Ace kicked at a rat crouched behind a crate. "And if you're wrong? What then?"

"I believe this is what is commonly known as a 'tight spot,' Mr. Barrett. Our choices are limited." She paused to jump over a puddle covered in green scum. "We can trust Shuhab, who knows the town like the back of his hand. We could try to hide on our own. Or we could fight. Mr. Davis and I have chosen to trust Shuhab."

Ace laughed, then crouched to traverse a low passage. "I'd choose to fight, any day of the week. I want trouble in front of me, not sneaking up behind."

Mickey snorted. "There's your trouble, Ace. You focus on what you can see. It's the one you don't see that gets you."

The cartographers stopped talking as they saw the final phase of their journey. They were in an alley—little more than a crack between buildings. Dim light filtered down; they couldn't make out much detail about their surroundings. Shuhab swarmed up the side of a brick building, using cracks and uneven bricks as hand- and toeholds.

Ace ran a hand up and down the wall. "I'll give you this, Margaret. There ain't no way a mob is getting up here. Trouble is, I don't think we can, either."

Davis examined both walls, then took off his pack. He pulled out a coil of rope and slung it over his head and shoulder like a bandoleer. "I think I can make it up with this rope. Once we've got a line to the top, we can get everyone to safety.

The guide started up the side of the building. Davis climbed slower than Shuhab. The boy climbed like a monkey, trusting his grip and slight build to top the wall. Davis tested each grip before committing, sometimes pulling back and trying a different hold. The din of the riots increased during his climb; the mob approached.

At last, he reached the top. He called out in river language; a small head popped out of a hole beneath the roof. Shuhab extended a hand and helped Davis clamber into the hole. The rope dropped, and Davis called out, "Start by sending up the ladies. Let's try it with packs on to save time."

Margaret called up. "Very well, Mr. Davis. Verity will come first; she is the smallest. If there are problems, having a lighter climber will reveal them most safely."

Ace tied a harness in the rope and put it on Verity. She called up, "I'm ready, Davis."

A voice came from the hole. "It will be fastest if I pull and you climb. If you slip, I can catch you, but you still need to do a lot of the work."

"Understood, Davis. Here I come." She began to scale the wall, faster and surer than Davis.

Once Verity entered, Margaret slipped into the rope. She moved slower, more cautious than Verity. Mickey went next. With three people pulling the rope, he soared to the hole. The noise of the riot swelled as he went up.

When the rope came down again, Ace could make out individual shouts somewhere nearby. He tied Davis's backpack to the line. "Get this up and out of sight. I'm coming as quick as I can."

Davis whispered down. "Not the pack—let's get you safe, Ace."

Ace shook his head. "No good. If the pack is there, they will look for us. Haul it up." With that, he started climbing. He struggled to climb while wearing a backpack. His feet dangled about six feet off the ground when footsteps echoed down the alley. The rope lowered in front of him.

He turned his face up and whispered. "Come on, come on—just a little more. Let me get a foot in the loop."

The rope slid down a little more; the bottom of the harness loop reached his knee. Ace gripped a stone tight and lifted a leg to put his foot in the loop.

He missed at first, kicking the loop aside. He tried again, got his foot through. His fingers ached; he couldn't grip the bricks forever. He lifted his foot; it was tangled in the rope. He couldn't free himself.

Davis whispered down to him. "Are you in? I can't see." The footsteps grew closer.

"No—it's around my ankle. I can't get my foot out without using my hands."

Davis swore. "I'm going to pull the rope up anyway. If your leg is through, you probably won't fall. When the rope is tight, grab it and hang on. We'll pull you in."

Voices could be heard in the alley now—someone was close.

Ace nodded, not daring to speak. He watched the slack in the rope slide past his face, felt the loop slide up his leg and catch around his thigh. One hand slipped off the bricks; he lunged out and grabbed the rope. The loop bit into his thigh muscle as it took more weight. He released his other hand, shook it, gripped the cord. The wall began to slide past his face.

The voices came closer; a hole came into view. Ace grabbed at the edge of the opening; hands grabbed his jacket and pulled him in. Davis saw two men wearing the green armbands of the Basmachi enter the alley as Ace's feet disappeared into the hole.

〜

Ace looked around the forgotten attic. The space had been walled off from the rest of the building years ago; now it sat, empty and forlorn. Sunlight slanted through cracks between shingles; dust and pigeon dung covered every surface. The only objects in the room were broken odds and ends, the kind of detritus that accumulates in out-of-the-way storage spaces.

Shuhab sat with Margaret, talking in low voices. Verity pulled the climbing rope back through the hole; Davis and Mickey panted, tired from the strain of hauling Ace through the hole.

Ace held a finger to his lips. "Quiet," he whispered. "Somebody below."

Everyone froze. They heard voices from below, a pair of men discussing something. Not discussing—arguing. They paused below the hole; none of the cartographers dared to move. One of the men said something, voice harsh. He stamped his foot for emphasis. The other responded just as loud. They stood and argued for one minute, two. Blood pounded in Margaret's ears; it seemed loud enough to give them away.

Footsteps sounded below; the men moved away. The argument receded; they left.

Verity sighed. "That was close. Could anyone make out what they were talking about?"

Davis nodded. "Looking for us. Someone told them a group of avrupoi—outsiders, meaning Europeans—had ducked down the alley. They couldn't agree which way we went, but they'll keep looking for a while. We should get comfortable; we aren't going anywhere until well after dark. Keep quiet, too. We may not hear the next group of searchers to come through."

They did their best to get comfortable in the bare room, then settled in to wait.

The afternoon crawled by. The sound of riots rose and ebbed as mobs roamed the streets. Now and again, footsteps sounded in the alley. Sometimes Basmachi strode through, bold and noisy in their search for foreigners. Other times, furtive steps marked someone fleeing the violence of the mob.

The sun sank low; cracks in the wall caused beams of light to slant almost horizontally through the attic. The sky went dark, but the noise continued for hours.

After sunset, the attic became pitch black. No light from the houses or the moon shone in. Verity waved a hand in front of her face—nothing. It felt like sitting in a cave. Still, no one spoke or moved.

The cartographers waited until after midnight before they dared to climb down from their hole. Davis went first, followed by Mickey. They reached the ground, then paused—listening again. They separated for a moment, checking for trouble up and down the alley.

Satisfied at last, Davis called up to the hole. "All quiet down here. Come on down and we can head for the gate."

One by one, the team slipped down the rope. Shuhab remained behind for a moment; the rope dropped down from the hole. The boy climbed down the side of the building, agile as a monkey. He whispered something to Margaret.

"He says we need to take the rope, lest it reveal his hiding place to the world."

Mickey grabbed the rope and coiled it, then stowed it back in his pack.

The narrow alley was as dark as the attic. Shuhab whispered again; Margaret translated.

"Shuhab wants us to link up—hand to shoulder. He says he can find his way to the gate by feel, but we might get lost. I'll put a hand on his shoulder; Mr. Davis, please bring up the rear. The rest of you, link up."

Quiet shuffling broke the stillness of the alley. Murmured exchanges and light taps against the wall helped the team orient themselves into a line. Everything grew quiet again.

Margaret whispered something; Shuhab answered. "Shuhab is at the head of the line; my hand is on his shoulder. Call out now, one at a time. Who is third?"

Ace responded. "I'm three. Who's on my six?"

Verity stood next. "I'm behind you, Ace. Next?"

"Right behind you, V," answered Mickey. "I guess Davis is the caboose?"

Davis squeezed Mickey's shoulder. "Right you are, Mick. We're all here—get ready to move." He said something else, in river language. Shuhab led the parade forward.

Silence reigned in Dushanbe tonight; no one moved around. The town felt like a drunk sleeping off a bender. The rioters had exhausted themselves with the effort of the day; everybody else took shelter, still fearful of coming out into the streets.

A full moon bathed the streets in silvery light when the team exited the alley. No torches or fires burned; neither were electric lights operating. No one knew whether someone cut the power or if those who had electricity hid it.

They moved through the streets quietly. Shuhab stuck to the shadows as much as possible; the team stayed hidden from prying eyes in the houses around them.

The orange glow of a fire suffused the air as they approached the gate. Shuhab whispered something to Margaret; she called a halt. "He says we are just around the corner from the gate," she whispered. "He wants us to stay behind while he scouts the gate for us."

They huddled together in the darkness, waiting for the boy to return. Faint sounds of conversation could be heard—someone ahead was talking.

Shuhab came back, spoke to Margaret again. "There are two men at the gates, around a bonfire. He thinks they are wearing basmachi armbands, but he's not sure."

"What's the play," asked Mickey. "Sneak, rush or move?"

Margaret and Shuhab held another conversation. "He says he doesn't know what we should do. He also says this is the only way out of the wall on this side of town. Mr. Davis, why don't you peek around the corner and assess the situation?"

Davis tiptoed to the corner of the building. He crouched low, then peered around. A stone wall twelve feet high surrounded the city. The wall dated to an age when Dushanbe was prosperous and the steppe nomads belligerent. The west gate was a square, ten feet high and ten feet wide. It once boasted a pair of wooden doors that could be closed and barred. Only one gate remained, slouched like a drunk against the interior wall. A revolution a century ago wrecked the gates; no one bothered to replace them.

A small fire lit the gate and wall with an orange glow. Two men with the woolen robes and green armbands of the basmachi stood next to the fire, sharing an earthenware jug—probably apak, the local moonshine. They stood in the center of the street, about ten feet from the gate.

Davis retreated to the team. "Two basmachi, alright. Right in the middle of the gate—no way around."

Ace tilted his head to one side. "We've got rifles, and shadow. If they stand in the firelight, we could put both down before they even know we're here."

"Too loud," said Mickey. "Gunshots would draw attention. We'd be spotted running out the gate, probably. Even if nobody chased us, someone would see and tip off the basmachi—they would track us right away."

"Misdirection." Verity spoke with a firm voice. "We need a misdirection—get them to look one way while we move in the other."

"Excellent idea, Miss Hester," said Marget. "How do we achieve such a thing?"

"What about the kid," asked Davis. "We send him to the guards with a fake story. They follow, we slip out the gate."

"Yes, that could work. I'll ask him," said Margaret. She turned to Shuhab and spoke for a moment.

Ace interrupted. "Hold up a minute. How do we know he won't sell us out?"

"We don't," said Davis. "We trust him, like we trust others around us. He's played us square so far—taking us to Yando, hiding us in the attic, leading us to the gate. He could have tricked us, or sold us out, or half a dozen other things. I say we trust him."

Margaret cut in. "I have another idea. Please allow me to finish negotiations, Mr. Barrett, and I believe we can come to a mutually acceptable solution." She turned back to Shuhab and talked some more. The team could just make out motions in the darkness, then the clink of a purse. Silver flashed in the moonlight. Shuhab turned and ran up the street, away from the gate.

Ace whispered a sharp challenge. "Margaret—why did our guide just take money and run away?"

"Mr. Barrett, please, trust me. He is going to approach the gate from a different direction to lead the guards away from us. I have made further arrangements to leave money for him outside the gate. He'll be paid more if we get away than if he turns us in. I implore you, please, be patient."

Ace grumbled but said nothing. The cartographers waited in silence. After ten minutes, they heard Shuhab shouting from the direction of the gate. Davis listened intently. "He's telling the guards he found a group of avrupoi up the street somewhere. He's giving pretty good descriptions of us." He peered around the corner at the gate again.

Davis could barely make out Shuhab at the opposite edge of the firelight, standing in another broad street. As he shouted, he waved the guards to come toward him and pointed up the road—away from the cartographers.

One of the guards shouted something at Shuhab. The boy responded, came closer to the guards. He waved them up the street again. The first guard turned to the second; they held a brief conversation.

At last, the guards left the fire and walked up the street, following Shuhab. No one watched the gate.

Davis returned to the group. "He's done it. I'll bet we need to get out in a hurry. I'm not sure how much of his story they bought. Come on, now. Move out—quick and quiet."

They avoided light on the way out, skirting the ring of firelight as much as possible. They crouched in the gloom next to the wall now, just a few feet from the gate. Only by exposing themselves in the firelight could they escape. Davis whispered final instructions. "Move quick through the light, then get back out of sight. Come around to the opposite side of this wall, then we'll check in and decide what's next."

One at a time, the cartographers dashed from cover. They crossed from dark to light to dark again. Davis went last. As he left the gate, a man shouted behind him. The guards were back.

Davis ducked into the shadows outside the west gate of Dushanbe just as the guards returned to their post. One shouted at him; both dashed after him.

Ace hissed a warning. "Trouble coming—everybody be ready to silence it." Steel glinted in his hand—the razor-sharp bowie knife.

The first guard came into the black, heedless of the danger. Ace met him, knife at the ready. The guard grunted as the blade slid home; Ace clapped a hand over the man's mouth to silence him.

The second guard came slower, more cautious than his partner. He reached the edge of the shadow and paused, still in the light. A hand grabbed the front of his shirt. He jerked forward into the darkness. A dull thump; the guard collapsed as if his bones had turned to water. Davis turned to Mickey. "I got him good with the blackjack. He'll be out for a while. Help me get him into the shadows."

The pair pulled him into the blackness behind the gate. They were out of Dushanbe and safe, for the moment.

"What now?" asked Verity. "Do we need to take care of this guy so he won't talk?"

"No." Margaret's voice was flat, hard. "We will not kill this man when he is helpless. Killing in a fight is distasteful, but necessary. Killing a helpless man is murder, and I will not countenance it. Leaving him may present a risk, but we will not commit murder. Bind his hands and feet, gag him, and hide him behind the gate. That should buy us more time even after he comes around." She turned to Mickey. "Mr. Charles, please assist me. We need to find a particular tree with a hollow branch and leave some silver for Shuhab."

In five minutes, they departed. The guards were hidden behind the gate; the hiding spot for Shuhab's money had been located and filled.

Davis was grim. "We've got to make some tracks now. Someone will notice the blood here, or the missing guards, or the one I blackjacked will come around. The basmachi will start looking for us soon. We need to be gone. Here's the order of march: Ace, you take point. Margaret is next, then Verity. Mickey, follow the ladies. I'll bring up the rear." He pulled out a coil of rope. "Everyone grab the rope—that will keep us together. Move us fast Ace. We've got to outpace the pursuit and get somewhere safe."

Ace glanced at his watch—half-past two. Four hours until dawn. He led the team off at a steady trot.

# Chapter five

The cartographers made good time to start with. Ace pushed hard; he wanted to put as much distance between them and Dushanbe as he could before the sun came up. The team maintained a base camp about fifteen miles outside the city—close enough for easy resupply yet far enough to discourage intruders. On this day, the cartographers aimed to cover the distance in four hours—in the dark.

After an hour of hiking, Verity stumbled and fell; she cried out as she went down. Mickey recognized the problem first.

"Ace—hold up. Verity fell; she needs a sec to get back up." Mickey felt the rope in his hand grow slack—everyone gathered together.

"How far do you think we have come?" asked Davis.

Ace shrugged. "It's been maybe an hour, but I can't see my watch to be sure. I hoped to cover four miles the first hour to make sure we're clear of Dushanbe before dawn."

Four miles sounds right to me," said Margaret as she pulled out her canteen. "The guild manuals maintain that four miles an hour are the fastest sustainable pace in darkness with full packs. We should be out of sight of Dushanbe now; we can take a short break. Everyone, have a seat and some water."

Verity groaned. "I cannot keep this up. I need sleep, and food, and time away from this damned backpack."

"No good." Davis was firm. "We have to get back to base camp as soon as we can. It's sheltered, and defensible. Unless the entire army of basmachi shows up, we can hold them off for a good long time. We can't afford to get caught out here in the open, though. Only two rifles and two pistols won't keep a mob at bay for long along the road."

"Should we maybe get off the road, take to the woods?" asked Mickey. "They'd not find us in the trees."

"No way." Ace's voice was grim. "We'd make terrible time in the woods in the dark. We could get lost, go back to Dushanbe, maybe even stumble into a camp of the basmachi. It's the road until the sun is up, or we hit camp."

Margaret chuckled. "For once, Mr. Barrett and I are agreed. We are safe enough on the road in the dark. Distance is what we need now. We will consider taking to the woods when we can see a path through them."

The team rested in silence for a few more minutes. At last, Davis stood. "Stow your canteens and grab the rope. It's time to move again."

Everyone grumbled but complied. Verity gasped when she shouldered her pack. "It's impossible. The pack is too much—I can't keep this pace with all the weight."

Mickey responded first. "I could take a little more if it would help. Pass me something, Verity." She handed him her blanket roll; he lashed it to his pack. Ace, Davis, and Margaret all took small items as well.

Verity smiled to herself. "Much better," she said. "I can make it, I think. Lead the way, Ace." They set off again at a more comfortable pace. The cartographers marched into the dark, resting twice more.

They saw a thin orange line to the east when Margaret called for a halt. "Look there—the break between the hills. Base camp is at the foot of the shorter hill, I believe."

Ace whooped. "You're right, Maggie. Half a mile more, and we can stop."

"Margaret, or Ms. Atherton, if you please, Mr. Barrett."

Ace laughed. "How's about I sleep the rest of the day and don't call you anything at all?"

Verity groaned. "Let's please keep moving. I want nothing more than to be finished with this wretched hike."

They set off once more, ready to rest after the arduous flight from Dushanbe.

～

The camp was quiet for the rest of the day. The team members staggered to their own tents and collapsed, exhausted. They gathered in the cook tent for supper. Everyone ate in silence; they were ravenous from the previous thirty-six hours.

Ace spoke first. "Think we should head for Daroot-Korgon first thing tomorrow? Doc and Alicia could use help mighty quick, I'll wager."

Davis nodded. "Sounds good to me. Margaret, what's the plan?"

The expedition leader paused for a moment to think. "I've not thought it through fully," she confessed. "But I concur with Mr. Barrett—we should move to Daroot-Korgon without undue delay. Perhaps not at first light, but soon."

"Why the delay, Maggie? Sooner we leave, sooner we rescue our folks," said Ace.

"Ms. Atherton, please. And we should delay long enough to develop a plan. How will we search for the missing doctors? How much ransom are we willing to pay, and how much hard cash should we bring with us? Are we willing to fight, and if so, under what circumstances? There is much to consider in our packing."

Mickey cleared his throat. "And the big question is, who goes? Davis is our fixer—he's probably best positioned to negotiate. Marg—I mean, Ms. Atherton—is our team lead. Should she also go? Verity should stay here, where it's safe. That leaves me and Ace—do we both go? Just one?"

Ace glared, defiant. "I'm in, no doubt. I want to get our people back, and if there's trouble, I want a big piece. Ain't no way I'll stay behind."

Margaret was just as firm. "I am the expedition leader. Whatever decisions must be made are ultimately my responsibility. I will not stay behind—I must go. Mr. Charles, you and Miss Hester ought to remain here in base camp, where it's safe."

Verity bristled. "Uhn-huh. No way. I will not stay behind, with the basmachi active, with both translators gone. If Davis and Margaret both go, I'm going, too."

Margaret raised an eyebrow. "Perhaps Mr. Davis should stay behind, then, to protect the camp."

"No way," said Ace. "He knows the bandits, and he's as handy with a rifle as anyone I ever met. If it comes to shooting, we need Davis out there."

"Maybe you should stay behind to defend Miss Hester and our camp, Mr. Barrett." Margaret wore a frosty expression.

"Me? Hell no, I ain't staying. Like I said, if there's trouble, I want in. I'm going, that's final." Ace crossed his arms over his chest and glared at Margaret.

"Well, it looks like everyone but Mickey has volunteered to go," said Davis. "Mick, you want to come help too, or would you rather hang around camp?"

Mickey looked at the four faces around the table—all resolute, ready to charge up the river to save Doc Z and Alicia. He wondered if they could sense his reluctance. "Well, we're probably all safer together than apart. I suppose if everyone else is going, I should tag along."

Ace slapped the table. "That's settled, then. Everybody goes. Margaret, you figure out the ransom angle. Davis, Mickey, and I will make plans for—other things. One way or another, we'll get our compadres back."

"Very well, Mr. Barrett." Margaret nodded her head at Ace, once, then turned to the rest of the team. "Everyone, prepare to travel fast. We will do no mapping or exploring on the way to Daroot-Korgon—this is strictly a rescue mission. Prepare to move quickly and quietly—we may need stealth to get past any basmachi or ordinary bandits on the way. Pack your things tonight, and reconvene at fist light in the morning to discuss the trip."

⌒

The cartographers gathered the following day for breakfast and a discussion of the trek. The field expeditions had not reached Daroot-Korgon, nor had Davis ever gone so far afield. The porters thought the trip took three days by foot but were uncertain. Margaret planned provisions for nine days to allow sufficient margin for the route and the possibility of detours or delays on the trip.

They set out at mid-morning; the road was deserted. The Basmachi activity kept the locals at home, avoiding trouble.

Just before they set out, Margaret turned to Davis. "Your thoughts on the route, Mr. Davis? Should we make haste along the roads and risk discovery, or should we take the slow and secret route across country?"

The fixer paused to consider the question. At last, Davis responded. "I think the road is straight, so we can see anyone ahead. It's quiet enough that we should hear anyone fast enough to catch us from behind. I say we take the road, but we should keep our eyes open and be ready to hide at a moment's notice."

Two days passed without difficulty. The Tajiks took cover while the Basmachi were active; the road stood empty. The trouble started on the third day.

The cartographers started the day's march at seven-thirty; the day was bright, and the air clear. After an hour's march, they could see something obstructing the road ahead. Half an hour later, they could make out a barricade across the path.

Davis examined it with binoculars. "Looks like wagons or carts, parked across the road. They can block traffic, but roll the carts away for traffic. They are built in a choke point—a steep shoulder of a hill on one side, the river on the other. No way around. Margaret, want a look?" He handed off the binoculars.

Margaret examined the block. "How many men did you see, Mr. Davis? I count nine."

"I counted nine or ten. One moved out of sight; I think a different one came back. I suspect there are at least twice as many out of sight. I didn't see guns, but we are so far away—I'm not sure we could make out rifles at this distance."

"Mmm…I concur." Margaret lowered the binoculars and thought. "It's too dangerous to try to force a passage. Could we go around, do you think?"

Mickey took the binoculars. He looked, not at the blockade but at the hill anchoring the flank of the position. "The ridge is steep and rocky. It's bare, too. We can't sneak over; they would spot us climbing and try—something. I don't know what. At any rate, the only through this valley is up the road, through the block. We'll have to back up and try something else."

Ace frowned. "What about crossing on the other side of the river? Looks like easy going over there."

Mickey shrugged. "We probably could sneak past on the other side, but we would have to cross the river. Crossing means boats, but nobody up here has one. Putting a boat into the rapids here is suicide. It's fight or turn back."

Ace started to say something; Verity held out a hand to cut him off. "Fighting our way through a fixed position is a low-percentage play. Even if we force ourselves past the barricade, and then escape any other basmachi around, we stand a good chance of losing several team members. I know it pains you to walk away, Ace, but walking is the smart play. It does us no good to sacrifice half the team to recover two."

"Mr. Davis," said Margaret, "do you believe there is any possibility we could talk our way through the block? Appeal to their humanity, perhaps? Or perhaps the barricade isn't manned by basmachi at all. Perhaps they are representatives of the army, or the provincial security forces."

Davis scowled. "Most likely basmachi, but maybe bandits. That doesn't matter. With as much cash as you're carrying, we don't have a prayer of getting through a legit checkpoint, either. Best case with the army or security forces is they relieve us of weapons and cash, then send us on our way."

Verity raised an eyebrow and looked at Davis. "And the worst case?"

Davis set his mouth in a hard line. "They take what they want, shoot us in the head, and blame our deaths on the basmachi." He stared at the distant blockade, then raised the binoculars to his eyes. "Time to go. I think they've seen us. At any rate, four or five watchers have come out from the barricade and are coming this way."

Ace grinned. "Finally some action. There's a nice grove of timber a couple hundred yards back, on the south side of the road. We could make a stand there—we can wipe out these clowns, easy."

Margaret scowled. "No, Mr. Barrett, we will strive to end this peaceably. We will most certainly not take a stand and 'wipe them out,' as you so… eloquently…put it."

Davis jerked his head back up the road, the way they had come. "Let's walk and talk. They gain slower if we're moving." The team turned and withdrew back toward Dushanbe. Davis continued. "Plus, the stand of trees you saw is no good, Ace. It's small, and set next to the river. We go in there, we're rats in a trap. We need something better."

Mickey gestured up the road. "I remember a big patch of shale half a mile up the road. It's on the outside, away from the river. It's around a bend, by a little creek there. We could get out of sight, leave the road without making tracks, and hide in the creek bed. I bet they pass right by us if we do that."

Margaret nodded. "Excellent plan, Mr. Charles. Please, lead the way. Everyone else—double time. We must move as if our lives depended upon it, because they do."

They picked up the pace, moving at the same ground-eating trot they used to escape Dushanbe. Davis glanced over his shoulder; the pursuers kept walking and chatting with one another. They wouldn't catch up soon.

Mickey's memory was spot on. In half an hour, they rounded a bend that took the cartographers out of sight of the pursuit. Fifty yards around the bend, a patch of black rock the size of a tennis court sat next to the road.

"There it is," he said. "Look—there are some big trees there, too. Those will give us some cover. When we leave the road, be sure to step on the main rock bed and not the little loose ones. We'll make it out of here yet."

They exited the road and made their way through a hundred yards of towering pines with little underbrush. The creek bed was a different matter; a thicket of willows and dense brush that grabbed at them and held them back. As the team forced a way through the scrub, they heard voices coming from up the road.

Mickey and Ace reached the creek first; Davis and Margaret arrived next. Verity was tangled in brambles, unable to move. Ace dropped his pack and went to her. Verity unslung her backpack and passed it to Ace; he tossed it down into the creek bed.

The voices grew louder, chatting and laughing in Mongolian. Davis grabbed Verity's hand and yanked hard. She stifled a cry as the briers bit through her clothes. She came loose, and the pair dived below the creek bed just as five basmachi rounded the bend.

The pursuers lacked discipline. They joked and laughed as they came up the road; two smoked. The cartographers crouched in the deep bed of the creek, using high earthen banks to shield them from sight. Only one carried a rifle; the other four were armed with sticks and axes.

Ace unslung his rifle and prepared to sight it. Davis grabbed his arm.

"Are you crazy?" said Davis in a whisper.

"No. Look—just five, only one gun. We can end this in ten seconds."

Davis shook his head. "No. Shooting will bring the whole bunch down. We wait—" He cut himself off, mid-sentence. One man looked their way, wearing a puzzled expression.

None of the cartographers moved; they hardly dared to breathe. The outlaw stared intently at the patch of brush for a moment longer, then shook his head. He moved on, resuming his chat with the others.

Half an hour later, the five investigators passed out of sight around another bend in the road. Davis sighed.

"That was too close. We need to sit tight here until they get tired of looking and come back this way."

Margaret nodded. "An excellent idea, Mr. Davis." She addressed the entire group. "Make yourselves comfortable. We shall be here until after nightfall, I think."

The five basmachi passed back by the concealed team an hour later; an hour after that, Margaret deemed it safe to talk again.

"I suppose we are safe, but I prefer to avoid undue risks. I believe our best course of action would be waiting until nightfall, then making another rapid march under the cover of darkness. Mr. Davis, your thoughts?"

Ace spoke first. "What about my opinion, or Mickey's, or Verity's? Why just Davis?"

Stsnding tall, mouth drawn in a frown. Margaret looked like a teacher disciplining a wayward child. "In the first place, Mr. Barrett, I do not need to inquire as to your opinion—it never changes. You wish to charge into the greatest danger, as rapidly as possible, and engage in maximum violence." Ace grinned and shrugged. "And in the second place, the services of Mr. Davis have been engaged by the Cartographers Guild to advise us on matters pertaining to safety and local difficulties. I have asked him because it is his job, just as it is your job to operate aircraft and repair equipment. If we had a geology question, I would ask Mr. Charles. And if anyone needed assistance with cataloging or preparing samples, I would dispatch Miss Hester."

Davis cut in. "You're right, Margaret. About waiting. I think we should stay hidden until after dark, then run like hell for base camp. We can cross the river there and work our way back up under cover of the trees. It will be slower, but safer."

Mickey and Verity nodded their assent. Ace scowled, then lay down. He made a show of putting his hat over his face, crossing his arms, and going to sleep.

Once dark fell, the cartographers exited their hiding place and started the march back to base camp.

—

The team marched all night. When dawn broke, Davis pushed the pace faster; they covered the return trip in a little less than twenty-four hours.

Late in the afternoon, Ace pointed at a hill about three miles away. "That's it. Base camp is at the foot of that hill. Another hour and we can sleep off this nightmare hike." His response was subdued; the long hike had taken its toll.

No one responded; sullen eyes glanced at the hill, then back at the road. "Just keep walking," said Davis. "We'll get home safe soon."

A sharp crack cut the evening air. Davis spun, looked back up the road. A dozen men in black followed them; each held a rifle. They all wore the green armbands of the basmachi.

"Run," he shouted. "Off to the right—make for the boats."

Margaret started to argue; Davis cut her off. "If they find the camp, we'll have to kill all of them. If we make for the boats, they can't follow."

Ace reached for the rifle slung over his shoulder; Mickey grabbed his arm. "Come on, Ace. Get under cover. Take a couple of potshots while it's safe. Don't stand here in the road and trade bullets."

Ace ran a hand over his face and rubbed his eyes like someone had just roused him from a deep sleep. "Good idea, Mick." He followed, the last of the team to plunge into the trees between road and river.

Davis and Margaret crouched behind large trees, ready to shoot; Ace followed suit. The basmachi were too far away for accurate fire—maybe five hundred yards. Davis fired twice, then spoke in a low voice.

"Don't waste a lot of shots—just make them get down. All we need to do is hold them up long enough for us to get to the boats."

Ace looked down the barrel of his rifle; he saw no targets. They all took cover while Davis spoke. He fired once anyway, just to scare them, then ran.

The boats were moored half a mile away through a belt of large pines. No underbrush hindered them; it felt to Ace like the team crossed the distance in a blink.

It was almost dark when they reached the pair of collapsible canvas boats brought from Baltimore. Each boat could hold eight people, plus gear—more than enough to ferry the five across the river.

Mickey stood in the river, pulling a boat into the current. Verity and Margaret were already aboard; Ace ran to join them. Davis grabbed his arm.

"Come with me to the second boat—we can't leave one for them to use." He turned to Mickey. "Launch now, Mick," he shouted. "We'll take the second boat across." Mickey nodded, pushed the boat into the current.

Ace tossed his backpack into the second boat. Davis worked the knot that tied the boat to a sapling. Ace pushed the boat off the shore and into the river.

A shout echoed from the woods; another answered farther upriver. The basmachi had arrived.

Davis's fingers fumbled with the knot; Ace stood at the bow of the boat, waiting to launch it into the water.

The shouts came closer; Ace heard footsteps as well. Davis gave up on the knot; he pulled a hunting knife from his belt. He pulled the rope tight with his left hand and sawed with his right.

Three fists emerged from the trees and shouted in triumph.

Severed fibers blossomed under the knife's edge. "Come on, Davis," Ace whispered. "Cut that rascal." Ace kept one hand on the boat; he drew his pistol with the other.

The bandits lifted rifles and began firing; Ace fired twice in return. The foes dropped back into the trees. "Any time now, Davis." Ace scanned the edge of the forest, pistol held ready. Davis sawed his knife like a madman. One fiber of the rope popped, then a second.

"One more, Ace. Make sure you've got the boat."

Ace gripped the boat and leaned back toward the bank. The last fiber broke with a pop, and the boat bucked toward the current. Davis leaped into the vessel; Ace gave it a shove and climbed in after.

Davis crouched low as he put oars in locks and started to row. "I've got the oars, Ace. Cover us with the rifle."

Ace unslung his rifle and pushed it over the gunwale. He removed his cowboy hat, lifted his head to look at the bank. Two basmachi advanced, rifles at the ready. Ace aimed at the closest and fired; the man dropped like a rock. Ace took aim at the second. As he squeezed the trigger, the boat hit a stone and lurched. The shot went wild; the bandit scuttled back into the forest.

A volley echoed from the trees. Splinters bloomed on the wood of the gunwale, too close for comfort. Ace had an idea. He didn't dare look at Davis or the other boat. He shouted, hoping to be heard. "Head downriver, toward the bend. Don't cross until we're out of sight. Make 'em think we're headed back to Dushanbe."

Davis grunted as he worked the oars. Mickey shouted something back; a volley from the bank drowned out his voice. Ace popped up and fired another round toward their pursuers. Long shadows of dusk stretched through the trees—darkness cloaked the forest. He ducked down and rolled on his back to see Davis. "It's nearly dark—a few more minutes, and we'll be safe."

A final volley came from the trees. The boats drifted around a bend in the river, out of sight of the pursuers. They were safe.

Bright moonlight guided their landing on the rocky bank. Margaret leaped out of the boat first, rifle in hand. "We must get the boats out of sight tonight. It would be best to do so without dragging them up the bank. I want to leave no sign that we crossed the river. Let them think we have returned to Dushanbe."

It took all five cartographers to lift each boat and carry it from the bank into cover. Mickey spotted a recently downed tree; dirt still clung to the roots in a mass eight feet tall. Behind that screen, the boats would be invisible from the river.

It was well past midnight when they finished hiding the boats. After that, the team collapsed where they stood, exhausted after their non-stop retreat from the roadblock nearly two days prior.

# Chapter six

*Daroot-Korgon*

Doc Z looked over the excavation. Not professional-grade, but the best that could be expected from a solo academic using bandits for labor. He possessed good digging equipment, knotted ropes for measuring, stakes for a grid, enough pens and paper to start a library. Titianus assigned eight laborers to the project—four bandits and four hill peasants. The men were indifferent to Doc's encouragement but feared Titianus's anger. Fear kept them in line well enough. A real archaeological team could have done better, but this crew was better than what the hack Schliemann inflicted on Troy.

One of the diggers stood and shouted to Doc. The man thought he had found something important. Doc walked to him. It was the young one—Doc couldn't recall his name. At any rate, the man was earnest and proud of every stone he found. This was probably nothing.

Doc squatted next to the excavation trench. A stone wall once stood on this site. The wall had collapsed centuries ago; the foundation had been swallowed by the ground. The excavators dug along the foundation, revealing the shape of whatever building once stood there.

He smiled, nodded. Pema—that was the name. Pema. He addressed the man in Pamiri. "Yes, Pema? Find something?"

Pema smiled, excited. "Look—here. Letters! Someone wrote something on this wall." Doc nodded, feigning interest. Pema stooped and swept the soil from a block. Most of the stones for this tower were square; this one was a long, narrow rectangle. It looked like a lintel for a doorway, but the placement seemed too low. Doc saw the markings now—it had been carved with something.

He hopped into the hole and looked at the carving and the stone. He brushed more dirt from the inscription; Pema had only uncovered a portion of it before calling him. He examined the carving, dug a little further, looked at the new letters. Something seemed off; he couldn't put a finger on it. What he could see looked like the inscription 'Entry to the House of That Which is Hidden.' A common inscription in post-Roman cult sites. After the empire fell, mystery cults tried to revive the glories of Rome through rituals and magic.

That was it. This site matched the glories of Rome, not the decay that came after. Every inscription, every artifact, the architecture, everything here screamed Roman Empire at the height of its power. Even the projection of power this far east could not have come after Rome fell. The phrase should not be here. It belonged on something two or four hundred years newer, made by people trying to revive something lost, something they didn't understand. An impossible inscription, in an impossible ruin.

He stood and stretched. He smiled and nodded to Pema. "Excellent work, Pema. Truly a momentous find. Wonderful." Doc looked around the dig site. Shadows stretched across the valley; evening approached. Time to be clever. He climbed out of the hole and walked around, examining the rest of the dig. He stooped again, chatted with another digger. He stood and shouted for everyone to hear.

"Excellent progress today, everyone. Time to close up and go for supper. I'll see all of you here tomorrow, bright and early."

He watched as the diggers exited the trenches and walked home, laughing and joking. Time to get to work, he thought.

He stooped in the trench and worked with great care. He uncovered the entire stone; his guess was correct. In Latin, the stone read 'Entry to the House of That Which is Hidden.' In post-imperial ruins, that inscription always marked a doorway. Scholars disagreed about what the portal symbolized, yet it always marked an entry into another room or tunnel.

Doc slid his hand into the soil along the base of the stone. He worked his fingers down, down, until he felt the edge of the stone. A little more now, he thought. Let's see what's down there. He hooked fingers under the stone— back, back, past where a wall stone should be. He flexed his wrist back, moved his hand up and down under the stone. Nothing. A door to—where?

He blocked up the hole with a large stone then covered the inscription with dirt. He would make sure no one dug here tomorrow.

He arrived at the hut, pondering the mystery. Alicia sat cross-legged in front of the low table; she had started eating without him. She smiled an apology. "Hope you don't mind," she said. "Long day. People are coming from miles around to see the great doctor from America. Life in the Pamirs is rough; there are lots of injuries to tend."

He chuckled. "As long as you saved me something, all will be forgiven."

She inclined her head to the table. "Plenty of everything. I may be a captive, but these folks still want me to eat good. Help yourself and give me news of the great dig."

He shook his head and sighed. "Strange. I found an inscription today matching a common post-imperial religious carving. It doesn't fit."

Alicia raised an eyebrow. "Why not? Maybe these guys were ahead of their time."

Doc chuckled. "No. It's like finding a subway sign in a medieval castle. It doesn't fit. I hesitate to tell Titianus. It's such a mystery—I don't want him to waste it, or blow it up, or something."

"But if you tell him, he'll investigate. Maybe even send someone to investigate the passage. Exploration could buy us lots of time."

Doc hadn't considered that. "It might buy us time, or it might get us killed. I just don't know."

"Any way to explore it without him knowing?"

Doc shook his head. "Not likely. For me to make a hole big enough to enter—he would see that for sure. Plus I need lights, or torches at least, to bring into the hole. He'll notice an excavation. It's either conceal it or reveal it."

Alicia frowned at Doc. "Let's sleep on it. Maybe things will look better in the morning."

~

Doc tossed and turned on his pallet. The inscription tugged at his brain. It belonged at a site at least two hundred years newer, maybe more. After Rome fell to barbarians, new religions appeared, trying to revive the ancient magic. Each one mimicked aspects of the mystery religions that flourished in Rome's heyday. The 'entry cult' built underground structures similar to below-ground constructions sometimes found in imperial outposts. The same inscription marked every temple: "Entry to the House of That Which is Hidden." It was always carved above a doorway, leading to a tunnel that opened in a large chamber.

The door/tunnel/chamber architecture was often found in Roman religious architecture; however, it was also common in modern buildings. The inscription—always written in Latin—was a different story. Dozens of post-imperial sites held such carvings. It had never before been found in actual Roman ruins. Why?

The thought whirled in his head, keeping Doc awake. Had the entry cult found this place and added the inscription later? Or could it be Roman—the source of the later copies?

He dressed in silence, trying not to bother Alicia. He found a couple of candles by feel. He put on his shoes, slipped out the door, and headed back to the dig site.

The sight of torches surprised Doc. Titianus stood there with half a dozen of his bandits.

"Ah, good evening, Dr. Zsezsnky. I am not surprised to see you here tonight. You saw the lintel stone and inscription?"

Doc nodded. "I did. The stone is part of the wall; the inscription seems to be original as well. But the ruins are so much older than the entry cult...." His sentence trailed off; the thoughts chased each other around his head again.

"Indeed. I have reason to believe this site, or other ones like it, are the source of the inscriptions used by the entry cult."

Doc furrowed his brow. "What reason? I've read some unorthodox materials, but that—that would be crazy."

Titianus chuckled. "There are sources that mention this inscription in an imperial context."

"What sources? There's nothing in the legitimate literature, or even the fanciful literature—"

Titianus cut him off. "How about the absent literature? It's in the Codex Tumulatus."

"The Tumulatus? But it's just a legend—no copies are known to exist, to ever have existed. It's a mythical book."

Titianus laughed now, loud and long. "Lost? No, only hidden. The Tumulatus and works like it were hidden before the empire fell. My...organization...has copies of many of them. We do not advertise the fact, nor share them with outsiders, for the same reason the last imperial wizards hid them."

"What reason? Why would you hide such treasures away?" This revelation puzzled Doc.

"Why? For the same reason the Romans did, of course. We wish to conceal the secrets of magic possessed by Rome."

Doc's eyes grew wide. Magic? That's another myth—just a word the Romans used to overawe barbarians who couldn't understand their technology or organization. There is no magic; there never has been."

"You believe as well as I do that magic is real, Dr. Zsezsnky. Sorcery is associated with doors inscribed Entry to the House of That Which is Hidden. We will now proceed to search the tunnel below. I expect we will find the first storehouse of magic to be found in a millennium."

Doc realized the bandits clustered around the inscribed stone. They were digging—opening the doorway to…what?

Something glinted in Titianus's hand—a pistol pointed at Doc's heart. "Dr. Zsezsnky, I am going to ask you to do the honors. The Tumulatus suggests a tunnel like this will have four traps—of earth, sky, bronze, and fire, if that means anything to you. You will explore this tunnel, identify the traps, and disarm them if you can. I will have my men assist you. Feel free to have them precede you; they will be useful in discovering the traps, if not disarming them."

Doc stared at Titianus, mouth hanging open. "Use the men to find the traps? But that would—they'll be killed. We could just get a long pole and try to set off the traps."

Titianus chuckled again. "You worry about killing these men? They are cutthroats and bandits—the scum of the earth. The world will be better without them. And as to your pole—the Tumulatus suggests the traps were made with magic. They will reset themselves, time after time. You can't simply trigger them then pass by. And don't think the traps would have rotted away, either; the magic protects against age as well. Come now, here is your torch. Happy exploring."

Titianus forced a torch into Doc's hand, then waved the pistol at the excavation trench. Doc had left the excavation as a shallow trench containing a wall fragment; he found a pit holding an empty door frame. The lintel, inscription still present, now marked the top of a black abyss. The torchlight cast an eerie orange glow into the hole; it did not extend deep into the tunnel.

Doc climbed down into the trench. The bandits moved aside as well as they could in the confined area. He approached the doorway and looked at the stones that formed its edges. Aside from the inscription on the top stone, it was bare. The hole held no door or even a sign that a door had been there. He ran a hand around the door frame, then extended his torch into the hole.

The tunnel looked like a dozen other excavations he had entered. The walls were made of smooth blocks of stone, all the same size and shape. Even after two thousand years, they remained vertical. The passage was about four feet wide; a vaulted arch eight feet high made up the ceiling. Smooth flagstones four feet square composed the floor. He took a single step forward, then another.

One of the bandits behind him muttered something; the other laughed. Someone shoved Doc aside hard; his shoulder hit the wall with enough force to leave a bruise. A bandit marched down the tunnel, torch held high. The man laughed in triumph.

Doc heard something—a subtle ping, barely audible. An orange glitter flashed in the torchlight; something swished. The bandit shouted, gurgled, and collapsed. An object rolled toward Doc's feet, then stopped. Doc extended his torch toward the projectile: the bandit's head. The men behind him gasped. Excited mutters echoed up the stone tunnel.

Doc retched as he backed out of the tunnel. He turned to look up at Titianus. Five shapes loomed tall above him in the orange light. The madman stood with four bandits at the edge of the hole, their feet level with his eyes. Four rifles pointed down at him. Titianus smiled faintly. "Please, Dr. Zsezsnky, continue your exploration. You might be able to outwit the traps in the tunnel. You will not outwit my riflemen."

"For the love of God, Titianus—be sensible. We need to study this tunnel, understand how the traps are still armed—"

Titianus squatted down and pushed the muzzle of his pistol against Doc's forehead. "We are going to explore the tunnel tonight. You will return to the tunnel, locate the traps, or die trying. Understood?"

Doc swallowed, then nodded. "Please—at least give me the tools. I need a pole to push ahead. And a rope, with a hook. We need to retrieve the poor unfortunate in the tunnel."

Titianus inclined his head slightly. He stood and shouted over his shoulder; torchlight moved here and there in the excavation. In a few minutes, Doc held a stout coil of rope with a grapnel attached and a pole made by removing the branches from a small pine tree.

He set out up the tunnel once more, slower than before. He held his torch close to each stone in the wall and floor, looking for inscriptions or other signs of traps. He reached the dead man. The flickering torchlight revealed letters incised in the wall just past the body. Doc hooked the grapnel on the man's coat, then turned back to the tunnel mouth. Once there, he handed the coil of rope to the bandits at the door. They dragged their unfortunate fellow out of the tunnel, passed him up out of the excavation.

Doc returned to the tunnel. Sticky blood pooled on the floor. He walked as carefully as he could until he reached the spot where the bandit fell. He stopped short of the text on the wall, uncertain about the trap that killed the bandit. He tested the floor ahead for a trip plate then used the pole to check for tripwires. Nothing. He stepped forward, repeated the process. Still nothing. Another step. He could read the inscription now.

He extended the torch. The letters glittered in the wall—bronze inlaid into the stone. Something else caught his eye. Just in front of the inscription, a seam between bricks looked different, wider than it should be. Doc squinted at the thin crack; he thought he saw a glint inside. He froze, studied everything around him: walls, floor, ceiling.

He didn't see anything, but he knew this was where the bandit stood when the trap went off. Doc extended the pole to touch the floor, right in front of his feet. He slid it forward slowly. The tip caught on something; he knelt down to look. As he did, the pole slipped further forward. Swish. Bronze flashed above his head; had he been standing, it would have hit his neck. He ducked without thinking. He turned his attention back to the tip of the pole; it lodged on the lip of one of the floor stones. The paver lifted half an inch from the one where he knelt. Doc nudged the floor stone again; another swish and flash. This one he expected. He stared at the crack in the wall, pressed the stone a third time. A bronze sword scythed out of the thin gap—the blade that decapitated the bandit.

Doc kept low and experimented with the pole. The floor stone was loose; any motion set off the trap. Like a tripwire, but harder to avoid. He called for assistance; two bandits came up the tunnel, flinching at every shadow or sound. He explained what he needed: split logs roughly the width of the tunnel, planks half again longer than the floor stones.

He laid one log, flat side down, across the tunnel just before the trigger stone. He tossed the other just past the trigger, used the pole to square it up. He laid the planks over the logs, making a bridge over the trigger plate.

He stood, started across the bridge, then paused. He knelt again and used the pole to test the plate past the trigger. The fix held; no trap sprung, even when he hit it with the stick. He stepped across the bridge and continued down the tunnel.

He could now read the bronze letters inscribed in the wall: a passage from an obscure Latin epic, describing how the hero fended off thieves. Odd to see that here.

Or maybe not—the hero used his sword to decapitate the bandits who attacked him. Oblique, to be sure, but a warning to those who knew what to look for. And a hint—the other traps would not be marked as traps, but there would be something to alert those who knew what to look for. If Titianus's warning was correct, this would be the bronze trap. At least three more traps remained.

Doc extended the torch down the hall; bronze letters glittered in alternating blocks down each side. Titianus mentioned four traps—bronze, earth, sky, and fire. The sword was the first, the bronze trap, next to the inscription about swords.

He looked down the hall again—at least a dozen more blocks of letters glittered along the wall.

# Chapter seven

Margaret roused the cartographers at noon. "I know we are all tired. We must persevere; Dr. Carambo and Dr. Zseszky are counting on us. Get some food, gather your strength, and prepare to march once again." She sought out Mickey. "Mr. Charles, a moment, please. I wish to make use of your geological knowledge before we move ahead."

Mickey nodded. He pulled a slab of dried beef from his pack and began to gnaw on it. He and Margaret strolled out of the shelter of the tree; she pointed toward the river.

"How much did you see of this side of the river last night, Mr. Charles? Do you know where we are?"

Mickey shrugged. "It was pretty dark. I'm not sure how far down the river we came. Why?"

"How much did you look at the maps of this side of the valley, Mr. Charles? Do you remember the lay of the land here?"

Mickey chewed his jerky and thought. "I know there's a stretch where the river flows pretty close to the valley wall, and the wall's pretty steep. Other than that, it's flat most of the way."

Margaret nodded. "You are correct. We need to discern whether we landed above or below that section of the valley wall."

"Why? Even if we are below it, there's a nice flat stretch of bank there. We can just march along the river for a while."

"No, Mr. Charles, we cannot. We must stay out of sight of the road and the basmachi. They must think we fled to Dushanbe; if they knew we were headed toward Daroot-Korgon, we would most certainly be captured or killed."

The geologist contemplated the revelation. "I think we can traverse the cliff, but it will be tough—and slow. Isn't there any other way?"

Margaret shook her head. "Crossing the cliff is the only way to reach Daroot-Korgon and find our missing members. I want you to contemplate a method for crossing the cliff while we march today."

Mickey raised his eyebrows and whistled. "You don't ask for much, do you?"

They marched through forest for an hour. The cartographers could hear the river and occasional sounds of activity from the opposite bank but saw no one.

The topography changed from the flat river valley to the steeper valley by mid-afternoon. Margaret kept them to the trees, even as the going became difficult. The terrain went from level to gentle slopes to steep ridges.

Margaret herself slipped first; her boot lost traction in loose gravel. She pitched herself forward, landing on hands and knees.

Mickey rushed to her side. "Are you all right, Margaret? Anything hurt?"

She struggled to her feet, using a sapling for balance. "I am uninjured, Mr. Charles. Just a bit of loose footing." She raised her voice to be heard by everyone. "Please, everyone, gather round as best you can."

One by one, the cartographers worked their way to Margaret and Mickey. Davis had hiked at the rear; he arrived last. He looked up at Margaret; the steep slope put his head in a position just below Margaret's waist. "All present, Margaret. What's the good word?"

She smiled with regret. "I am afraid I only have bad words, Mr. Davis. There is no safe path through the next mile or so. In order to remain concealed, we must traverse a steep section of the valley wall. Mr. Charles will be our mountaineering expert for the next few hours."

Mickey took a slight bow. "Bad news, folks. There's not much we can do here. I'll take the lead and rope off as much as I can. Everyone, go slow and careful; take your time, and keep a hand on something as much as you can."

Ace raised a hand. "Why don't we rope together? That way, if someone falls, we've got 'em safe and sound."

Mickey shook his head. "No good. It's worse to rope together—when one person falls, it jerks the line. The jerk usually pulls the second person off balance. With two people falling, the third doesn't have a chance. Then we've got a full disaster on our hands—like dominoes. Everyone falls together, boom, boom, boom. I'll go first and do my best to keep a rope with a fixed end available for everyone."

The geologist took two coils of rope. He tied one end of the first to his waist; the other end he fixed to a tree where the team gathered. He handed the tail of the second rope to Davis, then slung it over his shoulder.

As Mickey walked, he played out the rope that Davis held. Ace managed the slack in the line tethering Mickey to the tree, preventing tangles from tripping him up. His progress was slow; more than once, his foot slipped in the dry, loose soil of the hillside. His steps were sure, though; he never fell.

At last, Mickey made it to the end of the rope, then tied Davis's end fast to a tree there.

"Ace—untie the rope, coil it up, and bring it this way. Keep a grip on my rope in case you slip."

The pilot worked his way across the slope, one step at a time. With the rope to help him balance, Ace crossed faster than Mickey. He arrived with the untethered line and gave it to the geologist.

Mickey turned to the team behind him. "Next up! Come on now, one at a time. Everybody over here."

With that, Mickey lashed the rope around his waist to the tree, then started forward again. Ace realized Mickey would have the second rope ready when the team finished with the first.

They covered a mile that way, Mickey moving one rope ahead while the rest crossed behind them. The hill was steep but covered with trees. The cartographers moved slowly but stayed safe.

Everything changed when the trees ran out. Mickey stopped at the edge of a patch of scree five hundred yards wide. Fifty yards uphill loomed a steep cliff of bare stone. At the foot of the cliff, stretching down to the river, they faced a bare slope covered with loose rocks.

Mickey squatted in the trees, out of sight of the river. Once the team assembled behind him, he spoke. "Two problems. First, the slope itself." He pointed at the stone. "That scree is loose shale sitting on bare rock. It's tough enough to cross anyway—one wrong move and the whole thing comes down." He held up two fingers. "Second, there's no cover—no way to cross without being seen. Maybe, if we're lucky, they won't be watching and we can cross unnoticed."

Ace raised an eyebrow. "And if we're not lucky?"

Mickey shrugged. "Depends on how unlucky we get. Maybe we cause a landslide and the basmachi notice. Maybe we cause a landslide and all get killed. Maybe they see us, get a sniper across the river, and we're sitting ducks."

Ace made a low whistle.

Davis tossed a rock downslope. "What if we crossed at night? We'd have darkness to cover us."

"Ha!" Mickey grinned. "Crossing scree is bad enough in the daylight. Crossing at night would get us all killed." He paused and thought. "No, not all of us. Just the first to step out there. The rest would stay back here in the trees and wait for daylight."

Margaret gazed at the river. "What are the chances the basmachi are watching this patch? Would they really monitor out a scree slope on the uninhabited side of the river just to make sure we don't use it?"

"That's not a bad point." Davis wore a thoughtful expression. "They didn't see us land on this side, and we hid the boats. They most likely think we went to Dushanbe, or further down the river. They don't know we are going upriver, or why. There's a reasonable chance we could cross without being seen."

Mickey ran a hand over his face. "We could take the risk, but we need to be smart about it. No bright colors—Verity, hide your red scarf. Everyone wear gray or brown if you have it. Take off your watches, too, and your other jewelry. If anything catches the light and makes a sun flare, they might notice."

The cartographers removed their jewelry and bright clothing; they looked each other over for things they might have missed.

Mickey stood in the shade of a large tree and examined the slope with binoculars. After an age, he lowered the binoculars and scrambled up the hill to the base of the cliff. The geologist took out the binoculars and searched the slope again. Next, he examined the cliff itself, running a hand over the stone and looking at its texture. He tied a rope to a tree next to him and tossed the end down. At last, he called to the team.

"Up here, everybody. Our safest crossing will be here next to the wall. I think I can drive in some pitons to tie the line off. Those will help.

"I also think we should rest here tonight and make the crossing in the morning. The entire slope will be in shadow; the darkness will help hide us, at least a little."

Margaret nodded. "You all heard Mr. Charles. It's a cold camp here tonight, then we cross the rock field in the morning." Everyone grumbled but obeyed her charge. They settled in for a restless night.

Dawn bathed the far side of the river in golden light when Margaret roused the team. The sun remained out of sight behind the ridge; the deep shadow concealed the slope.

Mickey drove a piton into the cliff face. He made a rope fast to it. He tied a rope to the piton, put another coil of rope over his shoulder, then started walking.

His progress was slow. He paused to consider each step. A few times, he placed his foot, drew it up, put it elsewhere. At last, he reached the end of the rope and drove in another piton. He tied the second rope to the new pin and made himself fast.

Mickey turned and called to Ace. "You're good to cross. Move one at a time, and go slow.

The pace was excruciating. Margaret watched the traverse with concern. The line between sun and shadow across the river marched ever closer to them; she prayed everyone would be across before the sunlight reached their position.

They covered four hundred yards without incident; Margaret thought two more rope-lengths remained before they reached the shelter of trees.

Then disaster struck.

Mickey placed a foot on a stone that felt stable. He put his weight on it and stepped forward; the rock slipped, then gave way. He tottered for a moment, unbalanced. His foot slipped farther, and Mickey went down.

He made a dive uphill, getting his weight flat on the slope with his feet pointing toward the river.

Rocks bounced and tumbled down the hill; each strike loosened a few more stones.

Mickey himself slid down the hill on his back. Margaret realized he had dropped the rope—Mickey could not stop himself.

She wanted to scream, cry out, something—but she didn't dare. The landslide would be bad enough; shouting would confirm their presence to the basmachi.

Mickey managed to steer his slide somehow. He slid into a tree, wrapped his arms around it. His slide stopped.

Margaret took a deep breath; she realized she hadn't breathed while Mickey slid down the slipe. She looked at the rocks around him—the rockslide had also stopped.

Ace called out to Mickey. His voice was louder than usual, but not a shout. "Mickey—hey, Mick, buddy. You alright?"

Mickey looked out across the river, then turned to face upslope. "I'm good. That could have been a hell of a lot worse."

Ace laughed. "Any landing you can walk away from. Want me to come down with a rope?"

Mickey shook his head no. "Get everyone safe, then come down even with me through the trees."

Margaret looked at the situation again. The shadow line had reached Mickey's position; it would soon hit the top of the slope. "Continue, please, Mr. Barrett. We must get everyone out of sight without delay.

Ace placed the rope Mickey had been working with, then another. The second rope ended at a patch of bare stone thirty feet across; everyone crossed it without difficulty and got into the forest.

The sun continued its march. Ace and Verity rested under the trees when the sun broke over the top of the cliff. Margaret was crossing the last section of the slope while Davis remained out on the rope.

"I suppose this will have to do," said Margaret. "Two exposed during the crossing is poor, but it's better than five."

Ace scrambled down the hill to get closer to Mickey. "How you doing out there, hoss? Need anything?"

Mickey chuckled. "Thirsty. I've been sitting in the sun all this time. I think we're safe, though. I've kept one eye on the river and road—there's nothing there. At least, I haven't seen anything."

"You give any thought to how you are going to get over here?"

Margaret put a hand on Ace's upper arm. "Mr. Barrett, please. Voices do carry in this air." She spoke in a whisper.

Ace shrugged. He turned to face Margaret and spoke in a stage whisper. "Just how do you expect me to talk with Mick, Maggie? Semaphore? Telegraph? I bet stringing wires is louder than our little chat."

Margaret made a sour face. "Please, just keep your voice down." She turned toward Mickey and made a shrugging gesture, then pointed both index fingers at him. Her meaning was clear enough: do you need anything over there?

Mickey nodded his head. He signed wrapping something around his shoulder, then mouthed one word: rope. Margret nodded. She slid a coil of rope off her shoulder and held it up.

Mickey gave a thumbs up. He pointed at Margaret and mimed tying a knot around a tree. She secured one end of the rope around a tree and looked back at Mickey. He gestured at Margaret and made a throwing motion, then a gimme motion with both hands.

Margaret handed the coil of rope to Ace. "I am not much for sports, Mr. Barrett. I fear my best throw would come nowhere near reaching Mr. Charles. Would you do the honors?"

Ace chuckled. "With pleasure. I started throwing ropes when I was just a sprout back in Texas." He took the coil from Margaret. He checked it for tangles, then laid it on the ground. He knotted the free end around a rock. He stepped out of the trees and started swinging the stone around his head, gradually playing out more rope. At last, he gave a flick of his wrist and sent the rock soaring toward Mickey. The line played out, and the stone came to rest—thirty yards short of the geologist.

Ace scowled. Mickey smiled and put both thumbs up: good job. The geologist now pointed at Ace, to his own eyes, then downslope. Ace shook his head and shrugged. What? Mickey made the same motions again. He also pointed to Ace and Margaret, cupped his hands around his eyes like binoculars, and pantomimed looking at the road: see if the coast is clear. Ace and Margaret both nodded. Ace drew out his binoculars and started scanning the other side of the river. When he felt satisfied no one watched, he gave a thumbs-up to Mickey.

Mickey exited the shelter of his tree slowly, moving with both hands and feet on the ground. His movements were slow, deliberate. The slope was steep and slick here; he kept three points on the ground at all times. He often rejected a hand- or foothold; three times, his grip slipped anyway. He went both up and across the slope, hoping a slip wouldn't drop him past the rope.

It took twenty minutes for him to cross the slope; when he did, the end of the rope was ten yards down the hill. He went down with the same deliberation. At last, he reached the rope and tied it around his waist.

He moved faster once he was tied off but still took his time. Ace coiled in the slack, bit by bit until he reached out and grabbed Mickey's hand.

Mickey gave a huge sigh. "That was close. Let's stow the rope and make some tracks. If anybody did see us, they can be up here pretty quick."

⁓

"Mr. Charles, are you all right? We must examine you at once. If only we had Dr. Carambo…." Margaret's sentence trailed off. Tears glistened in her eyes. "I only meant that—"

Mickey cut her off. "I'm fine, Margaret. And we'll get Alicia back—her and Doc Z both. I'm sound as a silver dollar. Come on—we've got miles to make yet before we rest."

Margaret smiled and nodded. "Mr. Davis, what route do you suggest?"

Davis thought for a moment. "The soldier in me says we stick to the trees, keep under cover. I don't want the basmachi to see us and come over here. The city boy says we should get closer to the water where we can make good time." He shook his head. "I don't know. Anybody else? Mickey—you've spent a lot of time hiking in mountains, right? What do you think?"

Mickey stood, hands on hips, staring at the river and the hills in turn. "Hills are slow, and there's danger up here. The basmachi are worse, and we won't make any kind of time at all if we get ourselves killed. I vote for the hills."

Margaret nodded. "Two undecided, one vote for the hills. Miss Hester, your thoughts?"

Verity, still sitting beneath a tree, made a sour face. "I vote for the best hotel in Samarkand, if I can. But since that's out of the question, I'm with Mickey. Slow and alive beats fast and dead every day of the week."

"It's settled, then." Margaret was back in expedition leader mode, decisive and efficient. "We stay in the trees as much as we can. Mr. Charles, if you will, please lead us up the valley."

Mickey was the natural choice to lead the team through this challenge. He grew up on the northern Rocky Mountains; blazing a trail through the foothills of the Pamirs came as naturally to him as breathing.

Mickey had a knack for finding game trails leading in the right direction. The terrain was less challenging than the previous day, but the geologist set a brutal pace.


"Ahh!" Mickey heard a sharp shout behind him—almost a scream. He stopped, spun around. Margaret stood thirty yards behind him, also looking back. Davis was fifty yards further back, almost lost in the trees. He stooped over something—Verity.

Mickey dropped his pack, dashed back to check on Verity.

Verity crouched on all fours, gasping for breath; tears streamed down her face. Davis knelt over her, murmuring encouragement into her ear.

"What happened, V? Are you OK?" Blood pounded in Mickey's ears—he feared the worst for her.

Verity swallowed, loud enough for Mickey to her. "Nothing—nothing happened. I just can't go on. The pack, the pace, these hills—it's all too much for me."

Mickey didn't know what to do—what good could they do if everyone got walked to death before they reached Daroot-Korgon? But if they arrived too late—what then?

Margaret reached the team. Davis stood, dropped his pack, faced Mickey and Margaret. "I was right behind her—I saw the whole thing. She's been struggling with the pace for a while. She's exhausted. I saw her stumble—just trip over her own feet, like she's too tired to lift 'em. I've seen it before, in basic in the army. A guy—a girl, here, I guess—a girl gets worn out, feet feel too heavy. She couldn't lift 'em enough and went down on all fours.

Nothing a few days' rest won't cure."

Margaret nodded. "We haven't got days to rest, I fear. We do have to-night. We will make a cold camp here. No fire—I don't want to give the basmachi any help if they are looking for us. Bedrolls only. It's hardtack and dried beef for dinner. Everyone, eat and rest for the evening. We'll start as early as we can in the morning."

For the next two days, they marched at a slower pace. Margaret insisted Verity stay near the front, even having the assistant take the lead much of the time. Verity hiked slower than the others; putting her at the front of the party kept everyone marching at a sustainable pace. Mickey enjoyed the easier pace; it gave him time to observe—geology, plant life, even wildlife.

Early on the third day, they passed through a coulee between two ridg-es—the valley of a creek that fed the main river. Thick brush choked the bottom of the coulee; Mickey couldn't see much farther than the end of his arms. He ducked low to crawl under an overhanging limb too thick to move. The geologist saw a flash of yellow about six feet ahead, low to the ground. The creature dashed away before he got a good look.

It was big—maybe the size of a deer, but lower to the ground. His in-stinct said cougar, but that was ridiculous—no cougars lived in the Pamirs. None for, what, five thousand miles?

"Davis, Margaret—you both know these hills. Are there cats here? Any-thing we need to watch out for?"

"Don't ask me," said Davis. "I can handle politics, bandits, corrupt mer-chants, that kind of thing. Identifying wildlife is out of my league."

Margaret knew more. "Of course, tigers and leopards are native to most of Asia, from lowland swamps to the foothills of the Tibetan plateau. I be-lieve tigers have grown scarce here, but leopards are still about. At least here in the river valleys, up to perhaps ten thousand feet of altitude. Above that the snow leopard—"

Mickey interrupted. "Leopards are yellow, right? How big are they?"

Margaret sighed. "They are predominately yellow, with black spots. In this region—hmm. I'm not certain of the weight, but they are the size of a large dog. Perhaps a bit heavier, but shorter—lower to the ground, and longer. Why do you ask?"

Mickey chuckled without humor. "Because I just saw one. I thought cou-gar at first, but your description fits a leopard perfectly. I think he was just laid up in the shade here and didn't like us strolling by."

They reached the edge of the thicket; everyone stood and gathered together.

Verity shivered. "Are leopards dangerous? Should we be worried?"

Mickey shrugged. "Don't know. My only big cat experience is cougars in the Rockies back home. People say they're shy, but that undersells it. Paranoid might be a better word. I've only seen a couple, and then for the blink of an eye while they run."

Margaret cleared her throat. "There are instances of leopards preying on humans, but they are rare, and localized."

Verity raised an eyebrow. "Localized?"

"A single cat develops a taste for humans and preys upon them repeatedly. I believe there have only been a handful of cats that have done so, but those cats have each killed a great number—"

Ace cut her off with a glare. "What Maggie means to say is that it's rare for leopards to attack people, and when they do, it's focused on one town. We'll be fine, I'm sure."

"Hmm, yes, Mr. Barrett is correct." Margaret bowed her head a fraction of an inch. "This leopard is not likely a man-eater, and we have nothing to fear. We may proceed without concern."

They reached the steep bank on the far edge of the coulee. Ace located a trail leading out of the ravine. Ace scrambled up the steep bank first, without his pack. He lowered a rope to pull up his backpack. He untied the bag then fastened the rope to a tree. As he tied the rope off, Ace thought he saw a flash of yellow in the distance. Just a beat; he wasn't sure he had really seen something.

The rest of the team used the rope to assist their climb. The going was easier here; the thicket ended at the bank. Beyond the coulee, the ridge sloped upward at a modest incline. They were in pine forest once again. They could see farther than in the creek bottom, but trees still limited their vision.

Ace directed the team as they prepared to move out. "Mickey, why don't you take point with Verity for a while. Margaret and Davis, y'all go next. I'd like to ride the drags for a while."

"'Ride the drags,' Mr. Barrett? Whatever do you mean?" Margaret asked.

"It's an old cowboy term," said Ace. "It means I'll take the back end of the line for a while."

Margaret shrugged. "If you wish. Is there any reason for your request?"

Ace pursed his lips and let out a slow breath. "No particular reason. I'd just like to watch over everybody for a while."

Verity looked at Ace with hooded eyes. "This is the first time you haven't charged to the front, Ace. Are you expecting some action back here?"

Ace shrugged, looked away. "I'd just like to be at the back, is all. Everybody keep tight together. Let's move out." He watched the group start up the hill, unslung the rifle from his shoulder, and followed.

Three times that day, Ace caught a glimpse of yellow in the trees. Twice he thought he heard a quiet footstep.

Shadows stretched long when they stopped for dinner. Margaret glared at the rifle in Ace's hand. "Are doing a spot of hunting, Mr. Barrett? Or perhaps the sling is broken?"

Ace shook his head. "It's that cat, Margaret. He's following us, and I want to be ready."

"Don't be silly, Mr. Barrett." Margaret glared at him, arms crossed over her chest. "The leopard is most certainly not tracking us. He is most likely miles away by now; we have nothing to fear."

"Sling up your rifle, Ace," said Davis. "You're more likely to shoot one of us than the cat. Besides, we don't want to risk a gunshot—the noise might bring the basmachi to this side of the river to investigate."

Ace scowled. "Fine, I'll sling the rifle—but everybody sticks together. That cat is stalking us, I'm sure of it." He picked up a hatchet and walked to the edge of the clearing where the cartographers sat. He chopped down a sapling low to the ground. He worked his way up the small trunk, trimming the side branches. He cut the top of the tree to create a pole about eight feet tall. The pilot drew his bowie knife and lashed it to the end of the stick, making a crude spear.

"Really, Ace? You going to chuck that thing at this mystery cat?" Davis grinned.

Ace glared at Davis. "I've seen this movie before. The cat's out there. It wants us. I think it's going to come at us in the dark, and I want to be ready."

"Come on, Ace. Don't you have cougars down there on the Rio Grande? They are cowards—your cat is miles gone by now. I've never seen one that wasn't running away." Mickey shook his head.

"Sure, Mick, I've seen cougars turn tail and run. But this ain't a cougar, it's a leopard. I grew up on stories from the old vaqueros, the cowboys who spent their lives riding the chaparral and scrub brush. They talked about tigres—jaguars, in the U.S.A.—that would grab men out of camps in the night. Big yellow cats with spotted coats. I've seen it, too, one time. A cat killed my mule, then my horse, then tracked me. That's what worries me."

Mickey shook his head. "Old men trying to scare a kid, most likely. The other, with the horses—you just had some bad luck, nothing more. Try not to stick anybody in the dark with that thing."

They made a cold camp. Ace made sure there were no thickets close by. As they began to take out bedrolls, Ace directed their arrangement. "Make a star shape—heads to the center, feet pointing out. That way, if the cat grabs you, you might have a chance to yell. And put your backpack at your feet; maybe we'll get lucky and he'll grab the bag instead of you."

Davis and Mickey scoffed but did as instructed. Verity and Margaret also obeyed. Ace refused to lay in the star; instead, he sat with his back to a tree trunk, spear in hand.

Night sounds drifted on the air; insects buzzed, frogs croaked. A night bird gave a monotonous, whistling call. The four sleepers lay still; someone snored softly. Moonlight flooded the clearing where they slept. Ace sat, one hand on the spear, and peered onto the shadows under the trees. His eyelids grew heavy.

Ace's head jerked up with a start—he had drifted off. Something was different. What was it? All his senses were alert, striving to detect—what?

He realized then the night had grown quieter. Off to the left—no insect sounds over there. Was something moving through the trees? He strained his eyes—a shape moved in the shadows. Ace drew up his feet, lifted himself into a crouch. He still saw nothing. He gripped the spear; the remains of a small branch dug into his palm.

The silence drew nearer. There—in the blackness under a tree, Ace thought he saw a movement. He tensed, ready to spring. A shadow flowed from beneath a tree. It charged with incredible speed toward Verity's sleeping form, then the leopard pounced.

Ace leaped into action. He surged forward—the moonlight revealed the leopard, claws extended into a black mass, fangs bared. The cat yanked the object toward its head, bit down. Ace lunged. He sunk his spear into the cat's side; it recoiled from his thrust, freeing the spear point. The leopard spun to face him, snarling.

Ace thrust his spear at the cat; the beast swatted the point away. It jumped forward a few feet; Ace retreated, spear at the ready. The cat snarled again.

Something flashed in the darkness and hit the cat in the flank. The cat spun to face the new threat.

Ace stabbed again, plunging the spear into the cat's ribs. It twisted back around to face him; this time, the spear stuck in the cat. It was wrenched from Ace's hands. He scrambled back, stumbled, almost fell. A paw lashed out; his leg burned. Claws dug into his calf, pinning him in place. The cat yanked back; the pain grew worse. He saw another flash—a stick appeared in the cat's side.

Not a stick—a hatchet. Someone was throwing hatchets at the cat. It turned again to face the hatchet thrower. This spin brought the haft of the spear back around to Ace. He made a desperate grab for the shaft. His hands closed around the rough wood; Ace lunged forward, further impaling the cat on the bowie knife blade.

Ace got his feet under him and kept pushing. He knocked the cat off balance then used the spear to pin it to the ground.

Ace spoke through gritted teeth. "It's down! I've got it pinned with the spear—somebody, do something, quick." Another flash in the moonlight—a hatchet struck the cat in the head with a dull thump. It growled, shook its head, and grew still.

Ace leaned on the spear, still pinning the cat to the ground. He panted, head bowed. His knees buckled; he collapsed on top of the cat.

Verity rushed to his side. "Ace, oh Ace—are you hurt?" She knelt over him and looked up at the others. "He's hurt. I think the cat got him." Tears glistened on her cheeks in the moonlight.

Ace lifted himself to a sitting position. "I'm not hurt. At least, I'm not hurt bad. He clawed me a little, is all. Is everyone else alright? Did he get his teeth into anyone?"

Verity wiped her cheeks on a sleeve, then straightened her back. "I'm fine, thank you. The cat grabbed my pack, but missed me. Anyone else?"

Margaret and Davis stared at the downed cat, stunned by the sudden fury. Mickey flipped a hatchet in his hand. "I'm good. We used to play around as kids, throwing hatchets into trees and stuff. We talked about fighting Indians and outlaws and the like, but I never believed it would actually be useful."

Ace pulled himself back to his feet. He nodded at Mickey. "Thanks, Mick. Your tomahawks made the difference between me getting the cat and the cat getting me."

Margaret was all business now. "Mr. Barrett, did you say the cat clawed your leg? We must clean it at once. Guild guidelines say scratches from a wild cat turn septic in short order. If we don't clean it, you could lose you leg—or worse."

Davis rustled around in his backpack and pulled out a flashlight. "We've got to risk a little light to take care of your leg, Ace." He shone the light on a large rock at the edge of the clearing. "Have a seat here and let Margaret take a look."

Ace limped to the rock and sat. He extended his wounded leg; the light revealed his pants were in bloody tatters. "Damn," he said. "These were my favorite pants." He smiled without humor, teeth gritted.

Margaret set to work on the leg; three parallel scratches ran down the outside of his right calf. Two were an inch deep; the third showed the glistening white of his shin bone. Ace gritted his teeth and swore as she cleaned the wounds. The iodine disinfectant she carried burned worse than the leopard's claws.

The worst portion came when Margaret sutured the wound. "I'm so sorry, Mr. Barrett," said Margaret. "I know I'm not the healer you need. If only we had Dr. Carambo."

Ace chuckled through the pain. "If we had Alicia, we'd be safe in a camp, with a fire. And we could have used a rifle on that rascal instead of a spear."

Margaret finished with the stitches then bound a bandage around the leg. "I wish you could stay off your feet for a while, but I fear that isn't in the cards, is it?" She sighed. "I hoped for so much for this expedition. I wanted to make the first woman-led expedition from the Cartographers Guild a success and here we are—two kidnapped, chased by nationalists, attacked by a leopard…." Her voice trailed off.

Ace forced another laugh. "It ain't so bad, Maggie. I've took worse scratches off chaparral thorns back at home. I'll be fine." He turned to Davis. Hey, could you fetch me my spear? I need my knife back, and I'd like to have a good stick in hand tomorrow. You know, if we need a spear. Not to walk or nothin.'"

They rested as well as they could for the rest of the night, but no one truly slept. As soon as the eastern sky grew gray, everyone prepared to move.

Ace took the lead. "Slowest first, ain't that the rule? I'll wager dollars to donuts I'm the slowest today. My leg is a little stiff." He set off, hobbling. He used the spear shaft as a crutch, helping him balance as he hiked through the trees.

~

The expedition did not travel far the next day. Ace hobbled along slowly but couldn't rush. Twice, he bled through the bandage. Each time, Margaret insisted on stopping to dress and clean the wound.

The second time, she washed it with stream water. "It doesn't seem swollen or feverish," she said. I can't tell if it is red or not; the iodine colors the skin too much. It doesn't feel hot, either. That is a good sign. I think we have escaped infection."

Ace made a growling noise in the back of his throat. "It hurts enough as it is, Margaret. Do you have to go poking at it?"

"It is this, or risk infection, Mr. Barrett. I will not have you dying out here if I can help it. Are you fit to continue, or should we leave you here and proceed alone?"

Ace used the pole to lift himself to his feet. "I can walk," he said. "I'll walk any one of you here into the ground, if I have to. And I'm not going to miss out on helping Doc and Alicia. We're a team, and I'll be damned if I let a little scratch like this stop me. Come on, let's go." He set off once more, leading the expedition toward Daroot-Korgon.

On the fourth day, they began searching for the roadblock that stopped their previous effort to reach Daroot-Korgon. The team marched lower in the woods, closer to the river. About once an hour, they stopped to scan the road with binoculars. At the fourth stop, around midday, Davis spotted the blockade.

"Look—there. The Basmachi built the barricade at the foot of that steep wall. I can't quite see from here; we need to move a little." They withdrew into the woods and repositioned a few hundred yards upriver.

Davis dropped his pack and pulled out his binoculars. "Wait here. If we are close to the basmachi blockade, I don't think all of us should try to go look. A single person is less likely to be noticed." The team assented; Davis slipped through the trees.

He heard the rebels before he saw them. Voices carried in the thin air. He dropped to all fours and crawled forward, careful not to be noticed. He slipped behind a deadfall tree and peered over.

He concealed himself only a hundred yards from the blockade but across a deep section of the river. Three Basmachi sat on top of the barricade, talking loudly.

Davis scanned the clearing between himself and the river; he needed to know if they stationed anyone on this side of the river. He saw nothing, heard nothing. Davis knew competent troops would have stationed sentries on this side of the river, hidden from view. Judging by the guards' behavior, he thought no sentries watched from this side of the river. He withdrew to report.

Margaret and Mickey thought the roadblock was half a day from Daroot-Korgon by road. They guessed the rough terrain and Ace's leg would double the time. The cartographers worked diagonally across the ridge, moving toward Daroot-Korgon and away from the river. Everyone agreed it would be safest to travel at a distance from the river. Once they climbed halfway up the ridge, they stopped ascending and marched straight across the slope toward the head of the valley. They made another cold camp in the forest; everyone hoped it would be their last.

They remained in the woods high on the valley wall when they stopped for lunch the next day. Ace sat on a log, injured leg held stiff in front of him. "Mick, Margaret, do you reckon we're close to the Daroot-Korgon ford? I wouldn't mind a break from this hiking."

Margaret considered for a moment. "That seems likely. Mr. Charles, Mr. Davis, I believe it is advisable for you two to scout the ford. We three will remain here while you examine it."

Mickey and Davis agreed; they left their packs and started down the hill. Verity and Margaret sat, quiet and alert; Ace stretched out on the ground to rest.

It surprised Verity to hear footsteps only half an hour later; she was more surprised when they came from further up ridge—the opposite direction from Daroot-Korgon.

"Margaret," she hissed. "Margaret, listen. Someone's coming. I don't think it's Davis or Mickey."

Margaret cocked her head to one side, intent on the footsteps. She put a finger to her lips, nodded. The expedition leader rose to her feet and faced the sound. She rested a hand on the butt of her pistol. She listened again, then drew the gun. She held it low at her side, pointed at the ground—but ready for action.

The footsteps drew closer, then stopped. A voice called out—first in Pamir, then in French. Margaret responded in kind; the only word Verity understood was 'ainglais.'

The man switched to English then. "Yes, I speak English. I mean you no harm—please, don't shoot!"

Margaret squared her shoulders and tucked the pistol behind her leg to hide it. Ace stayed on the ground, eyes closed, but rested his hand on the rifle by his side. Verity never carried a gun; she fidgeted with the leather and stone bracelet on her left wrist.

A man stepped into view. He was short and thin, wearing the wool robe and fur hat standard in the Pamirs; his were stained and tattered. His bald head and wispy white beard gave him an aged look, but his skin was smooth. He could have been forty or eighty.

He held his hands out, palms forward—the international gesture for don't shoot, I mean you no harm. He made eye contact with Margaret, then Verity; each time, he nodded acknowledgment.

"Greetings, friends. You may call me Zaldron. I am a—let us say I guard things better kept secret."

Margaret's face showed no expression. "Why are you here? State your business."

Zaldron gave a slight bow and smiled. "My business may coincide with yours. Perhaps you have come to Daroot-Korgon seeking after the two foreigners who have been brought here against their will?"

Margaret nodded. "Yes—yes, we have—"

Verity dismissed her with a wave. "Perhaps. What foreigners are you talking about?"

Margaret looked at Verity with surprise. "Miss Hester, what are you doing? This man could—"

Verity came close to Margaret. She faced Zaldron. "Please pardon us for a moment, sir. We must confer, briefly." Now she turned to Margaret and whispered. "We don't know this man. He could be a kidnapper, or a bandit or anyone. We need to play our cards close to our vest until we figure out his angle. Don't give anything away if you don't have to."

She turned back to Zaldron, smiling sweetly. "Forgive us. You said something about foreigners in Daroot-Korgon?"

Zaldron nodded. "Yes, a pair of foreign scientists have been brought to Daroot-Korgon by another foreigner. The two are a man and a woman. He is tall and thin, with white hair sticking out every way. He has been leading a dig on some ruins near Daroot-Korgon. The woman has dark hair with tight curls. She is a doctor of some sort; I am told she stopped an epidemic in Daroot-Korgon, and has treated quite a few other medical matters. Since you are coming in secret, I thought it likely you were associated with the two captives and not the others."

Margaret nodded. "Yes, that sounds like our friends." She glared at Verity, mouthed "he's a friend" at the research assistant. Back to Zaldron. "Please, be seated. Tell us what you can about our friends in Daroot-Korgon."

Zaldron gave an overview of the situation—how Titianus came with a gang of thugs to examine the ruins; how he brought in Doc Z to expedite the search; how the village headman demanded a doctor's addition as the price of cooperation.

"What can we do, then?" asked Margaret. "Can we approach Daroot-Korgon and bargain for our friends? Or sneak in and steal them back?"

Zaldron shook his head. "Neither is advisable. Daroot-Korgon is fortified and guarded against bandit attacks. Now Titianus has added to the guards. He has secured the ford and the road leading into town; you won't be able to enter openly or by stealth."

Verity rolled her eyes. "If we can't get in, how exactly can you help us?"

Zaldron smiled. "Because I know where Titianus will be going soon, and the route he will take. You can't get your friends out of Daroot-Korgon, but you can take them from Titianus on the road."

Verity glared at him. "How do you know this? And what's your angle here?"

"I know it because I have ears in the village; I know what he wants. Because I know what he wants, I know where he will go. And an 'angle'—I don't understand. What does this mean?"

Verity let out a small snort of laughter. "Your angle, your approach—why are you telling us? What do you get out of this?"

He smiled now and nodded. "I see. My angle"—he emphasized the word slightly—"is that I need help. I do not wish for Titianus to reach the place he wants to go. I need to stop him, and I cannot do this alone. I require your aid for it."

Verity shook her head. "You still didn't tell me your angle. You told us what you want, but not why. What's so important to you about stopping this Titianus guy? And why should we help you?"

He opened his mouth to speak; before he could, the cock of a pistol stopped him.

Davis and Mickey stood twenty feet away; Davis pointed a pistol at Zaldron.

Margaret jumped to her feet and stood between Zaldron and Davis. "Stop—Davis—don't shoot. This is Zaldron. He knows where Doctor Carambo and Doctor Zsezsky are being held. He thinks he can help us get them back."

Mickey looked from Davis to Margaret and back; he swallowed. "Okay, sounds good. Davis—put your hog leg away, please? Margaret says we're all friends here. Just take it easy, okay?"

Davis lowered the pistol. His eyes narrowed, his expression hard. "How do you know, Margaret? What makes you so sure?"

Ace opened his eyes. "I've been playing possum the whole time he's been here, Davis. My rifle has been in hand the whole time. I trust him—if I didn't, he'd already be gone."

Davis nodded, then holstered his pistol. "What's the plan?"

Zaldron pressed his palms together in front of himself and bowed. "I thank you for your trust. I must warn you—the way will be difficult. The easy path is guarded by Titianus and his men; we must walk a dangerous path to reach your friends. What is worse, winter is approaching. Once we are through, it is likely the only way back will be through Daroot-Korgon."

Ace interrupted. "You mean the way back is through Titianus."

"Just so." Zaldron nodded. "If you follow my path, you must succeed or die. Are you willing?"

Ace, Verity, Margaret, Davis, and Mickey stared at one another in silence.

Ace broke the silence. "We've faced down riots, the basmachi, rockslides, even killed a leopard with a spear. Doc and Alicia are part of this team. I'll do whatever it takes to get them back, come hell or high water."

Margaret nodded. "Cartographers stick together. I will not abandon members of my expedition while hope remains."

Mickey licked his lips. "I'm in, too. They'd do it for me."

Davis and Verity shared a look. Davis closed his eyes and tilted his head back. He drew in a long breath, then let it out slowly. "Well. I wouldn't be much of a fixer if I walked away from a little kidnapping, would I? I've got my business to think about. I'll go."

All eyes turned to Verity. She crossed her arms over her chest and glared, defiant. "I signed on to be a research assistant, not a pulp novel heroine. Still, I don't want to be left behind. I suppose forward is the only direction I can go."

Zaldron nodded. "Very good. Gather your things; I will lead you to the place where you can regain your companions."

# Chapter eight

Doc held the torch over his head. He brushed his fingers over the symbols carved into the door. His mouth hung open; he breathed slowly. He moved slowly, as if underwater. Doc knew he was the first person to see this door, to read these symbols, in over two thousand years.

The tunnel stretched only fifty yards; it had taken Doc two weeks to cross. He found six traps after the sword blade—pitfalls, a weight swinging from the ceiling, even lightning bolts that struck at anyone who passed. He noted that one, to come back and find the ancient batteries.

Doc found the traps, one by one, studied them, overcame them. He felt pride in his accomplishment—beyond the first bandit who rushed up the tunnel, no one had died; no one even got hurt.

Now he stood at the last door: a stone slab five feet wide and twice as high, carved with symbols from Roman mythology. He looked at the final set of bronze letters set into the wall, then at the door. The story inscribed in the wall was a myth more ancient than Rome itself—how the warrior twins navigated the underworld, how they retrieved the stolen cattle of the sun god, returned them to the earth. How the cattle came back with horns flashing with silver fire—the gift of magic, the magic behind the myths.

Seven traps in the tunnel—seven locks on the final door. Doc prepared to unlock the door; his hand shook. He tried to use his pole, a shorter stick, even a knife; nothing worked. Something in the door recognized the life force in his hands; only living flesh would activate the locks.

Or the final trap, if he guessed wrong.

One by one, he touched the symbols. The warrior twins riding horses. The twins reporting the theft of the sun cattle. The constellation they used to navigate. The mouth of the underworld. Crossing the river of fire. Driving the cattle home.

Doc winced as he reached for the last symbol—the sign for magic. If he guessed right, the door should open. If he were wrong—he shuddered. At least he probably wouldn't know if he got it wrong. There wouldn't be anything left of him.

He stretched out his hand to the final sign, then paused. This is it, he thought. He closed his eyes then took a deep breath; he pushed his hand forward. The stone felt cool beneath his fingers.

Then—nothing. Doc opened one eye, then the other. He started to breathe again. He heard no sound; nothing moved. Shadows flickered in the torchlight.

He withdrew his hand from the door. He heard a whuff. The torch winked out; blackness engulfed him. Doc froze. He didn't know whether to duck, jump, or flee.

A faint glow lit the door in front of him. The symbols he had touched produced a pearly light. Dim at first, only enough to show the seven signs, but it grew. Soon the tunnel shined as bright as day, then brighter. Doc shielded his eyes. The light vanished; Doc blinked, seeing spots. He heard the grate of stone against stone.

The darkness vanished again, replaced by a soft golden glow. The door opened.

Beyond the door, he found a circular chamber about thirty feet in diameter. A single pillar over a yard thick stood at the center of the room. The carvings covered the column; the outer wall displayed alternating shelving sections and carved panels.

Six large pots sat in a circle midway between the outer wall and the pillar. They were four feet tall with a wide mouth and narrow base; Doc recognized them as storage jars for clay tablets.

He looked up. The ceiling was inset with a geometric pattern of glowing metal. Strange; another mystery to explore later.

Doc looked around the rest of the room, wary. The hall contained a lethal array of traps—would the room be the same?

He looked first at the doorway—no obvious tripwires or triggers. Doc squatted, brushed his fingers over the threshold and the floor beyond. Satisfied with his security, Doc stood and stepped forward.

He heard a shout from the mouth of the tunnel. He shook his head to clear his mind. He shouted back over his shoulder. "What was that?"

Titianus shouted again. "Well? Have you found anything?"

Doc paused for a moment. "I'm through the door, but the room beyond could be trapped. I'm looking for traps now."

"Very well. Be cautious, and touch nothing you find. Alert me as soon as you know it is safe."

Doc sighed. He continued his examination of the room. He made his way to the first jar—empty. Doc worked his way around the room; all the jars were empty. The shelves, too, had been stripped bare; only scraps of paper and broken bits of pottery remained.

Convinced the room was safe, Doc started to make his way up the tunnel when he noticed something—the corner of a parchment protruding from beneath one of the library jars. He knelt to examine it. Was it a trap? Or had the Romans hidden something of value beneath the jar?

He stood. To check for a trap, Doc walked around to the opposite side of the jar. Using both hands, he gripped the mouth of the pot and prepared to tip it toward himself. If the jar had been trapped, it would likely strike toward the paper. He closed his eyes, turned his face away. Here we go, he thought. One, two, three, pull. The jar leaned forward and came to rest against his chest.

Nothing happened.

He opened one eye, then both. He could see the paper clearly now; the writing looked fresh despite its age. He went to the other side of the jar and pushed it away from himself. He used a toe to pull the parchment out from under the pot.

He looked at the page; it showed a magnificent map of the mountains. He recognized the river and the valley of Daroo-Korgon. He saw a town marked about where Dushanbe sat now—some things don't change. He examined the rest of the map; he located the outpost where the dig was located. It showed a route deeper into the mountains. Where the road ended, it said—how did that translate? House of the Jade Mask. He noticed some text next to the route shown from the outpost. This road is false, it said; use the waybill of Bereem to find the true road.

This parchment was priceless. Besides being evidence of Romans in central Asia, it purported to show the location of a legendary treasure. Everyone believed the mask to be fiction; to find it would upend the study of the ancient world. This parchment must be preserved, protected. He couldn't let Titianus get his hands on it.

How? Titianus would search him when he came up from the tunnel; his captor never let Doc leave unsearched. The parchment couldn't be left in the chamber, either; Titianus would examine the room in minute detail.

The traps—the only secluded places in the complex Titianus wouldn't touch. The swinging weight was the place. He could trigger the weight from a distance with the pole and tuck the map into the recess holding the weight. That would keep it from Titianus until he could plan the next step.

He looked around the chamber. Clear marks showed in the dust around the jar he had moved—a dead giveaway to Titianus. He examined a second jar; nothing lay under it. He went on to a third, nudged it with care. The weight was off; it moved stiffly. He looked at the floor around it—small slits surrounded the jar in a radial pattern. A trap. He looked at the remaining jars. Two were trapped, one safe. He examined the floor again—every pot showed his tracks. Much better.

Doc picked up the map with reverence and went to the tunnel to retrieve his pole. He started back to the surface, careful to avoid the traps. He paused at the swinging weight trap. He examined the wall, tracing his fingers over the panel concealing the killer weight. He squatted just behind the trigger, map in one hand and pole in the other.

He extended the pole to the pressure plate and pushed down. The roof opened, the weight swung down—a great stone hammer to strike down trespassers. It swung through a full arc, almost touching the ceiling at the other end. It came back his way; Doc lunged forward, laid the map on the swinging stone. He pulled his hand back and watched the stone draw up into the ceiling. He looked at the panel again—no sign of the map.

Doc walked back down to the chamber to examine the wall carvings and shelves. The pattern of sixes extended from the jars to the shape of the room itself. There were six sets of bookcases alternating with six carved panels. The panels showed people traveling—hiking through mountains, crossing rivers. On one tableau, the travelers visited an outpost matching the Daroot-Korgon site. That panel displayed a label incised into the stone: Departure of the Seekers from the Outpost of He-Yardim. He-Yardim must be the ancient name of this place. He realized that was the first panel; the rest showed the journey to the sixth panel.

The final showed them reaching a gate carved into a mountain. This panel also bore a label. It translated as Arrival of the Seekers at the House of the Jade Mask.

After examining everything in the chamber, Doc started out of the tunnel to report to Titianus.

Doc emerged from the tunnel, blinking in the sunlight. Titianus sprang from the chair where he waited and grabbed Doc's arm.

"Well? What did you find? What's behind the door?" He trembled with excitement.

"A library chamber," said Doc. "Shelves and six library jars. It's empty but for some trash; the imperials cleaned the chamber before they sealed it up.

Watch the jars, too. Three of them are trapped, I think."

Titianus recoiled. "Trapped? How do you know? Which ones?" Titianus feared the traps in the tunnel.

"I noticed slits in the floor around one jar. I think it's some kind of blade trap, but I'm not sure. Three show the slits, three don't. I could move the three untrapped jars a little; they are all free of the floor. The three trapped jars are connected to something, but I didn't explore too far."

Titianus nodded. We'll figure out the traps soon enough. What else did you find? Any inscriptions on the walls? Any carvings?"

Doc nodded; he told Titianus about the carvings and labels. As Doc described the different scenes, Titianus grew more and more excited. When Doc mentioned the House of the Jade Mask, the kidnapper grabbed Doc and hugged him.

"Oh, fortunate day—do you know what this means? Do you know what you have found? But how could you? The mask has been occluded, hidden from the world for four thousand years. This mask is one of the greater treasures of the empire! It is on a par with the sword Excalibur, the lost ark, the great cauldron. The greatest treasures of the empire were lost, hidden away below the earth; the only items remaining are lesser items, trifles not worth hiding. Yet what objects they are—crowns, scepters, diadems. The magic supporting and sustaining the oldest kingdoms of the earth is contained in those lesser items. To find the great jade mask—I will rule the world!" Titianus laughed like a drunk man, capered like a full.

He stopped suddenly, face grave. "You should not know those things. Forget I said them—burn the mask and the lost artifacts from your mind. Forget them, do you understand me? I cannot have outsiders with that knowledge.

"Come now, let me search you, then we'll quit early again today. I can't be too careful, you know."

Doc nodded, his mind a thousand miles away. "Hmm. Indeed, you cannot." Doc lifted his arms for the search. He paid no attention; he pondered how to retrieve the map and flee the valley before Titianus could stop him.

—◡

Alicia returned to the prison hut that night to find Doc already there. He sat slumped on one of the low beds, face buried in his hands. She smiled to see him; even with the long hours she worked as a doctor, Doc usually arrived much later than she did.

"Well, this is a treat," she said. "It's nice to see you home early. Are you in trouble or did you make a big find today?"

Doc looked up, eyes worried. "I found something. No—I found everything." He told her about the chamber, the carvings, the purported House of the Jade Mask.

"Fantastic! You have the key to the find of the century—this expedition will go down in history." Her eyes were bright with anticipation.

Doc shook his head. "No—Titianus has the key to the find of the century. He talked about the mask, about what he could do with it—then he got angry, told me to forget his speech. Forget the mask."

"So? You can just play along, wait 'til we get out of here—"

"No, Alicia. You don't understand—Titianus was angry I knew about the mask, about his desires. I think he's done with me—with us. Since I know his secret, I think he will have us killed soon."

The blood drained from her face. "We've got to run. We'll break out, head down the valley. We can follow the river—this is the same river that flows through Dushanbe, right? We just follow the river to Dushanbe and we're safe."

"Won't work. He's got guards on the trail down, the road to the river, the ford itself. We head that way and we're going to get caught for sure."

She scowled. "What then? We can't stay here—we're sitting ducks. He could have us executed in the morning."

Doc thought about the map hidden away in the tunnel. He thought about the legendary jade mask, the lost city high in the mountains.

"We go up—deeper into the mountains. There's a map I hid; we can beat him to the city and grab the mask ourselves."

Alicia gasped. "Up the valley? But we don't have any equipment for a trek like that. I can get us supplies to get back to Dushanbe, but going into the mountains? We'll never make it."

"I know—it's a desperate gamble. But our choices are to wait here to be executed, run the gauntlet of guards to Dushanbe, or take our chances in the hills. At least the last gives us a fighting chance."

She closed her eyes, pressed her fingers to the bridge of her nose. "I suppose you are right, but those mountains—we don't have much of a chance."

In the distance, a yeti wailed.

# Chapter nine

Zaldron insisted they wait for nightfall before moving. The afternoon dragged on and on. Margaret started by checking Ace's bandage then examined everyone's packs. Verity pulled out a deck of cards and practiced—something. Not quite magic, but close. She shuffled, re-shuffled, drew, cut, drew again. Her fingers had a life of their own. Ace slept; he only moved to growl at Margaret as she checked his bandage a second time. Mickey pulled a battered magazine from his pack and read. Zaldron sat with his back against a tree, eyes closed. His breath was slow and regular; it was hard to tell whether he slept or meditated.

Davis was a caged lion; he paced the woods, back and forth, looking at everything and nothing. He spoke to no one. He said nothing to Zaldron but orbited the old man, keeping close—but not too close.

The air grew cool; the sky went from cobalt blue to indigo to purple. Night birds and crickets started to sing; still, Zaldron did not move.

At last, he stood as if summoned by a bell only he could hear. "Please, friends, it is nearly time. Eat and drink; you will need your strength. He made a gathering motion with his hands—come on over, join me. Margaret came and sat; Verity woke Ace and helped him approach the sage. Mickey tucked away his book and followed. Davis approached last; he didn't sit, but leaned against a tree, watching.

Zaldron pulled dried meat from inside his quilted jacket. "Please, prepare yourselves. This climb is challenging in the best of conditions. The ridge is steep, and the footing poor. To climb it at night will be a feat worthy of tales."

Ace raised an eyebrow. "If it's so tough, why don't we climb it during the day? They won't see us through the tree cover."

Zaldron made an odd motion with his hand—he held it palm down and flicked his fingers a few times. It looked like shooing a fly. "No. The slope will be watched during the day. We must reach the top and cross over tonight while we cannot be seen. There is no other way."

"What about safety?" Mickey leaned his elbows on his knees, interested in the old man. "Do we need ropes or staffs?"

The same dismissive wave. "No ropes. We have little enough to tie them to. We can use staves and ropes for the trip down tomorrow. For the climb up, it will be better to use hands and feet together."

Mickey raised his eyebrows. "Hands and feet? How steep is this hill? Are we suicidal to climb it in the dark?"

The corners of Zaldron's mouth twitched just a bit. "Suicidal? No. The ridge can be climbed without equipment, even in the dark. It is not easy, but it can be done."

Davis clapped his hands twice. "Come on, people. It's time. If we are going to do this, we need to get to it. Let's go."

Zaldron bowed his head briefly. "Very well. Let us begin the climb. I will lead; the injured one should come next. My hasty friend, perhaps you will walk at the back? You can call out if you lose sight of me, or if someone in front of you has difficulty."

The climb was brutal; Margaret had never faced a task so hard. They found tolerable footing—loose dirt, but no slick rocks—but struggled with the steep grade. It was steeper than a staircase, and endless. The easy parts could be climbed on her feet. Many stretches came close to being as steep as a ladder; those required hands and feet.

Zaldron set a steady pace; it would have been a brisk walk on flat ground. On the steep hill, it was merciless. Worse than the speed was the relentless nature. He refused to stop or even slow; he insisted stopping on the slope meant death.

Margaret's legs burned—her thighs were on fire, her calves ached. Her shoulders ached from the pack. Still they climbed, up and up and up. She heard Verity cry out, a little exclamation of fear and frustration. Likely the research assistant had slipped and fallen.

"Enough. Gather here, near me." The sage spoke in a low voice, but everyone heard him. "Here, all of you, drink—just a sip. This will fortify you for the climb." He passed around a small earthenware jug.

Margaret took the jug and smelled it—a harsh floral odor with earthy notes. No tang of alcohol. She took a sip; the icy liquid burned on the way down. It scalded her tongue and her throat. She felt the ice first in her belly; from there, it spread throughout her body. Her legs still ached, but the burning cold dulled it, separated her mind from the pain.

She passed the jug to Verity. Zaldron faced her now, looked deep into her eyes. He touched her forehead with one finger and said a word. Charok? Sharod? She couldn't quite make it out. Once he said it, her mind focused on the sage. She must please him—she had no choice but to obey. Only Zaldron's will mattered; scaling the height, getting to the top before day-break—that was crucial.

She began to ascend again. Her legs still burned; her back still ached, yet she longed to move faster, higher. Zaldron commanded her to climb, so she would climb. The aches did not matter; the difficulty did not matter. Zaldron mattered; she would please Zaldron.

Margaret shook her head. Where did those thoughts come from? She looked around for her companions. It was too dark to see them, but she heard footsteps. They were with her still, climbing like machines.

Someone stumbled again, fell down. Margaret rushed to help—Verity lay prone. She had to get the woman back on her feet, get her to climb again. Zaldron willed it—Verity must climb.

There it was again. What made Zaldron's approval so important? She barely knew the man; she didn't owe him anything. She could rest if she needed to; Zaldron couldn't make her climb all night.

She slowed down; her head began to spin. Cramps gripped her legs. She could not continue.

Zaldron approached. Sadness filled his eyes. "My apologies, but this is necessary. I would not perform such an action otherwise." He touched her forehead again, said his strange word once more. The pains dulled; a desire to please Zaldron filled her.

The climb took on a dream-like quality. The doubts in her mind subsided; the aches and pains dimmed. There was no Margaret; only the climb mattered, and the sage she had to please. Time ceased to flow; the climb might have lasted minutes, or a hundred years.

The moon hung low in the sky when the cartographers reached the crest. They stepped over and descended a short distance—enough to hide them from observers in Dan Qui.

They slumped to the ground, exhausted. Zaldron stood before them like a pastor before his flock; he made a strange hand gesture and said something else.

The dream broke; Margaret's will was her own once again. The aches and pains from the climb flared throughout her body.

Zaldron bowed. "My sincerest apologies to all of you. Titianus uses magic to examine the slope facing Daroot-Korgon each morning; he would have detected us had we remained there. I used an ancient…technique…to assist you in the climb. I do not like to use it, but it was necessary in this case."

Mickey snorted. "An 'ancient technique'? You're going to tell us you used magic to hustle us up the hill?"

Zaldron made his "no" wave again. "I most certainly did not tell you that. I said an ancient technique. Your mind went to magic."

"Use whatever word you want. It's nonsense by any name. If it existed, somebody would have shown it—it would be captured in a lab somewhere."

Zaldron inclined his head to Mickey. "That is one opinion. Yet there are a score of ancient dynasties around the world that possess such items. These rulers swear they owe their power—and their longevity—to the influence of such techniques as these."

"Yeah, they say that." Mickey chuckled. "Of course they say that; everybody wants to claim ancient roots. But you notice nobody proves it? They never let anyone test these artifacts. A bunch of countries claim to have artifacts they never even show. It's all a bluff."

"Perhaps," said Zaldron. "But consider this—if you possessed an object of ancient magic that supported your power, would you allow others to examine it? What if they damaged it or broke its power? Or what if they stole it to use against you? No one who possesses such an artifact will ever allow it to be tested."

Mickey rolled his eyes but said nothing.

Dawn broke behind them. The sun cast a rosy glow on the distant peaks of the great mountain range; the lower mountains and foothills were still cloaked in shadow. No one had the energy to talk; they sat in silence, eating and watching the progress of sunlight over the mountains.

As the sun rose, successive crests were highlighted—snow turned pink with the dawn, then the purple of distant peaks. Next came mountains black with trees; at last were ridges green with pine.

Most of the group watched the show like a movie, enjoying the majesty of nature. Davis stared at the ridges, intent. He reached into his pack and rummaged around for a moment, then withdrew a folded piece of paper. He opened the document, spread it on his leg, and smoothed the creases with a careful hand.

He extended his arms to full length and held the map at the top and bottom. He looked at the paper, the mountains, then back to the waybill.

Verity tilted her head and raised one eyebrow. "You can't take a photo with the paper, Davis." She smiled a little at her jest.

He shook his head. "No—I'm not trying to remember. I'm trying to match—look, this map almost matches the range of mountains out there."

This got Margaret's attention. "What did you say? You think you can read that map? But imperial waybills have never been deciphered. It's useless—treasure hunters have been following those waybills to their deaths for a thousand years."

When Margaret mentioned the imperial waybills, Zaldron's head snapped up. His eyes shined bright; his head cocked to one side, listening. He looked like a bird examining a new object.

"No, Margaret—look. It's not a map, not really. It's a picture of the mountains we have to cross. Look—the double line is on the first row of snow-capped peaks. The double lines match that one." He pointed at a double-peaked mountain between two taller peaks.

"The next crest—the first without snow—is the next line down." He pointed again, at a closer line of hills. "And it goes on. They match up, mostly."

Verity scoffed. "Maybe the distant ones. The closer rows don't match at all. See? The next couple of hills aren't on your paper at all."

Zaldron stood now, casting a keen eye over the paper. "Where did you get this waybill? What do you know of it?"

Davis shrugged. "Margaret copied it from some old man in Dushanbe." He jerked a thumb at Margaret. "She says it's nonsense."

"Just because you don't understand a thing does not make it nonsense. Is a book nonsense, just because a small child holds it?" He turned to Margaret. "Please, tell me what you can of this document."

Margaret sat up straighter, all business now. She might have been discussing expenditure reports with the directors of the Cartographers Guild rather than a copy of an ancient map.

"We obtained the document from a man in Dushanbe named Yando. He claimed it was a map to a Roman city called Emal Mora, obtained from a carving in Maywhon in Burma. I made a copy of his original rubbing, though I have no confidence in waybills."

Zaldron spoke in a low voice, more to himself than anyone else. "Yando? Found a waybill in Burma? I'll have to…." He trailed off, then remembered he was not alone. Now he said to Davis, "show me the correspondences. Let me see this discovery of yours." Davis showed him; Zaldron listened and looked; his face was grave.

At last, the sage spoke. "You have indeed brought the key to Emal Mora. Once we collect your colleagues from Titianus, we must seek out the lost city and the jade—" He cut himself off. "We must protect the things the city contains."

Ace shook his head. "I didn't sign on to hike through the mountains, much less protect some lost city. I'm a pilot—I want to get away from these hills where I have to walk everywhere and back to country where I can land a plane without killing myself."

Margaret dismissed his objection with a wave of her hand. "Mr. Barrett, you signed on to assist this expedition. If we have an opportunity to discover an unknown Roman city, we must take it. Come, Mr. Zaldron, please assist us. How do we recover our friends and find Emol Mora?"

—

"I still don't like this plan," said Ace. "The way to get Alicia and Doc back is to go into Daroot-Korgon and find them, not run around in the wilderness. Plus, this seems like a good way to get us all killed."

"We have been over this," said Margaret. She sounded like an exhausted mother telling her child for the thousandth time, no, we will not be getting ice cream today. "We cannot enter Daroot-Korgon safely, nor can we guarantee the saftey of Dr. Carambo and Doctor Zsezsky if we try to force an entry. This is the safest way."

Verity laughed. "Safest? Margaret, this has got to be one of the most foolish things we've tried on this half-baked expedition. We'd be better off in the hotel in Dushanbe, fighting with the basmachi."

Mickey rolled his eyes. "Rappelling is perfectly safe. Margaret goes first, to demonstrate. Zaldron is next, to assist her at the bottom. You and Ace next, and I'll come down with no assistance from the top. We'll be fine."

Verity peered over the cliff. "And how do we get back up if we need to?"

"The issue has been discussed, Miss Hester. We do not climb back up this way. We must deal with the bandits in the open; doing so will clear the route through Daroot-Korgon for us."

Margaret secured the rope around herself for rappelling. "Miss Hester, Mr. Barrett, the time for discussion is over. I am about to descend; I suggest you observe me closely so you can perform the descent properly when your turn comes."

She straddled the twin ropes dangling down the cliff and wrapped one behind each leg under her seat and around her waist. She crossed the lines across her chest, over her shoulder, and behind her neck. She ran the twin lines down her arm and gripped them in her right fist.

"See? Simple. The friction of the rope slows my descent; my grip on the rope in my fist controls my speed."

With that, Margaret leaned back into space with her feet planted on the cliff face. She descended the ridge at a moderate pace, placing her feet carefully and using the rope to control her speed.

Once at the bottom, she waved her left arm over her head and gave two thumbs up—the signal she had completed the descent with no problems.

Verity went next. Mickey helped her sling up properly. The assistant struggled with the rope; she had no idea how to harness herself to rappel.

"I thought you knew how to climb," said Mickey. "That's what your resume said. Seems like you'd know how to rappel."

Verity offered an apologetic shrug. "One of those things I never got around to. You know how it goes."

Mickey replied too late; Verity had already started down the face of the cliff. He shrugged; her resume didn't matter now.

Once they got the all-clear sign from Margaret, Ace stepped over the rope. "This is still a dumb idea, but I guess we're committed now. Half the team is down there with no way to get back up. Well, here goes nothing."

He leaned back and let the rope slip through his fist. He descended faster than Verity; Ace liked heights and speed.

Zaldron descended next. His quilted outfit was perfect for rappelling—the thick jacket and pants let the rope slide without biting into his skin.

Mickey went last. As the most experienced mountaineer of the group, he would make the riskiest descent. He lowered the packs first, one by one, to Margaret.

He wrapped himself in the ropes and began his descent. "Good times," he said to no one in particular as he descended. "Rappelling down a steep cliff with no help at the top or bottom. Great idea," he muttered.

Mickey's descended smoothly until he reached a little past halfway. He felt the rope shudder, just a twinge. It shivered again, slipped; his left hand snaked out, grabbed a clump of grass clinging to the cliff face.

The rope shuddered again—then snapped. Mickey jerked backward; his feet slipped on stone. Rope slithered past him through the air. His grip on the grass held—for how long. He anchored his right hand on a jutting rock and looked up. He pulled himself flat against the wall, just in time. The tree they used to anchor the rope whistled past; a few of the branches lashed him on the way past.

He heard the tree smash into the ground below. A voice called out. "Mr. Charles, Mr. Charles, are you all right? Can we assist?" Good old Margaret—formal even in a life-and-death crisis.

"I'm fine. I got ready—I felt the rope slipping before it gave. I've got hand-holds on the wall right now."

Even as he said it, the grass he held gave way. The sudden surge of weight on his right hand caused it to slip as well. His feet braced against the cliff; his weight leaned forward. Instead of falling, Mickey slid down the mountain.

He went perhaps a quarter of the way when one foot struck a jutting rock; it slowed him enough for him to get a grip on another.

He came to a halt forty feet lower.

"Still good up here. Man, I wish I had the rope. This is no good."

He looked at the cliff below himself. There—a little lower. Another foot-rest. He found a hold for his left hand and moved his weight down. A lower rest for the right foot, then move the right hand. He made another thirty feet like this.

He reached a point where he couldn't see much lower than his feet. He realized the slope was no longer vertical here—still steep, but it angled slightly.

He looked over his shoulder. "Margaret—how much further?"

The answer floated up in the clear air. "Fifty feet or so. There is an old rockslide below your feet. It's less steep; you should be safer now."

Mickey worked lower; the footwork was challenging because he couldn't see where to put them down.

When his waist reached the edge of the rockslide, he risked turning around. He thought he could face out and get a better view of the rest of the route.

Margaret was right—the rockslide was steep and loose but angled enough for him to sit and scoot himself down. Not dignified, but safer and simpler than the previous part of the climb.

He reached the base of the rockslide. The ground still sloped but at a manageable angle. He found sound footing as well; grass held the soil in place. The rest of the team clustered around him. Davis patted him on the back.

Ace beamed, lifting Mickey off the ground in a bear hug. "Any landing you can walk away from—I guess that goes for hill climbs, too, don't it?"

Margaret turned to Zaldron, hands on her hips. "Well, Mr. Zaldron. We have circled Daroot-Korgon and must now cross through the town—which you sat is too dangerous—to get back to our base camp. How do you rec-ommend we proceed now?"

Zaldron's serene expression never changed. "We must first locate your friends. To do that, we need to scout Daroot-Korgon itself."

Ace glared. "We could have scouted from the other side of town—without risking our necks on…." He gestured at the cliff. "On whatever that was."

Zaldron waved no. "Titianus expects trouble from the southwest—from the government, perhaps the basmachi, maybe even your team. Therefore he scouts the southwest with most of his men and magic. Nothing attacks from the northeast; he watches little in this direction. We can approach and find your friends from this side of town with much less trouble."

"Then what?" Ace bristled. "We've still got to get through Daroot-Korgon. You got a plan for that?"

Zaldron turned his palms to Ace and made a pushing gesture—take it easy. "Something will present itself, my friend. Let us face one problem at a time."

"So what's the plan here? Do we just waltz up to Daroot-Korgon and grab our friends?"

"No. We must proceed with caution. I said Titianus watches little; I did not say he does not watch. We must stay in the cover of the trees and work our way down the ridge to the creek. We can use the creek to approach Daroot-Korgon in the dark. I have still some friends there; they will assist us in locating your friends."

Margaret stepped between Ace and Zaldron. "Mr. Barrett, please. We are where we are. Mr. Zaldron has contacts in Daroot-Korgon; no doubt they can assist us in locating our missing associates. Let us proceed with his plan for the time being." She turned to the rest of the team. "Packs, everyone. It is time to march."

Ace grumbled, then shouldered his pack. They lined up and began to march down the slope toward Daroot-Korgon.

# Chapter ten

As soon as they decided to leave, Alicia sprang into action. She astounded Doc—she had provisions secreted in nooks and crannies all over the hut. A supply of flatbread came from a cupboard; dried meat was stored in a pot in the disused kitchen. She pulled oilcloth rain capes from under the mattress of her bed; a pair of native-style packs came from beneath a stone in the hearth.

"Not a bad haul, Carambo. Where did you get all this stuff?"

Alicia shrugged. "Here and there. The locals want to support me; I've helped lots of them. Everybody here is a relative of at least one patient; they appreciate what I've done. Omarah and the other ladies have brought me things we need to escape and hidden them away here in the hut. As long as we avoid the outsiders loyal to Titianus, we should be fine."

Doc whistled. "Impressive. Did you manage to get any weapons to go with this gear?"

"You know better than to ask that, Doc. I received no weapons because I asked for no weapons. You know perfectly well that I won't harm another human. If we carry weapons, we'll be tempted to use them. We'll have to use our wits to get out of here. Our wits, and a few other things I have ready."

"I don't like that. Besides humans, there are animals out there—tigers and leopards for sure. Bears, too, as we go deeper into the mountains. Maybe yetis as well."

Alicia laughed. "Yetis? Really, Doc, yetis? Maybe we should arm up for ghosts, too."

"Supernatural entities are another matter. But there are plenty of large predators out there. I wish we had a gun, or at least a spear."

"Well, you won't get one. We can get a hatchet, though. One of Omarah's nieces has been leaving a little hatchet unsupervised behind her hut. We'll pick it up on the way out of town."

Now Doc scoffed. "A hatchet? If you're close enough to use a hatchet on a tiger, you're already dead."

"I planned on using the hatchet for firewood. A nice campfire should keep the tigers back."

Doc rolled his eyes. "I'll keep my eye out for something better than your hatchet. We've got to be ready if we meet one of Titianus's thugs."

Alicia whirled to face Doc. She stared into his eyes, her expression hard. "You will do no such thing. I have spent the last three weeks healing the people of Daroot-Korgon. I will not permit you to harm them. If you pick up a weapon, I will leave you. Understood?"

"Now you grow principles? When your life is on the line? You didn't have any qualms about having us go armed around camp before."

She crossed her arms across her chest. "I talked about that with Margaret, before we left. Before I signed on, even. I dislike violence for any reason. I will tolerate it when used to resist unprovoked attacks—to defend our camp when bandits attack. Here, in Daroot-Korgon—this is their home, Doc. These people belong here; we are the outsiders."

"Outsiders who were kidnapped and brought here against our will. We have every right to retaliate. If anything, sneaking out and only fighting to cover our tracks is an under-reaction."

"I agree that we have been wronged. Even so, I will not participate in violence. We will depart quietly, with no fighting. If you cannot abide that condition, then I will part ways with you now and we can each find the way back to base camp alone."

Doc tossed his hands up in frustration. "You are going to get us killed, Alicia. You know that, right?"

She nodded. "'Greater love hath no man than this, to lay down his life for another.' I will not be a party to killing, even if it costs me my life. And don't worry—I do have some tricks up my sleeve. Just because I don't want to kill doesn't mean I want to be killed. There is a difference, you know."

"So do you want to share these plans with me?"

Alicia shook her head. "If there's trouble, just follow my lead. I think we can get away clean without trouble, especially headed up country away from Dushanbe."

Doc smiled, but his eyes stayed sad. "Except we have to steal something from the ruins first. I can't risk letting it fall to Titianus, not for any reason."

"How many guards, do you think? Are we talking about a whole team or just one or two?"

Doc described the nighttime security at the dig site. As Alicia packed their supplies into the packs, they discussed ways to circumvent the guards.

The first phase of the escape was easy. Alicia knocked on the front door; the guard unbarred it and opened the door a crack. The man was in his late teens—little more than a boy—and wore the clothing of a local rather than one of Titianus's outside thugs.

Alicia used Doc to translate a quick conversation. Did he live here Daroot-Korgon? Yes. Did he know who she was, what she did for the village? Yes—she saved his aunt from cholera and splinted the broken arm of a cousin. She needed to visit a patient to follow up on earlier treatments. Would he permit her to leave? Yes, but not her companion; rules were rules.

She shook her head—no. Both must go; he was carrying medicines for her. The boy raised an eyebrow, skeptical,  yet he allowed the pair to exit with no further trouble.

Once out of the hut, they kept to the shadows. The moon shone bright; they avoided its light as much as possible. Alicia guided Doc to a home at the edge of the village. Like every hut in the mountain village, twin heaps of firewood towered behind the building. The first pile was a tidy stack of wood already cut and split, ready to burn. The second, a messy heap of logs to be split. Alicia slipped out of the shadows and rummaged around in the pile of unsplit wood. After a moment, she pulled out a hatchet.

A dog barked within the hut; a woman's voice called out in Russian. Alicia answered in the same tongue: "It's me. I'm taking the hatchet and leaving." The voice replied: "Good luck and Godspeed."

Alicia faced Doc. "That was Omarah; she's on our side. Now turn around so I can stow this hatchet in your bag." With that, they left Daroot-Korgon.

The ruins lay silent; it surprised Doc to see no guards around. The pair moved with great caution but saw no one.

At last, they reached the mouth of the tunnel;  a yellow-white glow marked it. Someone just inside the mouth of the tunnel had a lantern. Doc and Alicia maneuvered until they could see down the tunnel. A single guard sat in the lantern's glow, staring out at the darkness.

There was no way around him—the man sat on a stool in the middle of the passage; it was narrow enough that he could reach out his arms and touch both sides at once without moving.

Alicia studied the setup for a moment. "Is he the only one, do you think? Are there more elsewhere?"

Doc shrugged. "I would think Titianus would post more, but maybe

131

not. If he doesn't trust his guards much—" He shuddered. The thought that these men were too bad for Titianus—they must be truly wretched, or wicked, or both.

"I can handle this guy, but we've got to be ready. My fix won't last long; we need to have ropes and a gag ready to go in a second." Doc nodded, took off his pack. He rummaged around and found the ropes. As Doc prepared, Alicia pulled a small stoppered bottle from her pack.

"Here—put some of this under your nose. You'll need it to get past what I'm planning." Alicia held out the bottle; she put a few drops of an oily substance on Doc's outstretched finger.

He rubbed it under his nose; it felt cold enough to burn. An overwhelming aroma of mint filled his nose.

Alicia spoke again, her voice a low whisper. "It's just mint oil. It will sting a little, but it will cover up the smell of this." She showed him something—a clay egg.

He knit his eyebrows together, not understanding the egg. "What's that?" he hissed.

"Shhh…just be ready. I'm about to throw it."

Alicia stood and tossed the clay egg in one smooth motion. It landed in the tunnel just short of the guard's feet; the egg made a hollow pop noise as is broke.

The guard looked down, puzzled by the sound. He rose and looked out of the tunnel—then fell to all fours, retching.

"Now—let's go." Alicia rushed to the tunnel, dragging Doc along for the ride. Through the powerful mint smell, he breathed something else, a sulfurous stench.

"Tie him up, Doc, fast, while he's still sick."

Doc saw the remains of the clay egg—broken clay, the white of an eggshell, and a sticky black substance. He understood then—Alicia threw a rotten egg coated with clay for security. The stench of the egg sickened the guard.

Doc wasted no time binding the man—wrists first, behind his back; Alicia lashed his ankles together. Doc gagged the man when he retched again.

"Where now? We're taking quite a risk here—let's not make it worse with delays."

Doc pointed up the tunnel. "The map is up there. You wait here. The tunnel is booby-trapped. I can get through them; it will be fastest if I don't have to talk you through, too."

Alicia nodded. "Move fast—be safe."

Doc navigated the tunnel with ease. He came to the swinging weight trap; his pole still lay on the ground where he left it. He tripped the trigger. The weight swung down, the map fluttered loose. Doc used the staff to slide the map toward himself, then returned up the tunnel.

Alicia stared at the guard. She held a stick poking his back; the man acted as if it were a gun.

"Doc—translate for me. This man is local; I think he's related to the headman. Offer to bring him with us."

"What? Why would we bring the guard?" He was puzzled by this turn.

"Titianus is ruthless. He'll kill the guard if he's found tied in the morning."

Doc relayed the offer to the guard. The man shook his head. No.

Alicia's eyes narrowed. "Why? What does he gain by staying?"

Doc looked down at the prisoner. He spoke again in Pamiri. "Can you keep quiet if I remove the gag?" The man nodded. Yes. "If you yell, my partner kills you. Understand?" Another nod.

Doc untied the gag. The guard worked his jaws for a moment. "I have family here. If I leave, Titianus hurts them. I cannot leave. Does anyone know you came here?"

Doc shook his head. "No. No one knows we're gone yet."

"Did you take anything Titianus will miss?"

"No," said Doc. "I hid something to keep it from Titianus. He won't miss it because he's never seen it."

The guard nodded. "The healer will be missed. She saved us from the rice-water sickness. I will not betray her. Untie me; I will clean up the egg and carry on as though I never saw you. I think the men of the village won't look hard for you. We have no love for Titianus, but you have served all of us. Go now, as fast as you can. Get as far away as you can, as fast as you can. We won't find you if we can help it."

Doc translated the statement for Alicia. She nodded. "Good enough. Let's get him loose and go."

As they turned the leave, the guard spoke again. "Be careful how you go. There are many guards watching the road to Dushanbe; that will be a hard route. There are fewer guards to the northwest, toward the mountains. They move around in both dark and light; you will have to walk with care to avoid them."

Doc made a steeple with his fingers and bowed his head to touch his hands. "Many thanks, my friend. Go in peace."

The guard returned the gesture. "And you as well."

—

They emerged from the tunnel. Everything was quiet; the guard had not been missed.

"What now?" asked Alicia. "Where do we go from here?"

Doc sighed. "I'd like to travel up the valley and look for the city described on the parchment, but I think you should have a say, too."

"Why not go back to the expedition and bring the whole team?"

Doc pursed his lips. "I'm afraid Titianus will beat us to the city."

"And if he does? What then? Are you afraid of losing out on the glory?"

"No." Doc shook his head. "I fear what he could do if he finds the jade mask."

"Why?" Alicia was puzzled. "Are you in this for wealth? Or glory?"

Doc laughed. "No, I'm in it for history for truth. But I'm afraid Titianus will use the mask to wreak havoc on the world."

Alicia laughed out loud. "You really believe in ancient magic, don't you? Do you really think Titianus will—what? Take over the world?"

"Probably not the whole world." Doc wore a somber expression. "But he could burn down cities, or enslave half a continent. The jade mask was supposed to be one of the most powerful artifacts made by the ancients. We need to stop him from taking it if we can."

Alicia stared down the valley toward Daroot-Korgon. "So we charge into the mountains, with a four thousand year old map, no supplies, and only a vague notion of what we're looking for?"

Doc nodded. "Yes. Plus, the map itself says it contains an error, and that we need some other document. But it's the only way to beat Titianus."

"So, we can risk our lives on a foolish quest to save the lives of millions of people—because of a legend, no less—or we can run to safety just a few days down river. Is that right?"

Doc looked down. "When you put it that way, it sounds silly. But, yes, that is what I'm saying."

Alicia nodded. "Well, we'd better get started, then. We can't save the world if the next shift of guards picks us up."

She turned and started walking up the valley, away from Daroot-Korgon.

—

Zaldron kept the five cartographers hidden in a copse of woods all day.

When night fell, he led them further down the slope to the bottom of the valley. A small creek, only a few feet wide, burbled toward Daroot-Korgon. This, he explained, would lead them to Daroot-Korgon.

"We must be careful. Even at night, Titianus will have sentries about. If you hear noise, if you think you see someone, freeze. Remain silent and still until the others have passed. The sentries may have…unusual…abilities to sense in the dark. They will certainly have weapons and instructions to kill intruders on sight."

The team moved out, careful to follow Zaldron's instruction. Twice, the full moon revealed guards patrolling; both times, the cartographers hid in the shadows without being seen.

Ace hated this kind of hike; stealth was never comfortable for him. His palms itched with the desire to draw his pistol and charge at someone. His mind wandered from the darkness to imagine Daroot-Korgon. Was it like the little river villages they passed? Would the huts be made from sheet metal and tar paper, or mud bricks, or something else? How many guards were there?

He was considering his odds in a gunfight with kidnappers when a hand grabbed his collar. "Ace—stop, dammit." Davis kept his voice low, but it still carried urgency.

Ace was puzzled. "What's going on, Davis?"

"Shh. Listen—sounds like someone moving, just ahead."

Ace froze, cocked his head. He didn't hear movement, but something. Did he hear someone talking? He closed his eyes and concentrated. It didn't sound like Pamir or Tajik, or even Russian.

Could it be English? The cadence sounded right, but he couldn't make out anything. He dropped to all fours, crept closer.

A female voice—it was English. Something about a map. Ace strained to hear. A masculine voice. It seemed familiar, somehow. Was that—could it be?

Ace spoke in a low voice. "Doc—is that you over there, Doc?"

The whispers cut off. Silence reigned for half a minute; not even the crickets made a sound.

The female voice answered, again in English. "Who dat?" The New Orleans accent came through even in the short phrase—Alicia.

"Alicia! It's me, Ace. We're all here; we came to get you." He dashed over and caught the doctor in a bear hug, lifting her feet off the ground. "It's good to see you. It's been a hell of a ride to get here."

Now Doc spoke. "Oh thank God! We've had quite the time lately."

"Shhh!" A forceful shushing in the dark. Margaret spoke. "Quiet, all of you. Let us withdraw up the valley to a safe place before we speak." They started toward the ridge, back the way the five had come. Spirits were high as they marched.

Sunrise found the complete team back at the foot of the cliff they descended the day before. The mood in the little glade of trees was joyous; everyone was thrilled to be reunited. Each team recounted their ordeal; Zaldron remained silent through most of the morning.

"Where now?" asked Ace. "Should we follow this cockamamie map of Doc's, or head back to base camp?"

Margaret looked thoughtful. "Let us see this map, Doctor Zsezsnky. I am intrigued, but I suspect a great deal of additional study will be required."

Doc Z laid out the paper he had recovered from the dig site. Everyone clustered around it, examining the ancient parchment. Margaret reached out a finger and traced the river. "I recognize the river. This town sits about where Dushanbe is; this outpost is should be around here, near Daroot-Korgon.

"I concur," said Doc. "I think we could find our way to the House of the Jade Mask with this. It would be easier if the road were better marked, but we can probably do it."

Davis frowned at the map. "What does this say, here at the bottom?"

Doc translated. "It says the road shown is fake, and that we need something called the waybill of Bereem instead."

"What's that? We need a second map to follow the first map?"

Doc shrugged. "The Romans liked their secrets. They didn't make many maps—not true maps, like we make, at any rate. They preferred waybills. Waybills are usually sets of lines; we don't know how they were used. Bereem is an ancient city. If I'm not mistaken, the ruins of Bereem are now called Maywhon. It's in the Malay archipelago, two thousand miles away from here. I don't know what the waybill truly is, or how it would help us."

Davis's head snapped up. "Bereem is Maywhon? Could this waybill of Bereem be a set of lines carved on a stone there?"

Doc gazed at the mountains. "That seems likely, though that doesn't help us now. We would have go back down to Dushanbe, return to the Black Sea, sail through the Suez and around India—it would be a month of travel, at least, before we could even search the ruins. Assuming we could get permits, and make our way to Maywhon and—"

Davis cut him off. "We met a priest in Dushanbe. He showed us a waybill that had been traced in Maywhon. He believed it is connected to the ruins of Emal Mora somehow, though he didn't know how."

Doc grabbed Davis with both hands. "You saw the waybill? Do you remember what it looks like? Can you draw it?"

Davis grinned. "I can do better than that, Doc. Margaret made a copy."

⁓

They clustered around the two documents. Ace shook his head. "I don't get it. How do the wavy lines help us read the map? How does any of this get us to Emal Mora?"

Davis looked from one document to the other. He used a finger to touch marks on one, then the other. "I think I've got it. We saw yesterday that the waybill matched the lines of ridges we could see from atop this ridge. Look—you can match this row to the next line of hills." He pointed at the waybill, then at the ridge that formed the opposite side of the valley."

"Look here. There is a slash on each line of the waybill. Now look at the map—see the little decorative towers?" He indicated details on the map. "Each one matches a slash on the waybill. We use the map, but we don't follow the road—we march point to point, so we cross each ridge at the slash."

Margaret scoffed. "The greatest scholars of the last two millennia have been unable to decipher such waybills. Do you really think you will solve the puzzle, with no training, no tools, in a remote valley in the roof of the world?"

Davis shrugged. "The scholars never examined the waybills here, where they can see what it matches. They also never had an actual imperial map to tie it to. If I'm right, we can find Emal Mora. Maybe even the jade mask. If I'm wrong, we hike back out of the hills and go home."

"This is foolishness." Margaret crossed her arms over her chest. "Even if we do have the key to Emal Mora, we're not equipped to follow it up."

Doc interrupted. "Titianus is equipped to find it. If we pass now, he finds the city and whatever's there."

"Really? You think we could find Emal Mora—an untouched Roman city?" Verity's face was eager, her eyes shining with excitement. "Can you imagine what might be there? What treasure we could find? We'd all be millionaires!"

Margaret scowled at Verity. "If we find Emal Mora—if—any items we find must be preserved for posterity. The most valuable will be removed to museums for safekeeping. We most certainly will not use the city to enrich ourselves."

Doc nodded. "She's right, Verity. We can't just loot the city. Don't worry, though. I'm sure the discoverers of Emal Mora will all be famous. If you really want money, I'm sure there is a way to profit off the discovery."

Verity blanched, shook her head. "I don't want to be famous. I don't want my face plastered all over the newsreels. I just want enough cash to live a quiet life somewhere, away from trouble."

"You don't have to worry about fame, or treasure," said Margaret. "We don't have the equipment to reach Emal Mora safely. We must return to base camp."

"Margaret, no—we can't turn. Emal Moa will be the find of the century—maybe the millennium! We can't just abandon the quest!" Doc's face was red; he waved his arms at the distant hills like a madman.

Mickey looked from face to face. "We're split. We should put this to a vote of the party. I'll vote to go back to base camp. Traveling these mountains could be deadly if we're not set up right—and we're definitely not set up right."

Margaret nodded. "I concur. Any expedition to attempt to locate imperial ruins in the mountains needs far more equipment and planning than we have available."

Doc shook his head. "I vote to go on. Emal Mora—the jade mask—we came here to expand knowledge, to connect the peoples of the world together. Finding a lost Roman city in Turkmenistan would be—we would connect—I mean, we can't just walk back and let Titianus at the city."

"You're wrong, Doc," said Davis. "You are talking suicide. We can get the glory later, when it won't kill us all. We should turn back. That's three against. Who's next?"

Ace chuckled. "I signed on to this outfit for adventure, mostly. I reckon there's more adventure in going forward than back—I'm with Doc."

Margaret raised an eyebrow. "Really? You would rush into danger just for the thrill?"

Ace grinned at her. "That's about the size of it. If I wanted to play it safe, I'd be punching cattle back in Texas."

Margaret looked at Alicia. "Dr. Carambo—surely you will be more sensible than these two. Please, cast the fourth vote for return."

Alicia closed her eyes and took a deep breath. She opened them, looked Margaret in the eye. "I can't, Margaret. You haven't met Titianus, seen what he can do. If there is a chance he could get his hands on something with real power—". She shuddered. "If Titianus is going to try to find Emal Mora, I vote to stop him."

All eyes turned to Verity. Margaret spoke first. "Miss Hester, please. You are sensible—don't make the mistake the rest are making. Vote to take us back to base camp."

Verity took her time; emotions played across her face. When she looked to the map or the distant mountains, avarice glittered in her eyes. Yet when she looked back toward base camp, something like fear crossed her face. Everyone was silent, waiting for her choice.

Zaldron broke the silence. "Consider what this could mean. Your friend knows Titianus; she knows him to be dangerous, grasping for power and harming those around him. You also know what lies before you. It is possible there are things in the city to interest you—items with value, yet no history. Things of no interest to museums, yet are useful to others."

Margaret drew herself up to her full height. "Mister Zaldron! Surely you are not proposing that Miss Hester should loot the lost city? To do so would be—it would—"

Zaldron held a hand up. "I do not propose anyone steal artifacts of historic value. Yet these mountains have long been renowned for their mineral wealth. They are the source of gold ores, gemstones—raw materials with some value."

Mickey laughed without humor. "Gold or jewels?. I'll bet those are long gone, if there ever were any in this lost city. Nobody would leave valuable stuff behind."

"But if we did—think about it," Ace said. "Raw diamonds wouldn't have any historical value, but on the market—wow. Even a couple could change our lives."

Verity pursed her lips. "I don't want to die on a wild goose chase, but—"

"There we have it," said Margaret. "Four sensible votes to return to base camp."

"Margaret, please, let me finish. I don't want to die—BUT I don't want to miss out on the score of the century, either. If Davis is right about the map—if he's right, there should be a marker or something on the next ridge. We should be able to climb the ridge, find the marker, and get an idea where the third one is. I vote this: we go to the next ridge and try to see where the map and waybill point us. If we find ruins, we should look ahead and see if the next ridge fits the waybill. If we can't match the ridge, or if we can't find the marked place up there—then we turn and go home."

Margaret's eyes went wide. She said nothing; her mouth gaped open and closed like a fish out of water.

Davis raised his eyebrows. "Well, I didn't expect that. The vote is cast." He turned to Zaldron. "You're our guide—can we cross the valley in the daylight, or should we wait for nightfall?"

The sage pursed his lips and thought. At last, he spoke. "I do not think Zaldron watches the valley too closely. His concern is with those who might enter the ruins he has claimed and steal from him; I do not think he will be worried about traffic away from Daroot-Korgon. We can proceed today."

# Chapter eleven

The cartographers reached the top of the next ridge a little before noon. Matching the contour shown on the waybill was challenging from the crest of the slope, but everyone believed they found the correct place on the peak.

They stopped to eat at the top of the ridge, enjoying the view. The sky was cobalt blue; the clear air let them see for miles. A few white clouds dotted the sky. Ace stretched out on a patch of grass and soaked up the sun. "I could get used to this. I feel like the king of the world up here."

Mickey laughed. "It's great, isn't it? You should come home with me sometime to Montana. I grew up with views like this in the Rockies."

"Maybe I will. Hell, even if we don't find a marker, it was worth climbing this hill for the view."

Mickey nodded. "You can say that again. By the way, how are we going to find the marker, anyway?"

Doc pointed to the west. "I believe it lies in that direction. As we climbed, I tried to keep our drift to the east, if drift we did. My idea is to make a line perpendicular to the ridge, standing ten or fifteen feet apart. We should be able to move in unison along the crest of the ridge and find a marker, if one exists."

Margaret nodded. "And if we search in that manner and find nothing, will you be satisfied?"

Doc shrugged. "I can't say. Let's search and see what's up here."

The team lined up as Doc suggested. They moved at a glacial pace, all eyes scanning the ground ahead. Three times someone called a halt to examine stones on the ground; three times, the rocks were just rocks.

Margaret called the fourth halt. "It pains me to say this, but I think I have found the marker stone."

Doc stood next in line. "Where? I don't see anything." His eyes scanned the ground ahead of her.

"There, in the midst of that rhododendron." She pointed to a large evergreen bush. "I can just make out a stone column. It's red—perhaps sandstone?

It doesn't seem to be the same type of stone as the rest of the ridge."

Mickey approached the shrub and peered into it. "Yeah, sandstone. It's an obelisk—definitely man-made, and definitely not native stone. It's got carvings on it. Hey Doc—come here. You'll have to get up close to read it."

Doc wormed his way into the shrub and began to examine the stone. He lost himself in the translation; he would not respond to their calls.

Ace grew bored with waiting and moved away to enjoy the view. He stood in silence for a few minutes, then called Davis.

"Hey—Davis. You got the binoculars? Bring them here. I think something is happening back at Daroot-Korgon."

Davis and Mickey approached. Davis pulled out the binoculars. "Where? What are you seeing?"

Ace pointed at the road leading northwest from Daroot-Korgon. "A column of men along the road. They are heading up the valley. I wonder why?"

Davis studied the road with the binoculars. "Yes, I see them. I can't make out much more than that. It could be this Titianus coming this way, it could be farmers headed to fields on this side of town. Hell, it could be guys out for a stroll on a nice day. I'm not sure."

Alicia approached. "Let me look. I met most of the people in Daroot-Korgon. Maybe I can recognize someone and guess what they are up to."

Davis shrugged and handed her the binoculars. "It's a little far to recognize faces, but knock yourself out."

She stared through the binoculars for a few minutes. "You're right about the faces. It's too far. I can recognize clothes, though."

Ace laughed. "You can't spot a face, but you can tell the cut of a man's britches from here?"

She shook her head. "Not enough to recognize particular people, but enough to tell Pamiris from the Mongols. Most of those men are wearing steppe clothing—bandit outfits, in this part of the world. And one of the men is tall, thin, and pale. That's got to be Titianus. There's no one else in Daroot-Korgon it could be."

Davis dropped to the ground. "Everyone, down. We don't want anyone in that expedition to see us. I hope we haven't already exposed ourselves here."

Everyone dropped to the ground, hiding behind rocks or scrub where they could. Davis frowned. "Zaldron—over here. You say you know this Titianus. Have a look at the column coming out of Daroot-Korgon and make a guess what he's up to."

Zaldron approached, dropped to the ground, took his turn with the binoculars. "They are moving slowly. Many are heavily laden, carrying large packs. If they were pursuing, the column would be smaller, carrying less. Maybe mounted—the only horses I see there are pack horses. I would guess Titianus is leading an expedition to find Emal Mora, just as we are."

Davis gathered the cartographers together. "Margaret, what's the play here? Do we keep to the open and try to outrun Titianus, or do we trust to secrecy to hide us?"

"I'd vote for staying in the open and running like hell," said Ace. "We've got a lead and a map—if we go fast enough, we should be able to beat him to Emal Mora."

Margaret raised one eyebrow at Ace. "Mr. Barrett, are you the expedition leader?" Ace said nothing; Margaret continued. "As Mr. Barrett said, because we have a lead and a map, we should have no trouble staying ahead of them. We ought to keep out of sight so as to avoid giving Titianus clues about our route."

Doc approached the group. "I've finished with the stone. I only wish I could make a rubbing to take with me—it would be best to have the exact text preserved."

"And what does the stone say, Dr. Zsezsnky?" Margaret looked like a schoolmarm lecturing a wayward student.

"It's written in a rare variant of Latin. It mentions the house of that which is hidden, and the waybill of Bereem. It also issues a great number of threats against those who stand in opposition to Rome, though I think we will be able to avoid that."

No one laughed at his joke. Margaret nodded, lost in thought.

"What about the next marker, Doc?" asked Alicia. "Can you find it?"

Doc nodded. "Yes. The column has some clues. Let's get the waybill and see what we can find."

They withdrew to the other side of the great bush hiding the stone. They bush hid them also from the eyes of Titianus's expedition. Doc held the binoculars now. He scanned the next ridge, occasionally looking down at the waybill and muttering. It took him five minutes to find what he wanted.

He pointed toward the crest of the next ridge. "There—see that?" He indicated a dip in the ridge, a low saddle they could cross with ease. "I think I see a stone standing there. We should make for that saddle next."

Davis took a compass heading; Margaret confirmed it. They started down the ridge, toward the next saddle and the next marker on the way to Emal Mora.

—

They made steady progress for three days. The Roman roads still existed, though they were overgrown with grass. The waybill guided the cartographers to the easiest climbs, the safest river crossings. They saw neither Titianus's expedition nor any other dangers as they hiked.

The weather shifted on the fourth day. Rather than the cool, dry breeze from the north, they faced a humid, gusty wind from the south, over the mountains. After the sun rose, they saw the clouds—great white pillars looming over the highest peaks in the world.

"I don't like the looks of that," said Mickey. "It reminds me of storm fronts blowing up back home. Clouds like those will drop bunches of rain, lightning, even chunks of hail. I wish we could find a dry place to hole up while it passes."

"Ha!" Davis cut loose a humorless laugh. "The closest dry place is Da-root-Korgon. Get ready to get wet, people, because there's no alternative."

They hiked through the morning, watching the clouds loom ever closer. The wind grew colder and harder. When they broke for lunch, everyone put on whatever rain gear they possessed. While they ate, the sky grew dark; the wind blew chill gusts around them.

As they stood to resume marching, the first raindrops fell. One or two at first, followed by a few minutes of steady rain—then the bottom fell out. Huge drops hammered down; the rain cut their vision to just a few dozen yards. Everyone was soaked to the bone.

The cartographers trudged through the miserable rain for most of the afternoon. No one spoke; it took all their will to keep putting one foot in front of the other.

Late in the afternoon, Alicia stumbled and fell. Ace rushed to her side; she shivered fiercely. He tried to encourage her. "Alicia—are you OK? Come on, keep moving. It'll warm you up."

She looked up at him from the mud, eyes wide. "I can't. It's so cold—we've got to get back—where are we? Oh, I just want to rest. Please let me rest."

Ace stooped beside her, put an arm around her shoulders. "Come on, Alicia. Hang on—we'll get you warm soon." He lifted his face and shouted. "Margaret—Mickey—over here. There's something wrong with Alicia." The rain seemed to swallow his shouts; he couldn't tell if anyone heard.

Doc Z arrived next, also shivering. "We can't do this much longer. Alicia and I don't have good rain gear—I fear hypothermia."

Mickey agreed. "Yeah, with this rain and wind—when you're wet, it doesn't take much cold to bring on hypothermia. We've got to find somewhere dry to build a fire for her and Doc. The rest of us could probably use it, too."

The team assembled around Alicia. Margaret took stock of the group with a quick glance. "Mr. Charles is correct. We must find shelter immediately. Mr. Davis, Mr. Charles—do either of you have thoughts?"

Mickey nodded. "I think I saw a rocky hill a little ways back—there may be a dry crevice there we can squeeze into. I'll go check. I just hope there's nothing else already inside it."

"Very good, Mr. Charles. Mr. Barrett, please accompany him. In this weather, two are safer than one. The rest of you, huddle together. Perhaps we can conserve heat through contact."

Mickey and Ace found the hill in about twenty minutes; it took another twenty minutes to locate a large cave to accommodate the entire team. The rain still poured as they prepared to head back.

Ace heard the hail before he saw it. It started with a few pock sounds from small pieces of ice hitting the ground. The pilot looked around and saw small, white pieces of ice bouncing off the dirt; it looked like they sprang up instead of falling from the sky.

"Bad news, Mick," said Ace. "You seeing this?"

"I am. We've got to hoof it and get everybody under cover before the hail gets dangerous." They ran then, legs pounding harder than the hail coming down.

They found the other cartographers in a compact heap, fighting the cold. Ace doubled over, hands on knees gasping for breath. Mickey was in better shape, though also panting.

"Found a cave," he said between breaths. "Half mile back. Big enough for all." He gestured at them to follow.

Margaret, Davis, and Zaldron stood immediately. Doc Z, Alicia, and Verity struggled to rise.

"We shall have to assist one another with this endeavor. Mr. Davis, please assist Dr. Zsezsnky. Mr. Zaldron, if you would be so good as to take Miss Hester." She guided the sage to Verity. "Mr. Charles, you and I will both have to assist Dr. Carambo."

The group covered ground slower than Ace and Mickey did alone. The group shambled toward the hill. The hail increased in intensity; sporadic strikes became a steady pelting with the ice pellets.

Ace walked hunched over, holding his arms over his head to ward off the worst of the stones. They stung but caused no harm.

Then he felt a hammer blow between his shoulder blades, like being pelted with a large rock. He looked back—he saw a hailstone the size of an egg. "Big hail coming in—pick it up, people!" He tried to run; his wounded leg burned with the effort.

The cartographers went as fast as they could. Sharp cries and swearing punctuated the pounding of the rain and hail as bigger hailstones began to land.

They reached the cave just in time; the sky opened up. Chunks of hail as big as eggs, then baseballs, fell thick and fast. Had they been unprotected, the chunks of ice would have beaten everyone to death.

Mickey poked around and found an old tree lodged in a vertical shaft. He and Ace broke it up with hatchets and soon got a fire going. They huddled together around the fire and dried themselves as best they could.

Mickey explored the cave by the light of the fire. Piles of dried vegetation here and there resembled great nests. He examined one of the nests; long, coarse hairs remained, left behind by whatever animal slept there.

Bones lay scattered around the cave; they were medium-sized, from stags or mountain sheep. Most of the long bones had been cracked open somehow, and the marrow sucked out.

The cave was the lair of a predator.

Mickey beckoned to Ace. "Hey, we need more firewood. Can you come out and stand watch while I gather some?"

The pilot nodded. "Yeah. You worried about whatever lives here coming back in the night?"

Mickey shrugged. "Maybe. I figure we're safe as long as we have a fire. I want to make sure it doesn't go out in the night."

Verity stared at the fire, drowsy. She sat against the back wall, a rifle across her lap. She was supposed to be watching the cave mouth; everyone else slept.

She heard—something. What made that sound? She missed the sounds of a big city at night, sounds she knew and understood. Not the sound of some animal shuffling in the cave mouth.

She leaned forward and tossed another log on the fire. Sparks swirled up in the smoke. The wet wood popped and hissed as the fire dried it.

She heard the shuffling again, growing fainter. Maybe the thing was pulling out, afraid of the fire.

Then came a sound that made the hair on the back of her neck stand up—something between a shriek and a howl. A second followed it, more distant. Then a third.

The others stirred. "What the hell was that?" Ace sounded angry.

"Language, Mr. Barrett. And I am uncertain what the noise was. I've not heard its like."

Another shriek—a chorus. At least three or four of the creatures lurked outside the cave.

"I know that sound," said Doc. "It is a creature the locals call the yeti, a great two-legged ape of the mountains. They are said to be quite large and fierce."

"Not too fierce for a 30-06," said Ace. "I'll take care of this."

"No!" Doc Z grabbed his arm, gripped tight. "Yetis live in family groups. If you harm one, the rest of the family will attack. They will pursue us until we kill them all—or they kill all of us."

Ace shrugged. "So? I've got plenty of shells—we can take them all out."

"No." Zaldron's voice was sharp. "They yeti are a clan unto themselves. They will all hunt us; they will attack from the dark, in great numbers. If you kill a yeti, none of us will return to Daroot-Korgon alive."

Ace scoffed. "Really? Some tribe of monkeys is going to wipe us all out?"

As if to answer, a stone crashed against the wall in the mouth of the cave. Flecks of stone from the wall peppered Verity. The stone itself caromed off the wall, crashed into the floor, and rolled to a stop next to the fire. It was nearly as big as Verity's head.

"Yes, really," said the sage. "Stories say yetis throw stones with uncanny strength and accuracy. I cannot speak as to the accuracy, but this stone itself speaks for strength." Another rock crashed into the wall. The cartographers all withdrew, putting a bend in the passage and the fire between themselves and the opening.

The yetis continued throwing rocks at a steady pace. The screams grew closer; the rocks landed with more power, as if the throwers drew near to the last chamber. After an hour, Verity saw an arm flick as a yeti threw a stone from just around the bend.

"Enough," said Ace. He stood and picked up his rifle.

Zaldron also rose and blocked Ace with his body. "You cannot. If you kill a yeti, we will never see a town again. It is possible we will die here in this chamber."

Ace shoved the sage's shoulder. "What then? The next rock will come from close enough to hit one of us. We don't leave this cave if we don't do something."

Zaldron nodded. "The yetis fear fire. Perhaps we could start another in the cave mouth?"

"Won't work." Mickey's expression was grim. "We're out of dry kindling; all we have now is wet logs."

They heard shuffling from the tunnel. Zaldron gripped the rifle in Ace's hands. "No shooting—do not harm the yeti."

Ace closed his eyes and rolled his head back, face to the ceiling. He shook his head and exhaled deeply. "Fine, then. We'll do this the hard way." He released his grip on the rifle, leaving it in Zaldron's hand.

Ace stepped around the sage to the fire. He grabbed the end of a log that protruded from the fire and wielded it like a sword. Three steps took him to the bend in the tunnel.

Black eyes glittered in the light of his torch—the first yeti dared to come around the bend, holding a stone the size of a volleyball in one massive hand.

"Hyah! Get back, you rascal!" Ace shouted and thrust the burning log like a sword. The yetis stepped back, startled. Ace stabbed again, hitting the beast in the center of its chest.

The yeti howled; the cry echoed off stone. In the cramped room, it felt like standing next to a train whistle. The monster dropped its boulder, stepped back. Ace swung his torch and hit the yeti in the cheek. It howled again, then spun and fled back up the tunnel.

The cave was silent for a few minutes. Ace remained next to the bend in the tunnel, torch in hand. The rest of the explorers sat around the fire, staring at the opening.

The yetis clamored then—roaring, screaming, hooting, bashing rocks or sticks together. They remained just outside the cave mouth. A loud clattering—the yetis hurled a mass of stones down the passage. The display continued for ten minutes. The beasts were afraid to enter the cave but would not give the cartographers peace.

Everything went silent again. Ace heard nothing but the breathing of the cartographers—and the yetis outside the cave. He closed his eyes and strained to listen, to detect the next monster coming down the tunnel. After ten minutes, he heard it—the quiet shuffle of the beast coming down the tunnel.

Ace took a deep breath, surged around the corner, thrust out the torch. The yeti loomed in front of him, spotlighted by the torch. It was enormous—at least nine feet tall, with broad shoulders and long ape-like arms. Long, shaggy hair covered the monster. Each massive hand gripped a stone as big as the pilot's head.

His heart pounded; blood rang in his ears. He froze for a brief instant. Don't stop, he thought. Make him afraid; don't give him a chance to see your fear.

Ace shouted and lunged forward, waving the torch. The yeti recoiled and took a half-step backward. The pilot pressed the attack, swinging the flaming brand in great arcs as he charged the monster.

The yeti reared back its head and roared. Ace felt the sound as much as he heard it. He took one more step and thrust the flaming torch into the beast's face. The roar cut off as soon as the flame made contact. The monster took another step back, then turned and fled. A chorus of howls welcomed the yeti back into its tribe. A flurry of stones crashed into the tunnel mouth; Ace beat a hasty retreat.

The pattern continued for most of the night. A flurry of stones, silence, a yeti advancing into the tunnel. Ace greeting the invader with a torch to chase it back, followed by another volley of stones.

The assault continued all night. The yetis screamed and roared, threw rocks at the opening, but ceased trying to enter the cave. The cartographers kept the fire burning, but the woodpile shrank at an alarming rate.

It was still dark when Margaret put the last log on the fire. "Let us hope this will last until daylight. Otherwise…" Her voice trailed off; no one wanted to contemplate what would happen if the fire went out.

Ace awoke with a start—he had fallen asleep as the fire went down; so had everyone else. He peered down the tunnel, fearful of what might lurk there.

Mickey stirred, opened his eyes. He bowed his head and sat still, listening. He raised his face to Ace. "All quiet. You reckon they left, or are they sneaking up the tunnel now?"

Acee shrugged. "Only one way to find out." He stood and hefted his rifle.

"Don't you remember what Zaldron said about shooting a yeti?" Mickey's eyes were wide, his face pale.

Ace looked around for a torch; he realized all the wood was gone. He shrugged. "Yeah. Wish I had another torch, but…." His voice trailed off. He shrugged again, one palm up. What else can you do?

Ace shouldered the rifle but kept the muzzle pointing toward the ground. He edged around the fire, started up the tunnel. Nothing. Mickey watched him disappear around the bend in the tunnel. Silence.

Ace emerged a moment later, grinning. "Day's breaking outside and the rain has stopped. The yetis must've got tired or something—I can't see anything moving outside."

Everyone awoke; they ate a quick, cold breakfast. No one wanted to talk just yet; they re-packed their packs, putting away the clothes that had dried in the night.

Ace broke the silence. "Well? What's the plan for today? Do we wait here for the yetis to eat us, or do we go meet them?"

Zaldron gave this some thought. "Most tales of yetis suggest they are shy during the day; I cannot recall a tale of travelers attacked by the beasts in daylight."

Margaret raised an eyebrow. "So are we safe? Will they pursue us?"

Zaldron waved his hand in the no gesture he used. "I think not. We will vacate their lair and move away; we have done them no harm. No story I have heard makes me think they will pursue us." He paused, then spoke again. "Although I do think we should avoid this place on our return journey—it is likely they will guard this place to keep us from moving in again."

They left the tunnel without incident, though everyone but Zaldron held a weapon at the ready. They marched away safely, one day closer to reaching the lost city.

# Chapter twelve

When they left the cave of the yetis, the waybill showed three more lines of ridges to cross. They covered two that day; the cartographers camped in the evening in the shadow of what should have been the final ridge. They speculated about what might be on the other side of the ridge—nothing? A thriving city? Ruins of a lost city? No one could say. They stayed up late into the night, discussing Emal Mora.

They awoke feeling jovial; this would be the end of the search, one way or another. The climb up the ridge took half the morning. Like the previous ridges, the remains of the Roman road still extended through the soil. A path had been cleared and leveled up the face of the hill, using a series of switchbacks to lessen the slope.

The eight searchers reached the top of the ridge around the middle of the morning. No one spoke as they looked down into the next valley, scanning the area for remains of a city.

At first glance, the valley looked like the dozen others they crossed since leaving Daroot-Korgon. Towering, widely-spaced pines covered most of the area. They could make out the course of a creek along the bottom of the valley; willows and thick brush crowded out the pines along its banks.

Everyone stood and looked at the valley, wondering what the trees concealed. At last, Ace broke the silence.

"Well? Shouldn't there be a city down there, or some ruins or something?" He stooped for a pebble, tossed it down the ridge toward the city.

Verity sat down, leaning against the trunk of a towering pine. "Maybe the maps are wrong. Wouldn't be the first wild goose chase based on an old map."

Doc Z made a grumbling sound in the back of his throat. "It's there, I know it. The chamber, the map and waybill…There has to be something down there, there just has to be."

Mickey stared out into the valley, squinting. He reached out a hand to Davis without moving his head. "Binos, please. I think I see something." Doc, Davis, and Margaret crowded around Mickey. Davis removed the binoculars from his neck and pressed them into the geologist's hand. Mickey kept his eyes fixed on the same point as he lifted the binoculars to his eyes. The geologist stared at the valley.

Finally, Mickey pointed into the valley. "There, about two o'clock. Just short of the creek—I think I see a spire or something."

Mickey stared through the binoculars, intent on the view. "Yep. A stone tower or spire—I can just make it out through the trees." He handed the binoculars to Davis and tried to guide his gaze to the stone.

Margaret raised her own binoculars and peered through them. "I believe I see it, Mr. Charles. It is a square tower, a series of arches holding up each level, yes?"

Mickey nodded. "Yes, that's what I saw—a square stack of arches. There's something down there, all right."

Doc peered down at the valley, shaking his head. "What you are describing is the principium, the central watchtower from an imperial army camp. I'm no good at spotting stuff from a distance; I wish I were better. Still, the principium gives us an idea where the center of the city should be."

"If we do find this principium, Dr. Zsezsnky, do you think you can guide us around the town based upon it?" Margaret gave him an appraising look.

Doc nodded. "Most likely. Roman army camps were standardized for a thousand years or more."

Verity looked at him, eyes shining. "And the treasures? Do you think you could lead us to the treasure store?"

Doc shrugged. "Maybe, if there are any. Valuables would have been kept in the praetorium—the commander's office. Military items—weapons, that is—would have been in the quaestorium. I can find both. Whether there is anything worth finding there is a different question, though."

Margaret made some notes in her journal, then pulled out a compass. "Let us note landmarks and take compass bearings before we seek out the principium."

It was well past noon when the cartographers reached the stone tower. An ancient roadway switchbacked down the hill; they hiked it without incident. After an hour, they started seeing flattened stones in the roadbed, carved stones marking waypoints within the valley, and even the occasional Roman statue overgrown with brush.

They skipped a lunch break, opting to eat on the move. By mid-afternoon, the team arrived where Margaret expected to find the principium. They did not see a tower; thick brush limited visibility to a few feet. The trees likewise towered above them, blocking their ability to see any ruins.

Margaret, Davis, and Mickey conferred. They agreed the tower should be very close, now; it was just a matter of finding it.

The others removed packs and wandered around, looking idly into the brush. Verity looked at one clump, then dug into her backpack. She pulled out a hatchet and cut down a small sapling, then limbed it to make a pole.

Ace looked at her, one eyebrow raised. He said nothing, but the implication was clear: what are you doing?

Verity shrugged without stopping her work. I don't know; I'm just keeping busy.

The research assistant approached the thickest clump of brush and pushed her pole into it. Clunk—the sound of wood poking stone. She moved a yard to the side, tried again. Clunk. She did it twice more, with the same results. She attempted a third; the pole slid deep into the leaves with no resistance. Another yard to the side, another thrust. Clunk.

Verity whistled and waved to the team. "Guys—I think I found the tower—and a door."

They worked for an hour, chopping at brush and creepers. It quickly became apparent that Verity had found a doorway set in a stone wall. They couldn't see the top of the wall; the towering trees concealed it.

At last, they could make out the shape of the wall. Doc looked it over, then turned to the group. "This appears to be a principium of the standard type. The base is a building of two or three stories—the imperial headquarters. The watchtower will extend two or three stories more above the building."

The doorway gaped dark in the wall. The wooden door that once closed it had long since rotted away, though the stonework was still sound. They entered with caution—the first humans to do so in nearly two thousand years.

Ace shined a flashlight up into the gloom. A maze of timbers sagged above them. "You think the upper floors of the tower are still sound Doc?"

"Who can say? The stone is good, the wood is questionable. It depends on lots of things—what kind of wood they used, how dry it's been, the size of the timbers. There's no way to say." Doc used his light to examine the floor of the room. It was covered in dirt and littered with debris, the residue of two thousand years exposed to the weather.

They entered with caution. The antechamber was bare of any imperial artifacts; the only contents were natural detritus. The roof seemed sound;

the back wall stood undamaged, a thick oak door closed against intruders.

Doc examined the door, rapped it with his knuckles. "Oak, probably six inches thick. The wood seems sound—I'll wager it takes days to break this down."

Verity approached and ran a hand up and down the door. She pushed it gently at first, then with more force. "Yep, this door would take a battering ram to knock down. Good thing the Romans weren't very good with locks."

She reached into a pocket and pulled out a slim roll of leather. She looked at the door again, found a slit cut into one side. She put her eye close to the slit and shined her light through. Verity moved her head and the light this way and that, examining whatever held the door closed on the other side. She nodded a little, talked to herself.

She handed her flashlight to Doc, then positioned his hand. "Here, hold it just like this." She stooped down and opened the roll on the ground. She withdrew first a flat piece of metal with short barbs extending from one side like a comb, then a coil of fine wire and finally, a thin metal bar with a spike jutting backward.

Verity placed the flat piece of metal across the slot in the door so the spikes bit into the wood, then pounded it in with the heel of her hand. Next she lowered the end of the wire through the slot above the piece of metal. Finally, she slid the bar through the opening and played with it for a moment.

Satisfied, she pulled back on the bar with one hand, and up on the wire with the other. She grumbled under her breath, then swore. Verity kept working with the wire and bar.

"Ace, come help me," she said, not taking her eyes off the tools. "Bring your knife."

The pilot came to her side, bowie knife in hand. "What is it, Vee?"

"Slide your knife through the slot, about four inches under this bar." He did so; six inches of steel slid through the slot, then stopped.

"I hit something, Vee. What should I do?"

"It's the bar holding the door closed. Push with your blade, but be careful. We have to work together to move the bar out of the slot without dropping it."

They worked, gently, for a few minutes. The bar and blade extended further and further into the slot. At last, Verity called for a stop.

"I think we're clear of the braces holding the bar in place. Keep pushing with your knife while I pull the bar loose."

She gave a quick shove on the bar. The wire came loose; the bar clattered to the ground on he other side of the wall.

Verity returned the wire and bar to her tool roll, then pulled out a thin, T-shaped rod with a loop on the end. She tied a cord through the ring, slipped the head of the T through the slot, turned the tool ninety degrees.

"Now comes the tough part," said the research assistant. "This door is probably stuck pretty tight, if it really has been closed for two thousand years. My little tool may not be strong enough to get it all the way—we have to be gentle."

She tugged the cord tied to the T-tool, gently at first, then harder; the door held fast. Verity wrapped the line around her hands, braced her feet, and strained against the door. It held fast for a moment, then moved half an inch. The bottom of the door grated against the stone floor; it moved with difficulty.

Verity paused for a moment to catch her breath, then pulled again. Another inch. She tried a third time; the door refused to budge.

"Lemme take a poke," said Ace. He took the cord from Verity and gave a couple of firm yanks. "This bit of rope ain't very strong. Should we fasten something stronger to the bar?"

Verity shook her head. "No. This cord should break before it damages the bar; we can always tie a new cord and keep pulling. Using a stronger rope might break the bar; then we'd have no way to get through the door."

Ace nodded, then pulled on the cord. He fought the door for ten minutes, and managed only another half inch. Davis, Mickey, and Doc Z all took turns as well. The first stars shined by the time they decided to break for the day. The door had still not opened enough to allow for the use of a crowbar, much less to permit entry.

Spirits were high that evening; everyone was confident they would open the door in the morning.

"What do you think we'll find in the tower, Doc?" asked Ace.

Doc shrugged. "Hard to say. The principium likely contains both the commander's safe and the armory; it is the most likely place for valuables to have been stored. But that was two thousand years ago. Now? If the Romans left this place—I mean deliberately abandoned it—they would have cleaned out any valuables. And if someone sacked it..." His voice trailed off.

Verity shook her head. "It hasn't been sacked, Doc. That much is obvious."

He nodded. "Yes, the door is still intact—still locked, even. Most unusual. Most imperial ruins have been despoiled by looters long before modern researchers reach them. Even those that haven't been looted were cleaned out by the Romans themselves. To find a door still locked—this is extraordinary."

Margaret sat up a little straighter. "Ought we to open the door at all? Might it be better if we left it alone and let experts open the door later?"

Davis shook his head. "Not if Titianus is looking for the city. We'd just as likely come back to find the door battered down and the ruins looted. At least we can preserve whatever is here for posterity."

The mention of Titianus cast a pall over the group. The talk died down then; one by one, they slipped off to bed.

Dawn renewed their optimism—for a moment. As they clustered around the campfire, drinking coffee and eating breakfast, they heard sounds from the heights above. Voices carried down from the top of the ridge—the shouts and laughter of a large group of men. They scanned the ridge line, but saw nothing through the trees.

Margaret pursed her lips in thought. She nodded to herself, then spoke. "Mr. Charles, you are the best woodsman among us. I would like for you to investigate the sounds we are hearing. Take care not to be seen, particularly if you think we are being visited by Titianus or even ordinary bandits. Mr. Davis, please accompany him as a backup. Both of you, remain concealed and avoid violence if you can. Find out what we face and return here; we will decide what to do next once you return.

"The rest of us will stay here and attempt to open the door. We all must remain as silent as we can, at least until we know more about what we face."

Everyone nodded, then went about their assigned business.

The remaining team members set to work on the door. They took turns, each pulling the cord until the line bit into skin; then they traded. Alicia watched Doc Z struggle with the rope. He sat on the floor, feet braced against the door frame, straining with the thin cord.

After a few minutes, Doc dropped the cord and rubbed the red marks on his palms. He leaned forward to examine the door frame. He tested the tiny opening with the tip of a crowbar. "Just a little more," he said. "Maybe half an inch and we can get the bar into the gap." He stood and handed the rope to Alicia.

The medic tugged at the cord, tentative at first, then harder. The rough fiber bit into her hands. "Doc, you know I need to take care of my hands, right? I'm a doctor, not a field hand."

Doc was too intent on the crowbar to answer. Instead, Margaret who spoke up. "Yes, Dr. Carambo, we know your story. And we thank you for your service. However, we have all taken our turns pulling on the door; now it is yours. Please, just a little more so that we can bring the crowbar into play."

Alicia set her feet and yanked hard; the door scraped against the stone floor.

Doc grunted and shoved the crowbar into the gap; it slid forward. "Yes! We're in with the bar. Verity, you can take your tool back now."

The research assistant removed the t-bar from the door and began to wind the cord up. Margaret looked at her with suspicion. "Miss Hester, why exactly does a research assistant on a mapping expedition carry a set of house-breaker's tools?"

Verity shrugged. "They're handy. Sometimes I need to research things behind locked doors. Times like this, for example."

Margaret raised an eyebrow. "Oh really? Do tell me, which of your previous jobs have required you to break into locked buildings?"

Verity smiled sweetly. "You know, just…jobs. Little things, here and there."

The squeal of the door ended the conversation. Doc heaved at the crowbar; the door lurched six inches open. Ace grabbed the edge of the door and yanked. The combined efforts of the two men forced it open another foot—wide enough for a person to squeeze into the chamber beyond.

Doc was already disappearing into the black gap, with Ace preparing to follow.

—

Mickey and Davis prepared for a short excursion: one canteen apiece, a bit of dried meat, and rifles. They left their backpacks and other equipment at the camp site. They intended to move fast, stay quiet, and observe without being seen.

The cartographers' camp sat on the west edge of the massive thicket hiding the base of the principium; the group on top of the ridge was to the northeast. They set off to circle the brush. After fifty yards, Mickey noticed a break in the trees extending straight to the north—likely an old road.

They followed the path north; the scrub opened up. They walked through an ancient pine forest, with towering trees looming above the ruins of Emal Mora. To the right were the crumbling walls of a long rectangular building; to the left, a mixture of pits, small towers, and piles of rubble marking old workshops.

A hundred yards along, they crossed another old road that intersected with theirs a a right angle. Beyond this road, they saw small hillocks in neat rows. They reached a wall next—tumbling down, missing in places, but clearly the wall that once protected the settlement. Outside the wall, the trees were just as grand, but the ground was smooth—unmarked by human habitation.

They paused at the old gate. Mickey cocked his head toward the sounds coming from the northeast. The voice still carried from atop the height; he also heard the ring of an ax chopping on a tree.

"Whoever is up there, they don't care about being secret," he said. "You think we'll get lucky and catch them without guards?"

Davis shrugged. "Maybe. Sounds like there's a bunch of them. I hope they aren't too spread out—that could make it hard to get a count and figure out who they are."

Mickey nodded. "True. Well, let's head that way and see what we can see. Follow me and try to keep out of sight."

They started hiking. At first, they headed due east along the bottom of the valley, parallel to the top of the ridge. Thick timber along the valley floor kept them from being seen from above. They went about two miles in that manner before settling in directly below the newcomers.

Mickey signaled Davis to stop, then indicated Davis should put the trunk of a massive pine between himself and the the crest. Once Davis was hidden, Mickey began to stalk the invaders. He moved deliberately, placing each foot with care. He made the maximum use of cover in order to stay concealed.

It took an hour for the pair to cover two miles from camp to the foot of the ridge; it took another hour to cover three hundred yards to see the invaders.

Mickey froze as soon as he glimpsed motion from upslope. He got his first sight of the invaders—a fat man, dressed in Mongol garb. Mickey gazed at the man, intent on picking up every detail he could. Most of the clothing was from the steppe, but not all. He wore the boots of a river merchant, the belt of a bureaucrat. His wool hat had come from the foothills. Someone upslope shouted something; the man turned and answered. When he did, Mickey got a clear look at the rifle slung on his back—a Lee-Enfield, still shiny and new. Not just a bandit, but one carrying a stolen rifle.

The bandit wandered off; Mickey stole ahead to the shelter of a large tree. From his vantage point, he counted at least a dozen other men—all wearing steppe clothing supplemented with valuable items taken from others, and all carrying rifles.

There could be no doubt—these men were bandits. He decided to start back down the ridge to meet with Davis when a sharp shout called all the bandits together. Mickey watched just a little longer. The man who had shouted was European, tall and thin with red hair and beard. He wore the wool robe and flat cap of the hill folk. Mickey recognized Titianus from the descriptions Doc and Alicia gave. That clinched it for him; time to get back down the hill.

Because the bandits all gathered around their leader, Mickey took some risks to move faster. He covered in fifteen minutes the distance that had taken an hour earlier. He approached the huge pine where he left Davis, then called out, "Davis—it's me, Mickey. I'm coming in."

Davis peered around the trunk, recognized the geologist. "Thank God. How did it go? Did you see anything?"

Mickey nodded. "Bandits, at least a dozen, all with rifles. The guy in charge looks like this Titianus character who nabbed Alicia and Doc. We gotta get back to the team."

"How fast do you thin we can go?" asked Davis. "Can we run, or do we need to sneak it back?"

Mickey shrugged. "No good choices. There's enough of them that we'll get spotted if we run, but if we sneak, somebody will beat us to the camp."

Davis looked up the hill. "They aren't close yet. Think we can get a little lead now, while they aren't looking?"

Mickey followed his gaze. He cupped a hand behind one ear, then froze in place. "He's still talking, I think. We've got a little window—go fast, but keep quiet. Maybe don't run—just a fast, quiet walk."

They set off for camp; they walked faster than they had in the morning, but still took care. They covered a quarter of a mile before hearing the bandits moving around behind them.

"Slow down," hissed Mickey. "They will spot fast movement—move nice and easy now. We've got a lead; we need to make the most of it."

Mickey and Davis covered another half mile before they heard the shout. Mickey turned toward the source of the sound; one of the bandits was there—pointing right at Mickey and Davis. The bandit shouted again, then unslung his rifle.

Davis had already knelt and shouldered his rifle. The bandit fired; his shot went wide. Davis did not miss—he fired once; the bandit spun and fell. Shouts echoed from the ridge.

"Now it's time to run, Mick. Let's get moving." The pair dashed off, sprinting for the principium and the rest of the team.

Mickey grabbed his companion's arm. "Hold up, Davis. Look there—" He pointed at the ruins; a pair of bandits were searching the ruins ahead of them. Mickey pointed at a stone structure nearby. "Let's slip in there and try to wait them out."

The pair ducked low and dashed toward the building. Davis stumbled, fell with a grunt. The bandits turned; one shouted something. Davis scrambled to his feet and sprinted. A rifle barked ahead—once, twice, three times.

They ducked through a low arched doorway. They found themselves in a roofless room twelve feet in diameter. Six foot stone walls sheltered them from view.

Mickey looked at Davis. "You okay, buddy? Did they hit you?"

"I'm fine. Those guys can't shoot worth spit. What now? We're safe, but I'm afraid we're stuck."

Mickey shook his head. "I dunno. If we try to head back to the tower, one of those guys might get lucky with a rifle. If we stay put, the team is in trouble."

Davis glanced out the door. "Maybe they heard the shots. At least they will be alert, even if we don't report back."

More gunshots sounded outside; bullets spattered against the back wall of the tower. Davis shouldered his rifle and looked out the door. "Looks like we're here for a while. Best get comfortable." He sat on one side of the door and settled his back against the wall. Mickey did the same on the opposite side of the doorway.

~

Doc shined his flashlight around the room. It was pitch-black; the only light came from the open door. He took in what details he could with the small beam of light.

Ace stood right behind him. "What do you think, Doc? Did we hit the

160

mother lode here?"

"I'm not sure, Ace. I expected either a command post or a muster room here—either of those should have windows to let the occupants see outside, or at least arrow slits. This feels more like a storage room."

He moved the light around the room methodically; it was a square chamber roughly matching the base of the tower. The space was empty; no doors or windows could be seen.

Verity and Margaret joined them now. Four flashlight beams roamed the room, seeking details about the city and the empty tower.

One beam came to rest on a wooden panel set into the stone floor. Verity asked, "what's that, Doc? Why is there a trapdoor here?"

"An excellent question, Verity. I've never seen or even heard of a principium with a basement. This is most curious." Doc crossed the room to look at the panel. "It does look like a trap door. Perhaps we can get it open?" He pulled at the ring set into the door; it moved half an inch, then caught against something.

"Barred," said Verity. "Whoever locked the door behind us locked this one as well. Let's get to work and get this one open, too." Verity unrolled her tools and set to the second door; this one proved easier to open than the first.

Doc shined his flashlight through the trapdoor. "Marvelous, simply marvelous. A principium sitting over an underground passage—" He went silent as something glittered in the beam of the flashlight. "More light, please—right there where my light is hitting."

The other cartographers clustered around, shined their flashlights down the tunnel. Roman armor glittered there, still encasing the bones of the man who had worn it.

"Well, that tells us who barred these doors," said Verity. "Poor guy locked himself in and never got out."

"He must have been protecting something," said Margaret. "I wonder what was so valuable that he had to seal himself in and die for it?"

Ace squinted as he looked at the armor. "Why is he wearing his armor? If you wanted to lock yourself in and just…die…you wouldn't need the armor. Or you'd take it off once you got the door safely sealed up, right?"

Doc examined the tunnel. Rusty iron rungs led down one wall into the tunnel. He squatted to look at the first rung; it seemed sound. The archaeologist climbed down the ladder, testing each rung as he went. Once down, he took a few steps toward the bones.

"Most unusual," he said. "I don't see the man's head anywhere—just the body."

"Doc—freeze." Alicia's voice was hard. "Don't move a muscle. What if a booby trap got his head? You spent so much time on the traps in Da-root-Korgon—do you think this spot could also be trapped?"

"I suppose you are right," Doc responded. "This presents us with quite the conundrum. We need to get to the end of this tunnel before Titianus arrives—but haste might kill us."

"Perhaps the traps will stop Titianus—or whoever else is out there," said Margaret.

Alicia shook her head. "No. Doc and I have seen what he's like. If he needs to, he'll just send his men down the tunnel, one at a time, to find the traps. He'd start with us, though—Titianus would rather sacrifice captives than his own men, but he'll stop at nothing to get what he wants."

"We've got to get out of here," Verity said. "We cut and run now, while we can. Otherwise, we are just deciding if we want Titianus or the traps to kill us. Let's go before he gets here."

"Stop." Margaret's voice was flat. "In the first place, this expedition will go nowhere until Mr. Davis and Mr. Charles have returned. In the second place, we will not allow Titianus to loot Emal Mora, or to steal the discovery we have rightly made. We must find a way to get through the traps, or to defeat Titianus. Dr. Zsezsnky, what do you need to proceed?"

Doc opened and closed his mouth a few times without making a sound. He paused, thought, then responded. "I will need rope, a pole, flashlights, chalk if we have it, perhaps a torch. Some other things may come up—perhaps Verity can assist with her lockpicks...I mean, her unusual tool kit?"

Alicia scowled. "Margaret, this is ill-advised. If Titianus catches us, we're all in danger."

Margaret nodded. "I know. But think of this: if he catches us, and we have found something, we possess leverage. In the worst case scenario, perhaps we trade one treasure for our lives. Perhaps we can find a way to retain something we find here."

Alicia shook her head. "No, Titianus won't allow that. He'll take everything we have. He'll probably kill us anyway."

Verity held up a hand. "Pardon me, but if it comes to carrying out stuff under his nose, I have some experience. I could tuck away a few small things right now, if we need to. Give me enough time, I can work up more. We can get things past him without a doubt."

Margaret raised an eyebrow. "It seems you possess many skills beyond the conventional research assistant, Miss Hester. We must discuss them at length once we are safe."

Verity's smile was brittle. "Certainly, once we have escaped, we can talk about my skill set. Until then, I believe Doc needs me." She turned and followed the archaeologist deeper into the ruined building.

Doc shined his light along the tunnel, examining the walls and floor with care. Ace returned with a pole about eight feet long and as thick as his wrist; Doc used it to probe the floor ahead. Satisfied at last, Doc set off down into the dark.

The passage was low and narrow, five feet high and not quite as wide as his shoulders. The walls and ceiling were rough stone; tool marks still showed in many places. Rock chips and rubble covered the floor, but he could feel hard stone beneath his feet as well. It ran straight for perhaps ten yards before a curve blocked his view.

Ace peered down from above. "What do you think, Doc? Is it passable?"

Doc squinted down the tunnel. "I'm not sure. It's cut into stone, so the traps may be more visible. On the other hand, it's so small, we will have trouble passing through. There's no way to avoid traps—we can't go around or hope to get lucky; we'll have to find and disarm all of them." He probed ahead with the pole, then bent to examine the floor. "Best if you and Verity stay topside until I call for you."

He reached the bend before finding the first trap. The top of the tunnel narrowed at the turn; it would force an intruder to lean into the wall at the curve. There, a trigger protruded slightly from the wall. Doc stepped back as far as he could and pressed the trigger with the pole. Three blades flashed: at shoulder and knee height from the left, and at waist height from the right.

He examined the trigger and the blade slots, marked them with chalk, then retreated up the tunnel. He conferred with Verity; she dropped into the tunnel and proceeded to the trigger. Verity unrolled her tools and selected a thin strip of spring steel. She slid it beneath the trigger, tapped it lightly with a hammer. She withdrew to where the pole sat and tested her work; the mechanism was jammed.

They proceeded this way for an hour, Doc exploring and finding traps, then calling Verity to disarm them. They cleared fifty yards of tunnel, curving in a shallow S. Doc could see the tunnel grow wider in about ten yards;

163

he suspected he would find at least two more traps between himself and the chamber ahead.

More gunshots sounded outside the ruins; bullets spattered against the back wall of the tower. Davis shouldered his rifle and looked out the door. "Looks like we're here for a while. Best get comfortable." He sat on one side of the door and settled his back against the wall. Mickey did the same on the opposite side of the arch.

Mickey stared around the hut. The stone walls were thick enough to stop bullets; they were also too high to climb. The top of the wall was ragged; the building had once been much taller. Rubble filled the floor—the remains of the top portion of the building. He glanced at Davis. The fixer leaned his head against the wall, eyes closed.

A shot rang out. The bullet slapped against the wall; Mickey flinched. The doorway was off limits until dark.

He noticed the floor wasn't level; Davis sat near a bowl-shaped depression. Mickey raised himself to a crouch, took a deep breath. He lunged across the space and took shelter next to Davis. Shots rang out; some hit the outside wall, while others crashed into the rubble floor of the room.

"Why the hell did you do that?" Davis was alert now, glaring at Mickey.

"There is a hollow here in the floor. I want to look at it—maybe there's a way we could slip out of here and get back to the team."

Davis nodded. "Good thinking. Just warn me next time."

Mickey dug at the rubble. In a few moments, he uncovered a cavity big enough to curl up in. He wrestled with a stone the size of his head; it slipped from his grip and fell back into the hole—then kept going. It dropped into blackness, landing with a dull thud somewhere out of sight. Mickey saw a hole leading to darkness under the building.

He leaned into the hole, striving to pierce the darkness. "What do you think, D? Wait for night or dive under the town?"

"Mmmm...hard to say." Another shot rang out, scattered stones inside the hut. "Sooner or later, one of those guys is going to get us with good angle or a ricochet. Dark is a long way off. On the other hand, we've got no idea what's down there. Could be a highway back to the tower, could be a dead-end. Could be full of snakes."

Mickey pulled out of the hole. He grunted, ran a hand through his hair. "Damned if we do, damned if we don't." He shook his head.

Shots came in a volley. The bandits dispersed across the landscape; the bullets hit in a fan pattern on the floor. Mickey jumped back against the wall. "I'm for going. One of those guys will get a jump on us sooner or later. Better the hole than getting shot."

Something clattered on the ground outside. A wave of sound crashed over them; smoke and dust swirled into the doorway.

Davis stood up now. "That's it. This hut won't do anything about grenades. We've got to get down, now. Dive in; I'll follow."

Mickey rolled onto his stomach and slid his feet into the hole. He eased himself down; he pointed his toes down, seeking a place to land. He worked his way down the hole—waist deep, chest deep.

His grip gave way; Mickey scrabbled at the bottom of the cavity. He found no purchase. His body accelerated down. His head whipped up and crashed against the top of the hole. The geologist braced himself—then landed in a heap.

Davis called down. "Mickey—hey Mick, you okay down there?"

Mickey concentrated on his body, moved his feet experimentally. His front hurt where it scraped down the lip of the hole. His head ached from banging on the top. His feet and legs ached from the hard landing. Everything worked, nothing seemed broken.

"I'm fine, I think. The hole isn't that deep—maybe eight feet. I hit hard, but everything is fine. Come on down—I'll help spot you."

The hole grew dark as Davis lowered himself. Mickey stood and reached up his hands to brace his companion. Davis released his grip and landed lightly on his feet.

A dingy beam of light shined from the hole into the tunnel. They found themselves in a shaft three feet wide and perhaps eight feet deep. It extended two directions—toward the tower, and away out of the city.

Davis looked up the tunnel both ways. "What do you think? Back toward the center?"

Mickey nodded. "Yeah, that seems best. If we are lucky, this will connect to the tunnel Doc found."

"Lucky, maybe. Didn't Doc think there would be traps in the tunnel?"

Mickey shrugged. "Yeah. A chance of traps is better than grenades, though."

Davis inclined his head a fraction. "True. Who goes first?"

Mickey rubbed a hand over his face. "I'm closer. It's easier for me to lead than for us to switch."

Davis raised an eyebrow. "You sure? Well, lead on. I'll take point in a bit, if there is a chance to switch."

Mickey nodded and set off into the darkness.

～

Ace watched Doc, Verity, and Zaldron disappear down the trapdoor. He turned to face out of the tower; he saw little but the scrub.

"What now?" he asked Margaret. "Do we just sit and twiddle our thumbs?"

She sighed. "In a normal situation, we would all pursue our own daily tasks—the routine of camp life and exploration. Under these circumstances…."

Alicia cut in. "Under these circumstances, we wait. We've got three people underground, unaware of what's going on above. We've got two out scouting. We three just stay put, ready to help either team."

Ace rolled his eyes and looked at the ceiling. "I hate waiting. I want to be in motion, to make something happen. This is—" The sound of gunfire cut him off. He snapped his head toward the door. "Sounds like Davis and Mickey are in trouble—we've got to go help."

Margaret grabbed his arm. "No, Mr. Barrett. We wait. Rushing toward the gunfire puts the rest of us in danger."

He pounded a fist against the wall. "Standing around here puts Mickey and Davis in trouble. We've got to do something." He glanced up at the broken and rotted timbers that once lined the tower. "I'm going up—maybe I can figure out what's happening out there." He slung a rifle on his back and started climbing.

Half-rotted timbers crisscrossed the tower above. In places, the ceiling remained almost whole; in others, only a few support timbers survived. Ace took his time and tested each beam's integrity before committing his weight.

Margaret shook her head below. "Mister Barrett, climbing the tower will do you no more good than leaving. Anything you try to assist our scouts will reveal our position—I insist you come down at once."

Alicia chuckled without humor. "It's worse than that, Margaret. He'll probably bring the whole mess of logs down on top of us." She turned her face up to Ace. "You're gonna get us all killed, Ace. Come back down."

Ace reached an arched window thirty feet off the ground. Whatever glass or cover the window once had was long gone. A cool breeze played across his face. He looked out, scanning the hills around the town. Outside, all was quiet.

Ace saw motion in the trees a hundred yards from the tower. A group of men emerged—bandits, by the look of them. He called down in a low voice. "Half a dozen bandits are coming. You two, get behind the door and lock it. Maybe they won't notice if we're quiet."

More bandits emerged, followed by the tall European they had seen before. The bandits hesitated, scanned the clearing around them. The tall man said something, then pointed straight at the tower. Everyone moved; some bandits fanned out to scout around the plaza. The leader and a handful of others strode toward the principium.

"Move it," Ace hissed. "That Titianus fella is coming right this way. Get under cover—fast."

Alicia and Margaret complied, pulling all the extra packs and equipment behind the door, then pulling it shut. Ace heard the heavy bar thump into place. He froze, hardly daring to breathe.

Titianus and his minions went straight to the tower entrance. He posted sentries at the door. Once they were in position, Titianus turned his full attention to the round room. He walked a circuit, trailing the fingers of one hand against the wall. He stopped at the door. Stepping back, the villain stared at the door for a moment. He knocked on it, listened to the solid thunk sound. He closed his eyes and placed a palm in the middle of the door. There he froze for a few seconds, his breathing slow and regular.

Ace kept still, praying under his breath that the men would move on. Only the footsteps of Titianus broke the silence.

~

"Doc! Doc—hurry up! We're about to have company." A whisper echoed down the tunnel. Doc retreated to the first bend.

"What was that?"

Verity's head hung down from the trapdoor. "Titianus is here, in the tower. Margaret and Alicia are locked in here with us; they said Ace is hiding up high in the tower."

Doc shook his head. "This will be very dangerous. Verity, come on down. I'll have you wait about ten yards back. When I find a trap, we'll have to find some way to pass in the tunnel without coming back here to switch places."

He resumed work, found another blade trap seven yards from the chamber. He pulled back and got down on all fours; Verity clambered over him and wedged the trap shut.

"That was my last shim, Doc. Do you think there are more traps to block?" She climbed over Doc again, doing her best to avoid hurting him.

Doc's voice was muted while he faced the floor. "Probably. I expect there is one more at the door to the chamber. Beyond that, I'm not certain. It seems unlikely the chamber will be safe, but anything more I can't say."

Doc probed his way forward. He did indeed find one more trap trigger, this one at the door to the chamber. He marked it with chalk, scribbling hard on the wall to make the mark obvious.

He shined his light around the chamber. The room was thirty feet in diameter. In the center of the room stood a chest-high pedestal carved of white stone; something made of green jade sat on top. He examined the floor at the doorway, then probed it with his pole.

A series of pops rattled above him; Margaret shouted down the tunnel. "Doctor Zsezsnky, if you can, please hurry. Titianus's bandits have found the door to this chamber."

"Going as fast as I can, Margaret." His attention stayed on the floor. He placed one foot into the room, tested the stone, then stepped forward. He repeated the performance with the next flagstone. Shots rang out again as he took a second step forward.

Verity now stood at the entrance to the chamber. "Doc, if you don't hustle, we don't get the mask, no matter what. If we get pinned down, Titianus will take the mask."

Doc shook his head. "We can't rush this, Verity. If we trigger a trap, Titianus and his bandits won't be a problem." Another exchange of gunfire came on the heels of the remark.

Verity grumbled in the back of her throat, then stepped into the chamber. She walked around Doc Z, then strode to the pedestal with confidence. She shined her flashlight on the pedestal; a face looked back at her.

The mask was brilliant green; it caught the beam of her small light and seemed to amplify it. In the dark chamber, the jade seemed to glow as if illuminated from the inside. Veins of white stood out here and there. Gold stripes like warpaint glistened from the cheeks.

She reached out a trembling hand and lifted the mask. Something on the pedestal shifted; she felt a click beneath her feet.

"Doc? I've got the mask, but something just moved under my feet. What do I do?"

"You have triggered a trap of some kind. Since it hasn't fired yet, I surmise that it will go off when you move away from the stone. Stay still until we have a plan. Hand me the mask first so we can get it to safety."

Doc took two careful steps forward, then stretched out his hand. He took the mask and retreated back up the tunnel to the last blocked trap.

He shouted up the tunnel. "Margaret? We have the mask, but Verity has stepped on a trap. She's unhurt for now, but things could go bad in a hurry. If they do, you can retrieve the mask safely—just avoid the chalk-marked triggers."

He turned back to the chamber. "The trap is likely in the pedestal, or in the floor. Your best bet is to get up and out fast, before it can hit you. Thoughts?"

"Should I jump? Dive and roll? Fly?"

Doc laughed. "Flight would be fantastic if you could manage it." He shined his flashlight up, around the chamber. It extended perhaps three stories high—the top was probably a tower of some kind in the city. Wooden beams crisscrossed the space above, providing support.

"What about those?" he asked. "We could place a rope over a beam; maybe you could swing out."

Verity looked up, then swallowed. She nodded. "You could help—we toss the rope over, I grab one end and pull myself up, you grab the other and yank down. Maybe the combination will be enough."

Doc took a coil of rope and tied a monkey-fist in one end. He cast the rope without success, then again. On the third try, the knot arced over the beam. He lowered the line until the knot hung at waist level, halfway between them.

Next, Doc used the pole to swing the knot to Verity. "Ready?" he asked.

"No—let's test it first. We should both tug on the rope to make sure the whole beam won't come down on us."

Doc chuckled. "Good idea. It would be quite a trap if we collapsed the whole tower on our heads, though."

Verity took a deep breath. "I'm too pretty to die like that, Doc. Let's just pull on three—one, two, three."

Each explorer tugged on the rope; the beam held. Gunfire rattled above them again.

"Ready to go from frying pan to fire, Verity?"

∼

At last, Titianus moved on, completing his circuit of the room. He reached the doorway and stopped. He glanced up, then back at the door. He said something to the guards in a low voice.

As he spoke, the beam Ace gripped broke with a sharp crack. He scrambled for balance and bit back a swear word. He swung his weight forward, then threw one arm through the window opening. The crook of his elbow caught the windowsill; he froze again. His head and shoulders extended outside the tower; he could no longer see anything happening below.

Titianus called out. "You must be the pilot Barrett I have heard so much about. Please, Mr. Barrett, come down. I wish to speak with you."

Ace shook his head. "No way. I'm just fine up here."

Titianus cleared his throat like a disapproving schoolteacher. "I must insist, Mr. Barrett. If you do not wish to come down, my men would be happy to knock you down with a bullet. Your death would spoil our conversation, but I cannot have you hanging about the top of the tower as we search." He said something to the guard in a low voice. Ace heard soft footsteps, followed by a metallic click.

"I do not think you can see him, Mr. Barrett, but my man has a rifle aimed at your back. Perhaps you also heard the sound of him releasing the safety catch of the rifle? Come down now or be shot."

Ace sighed. "All right, all right. I'll come down. Hold your horses." He bent his knees and lowered himself out of the window. The descent took longer than the climb; working down through the rotten timbers was more complicated than going up.

At last, he swung his feet down from the lowest timber and dangled beneath it. His feet dangled about a yard from the floor. He let go, landing lightly.

Three rifles greeted him, pointed at his heart.

"Thank you for dropping in, Mr. Barrett. Where is the rest of your expedition? Where are Atherton and Zsezsnky? You must assist me in locating your team."

Ace shook his head. "Nope. Not gonna tell you a damned thing. Barrett, Roger M. Formerly lieutenant of the Army Air Corps, now pilot and photographer for the Cartographers Guild. Got no serial number any more. That's all I have to say to you."

Titianus rolled his eyes. "You military men can be so tiresome. You will do as I command, or I will make you wish you had. Tell me—where are Atherton and Zsnezsky? What have you found here in the lost city?" His voice rose in pitch, becoming a shriek. "Where is the mask? Tell me at once!"

"We haven't found a thing—we only got here a couple of hours ago. Everybody is split up, exploring the town. We're all supposed to meet up at the—" Ace struggled to remember what Doc said about the layout of the camp. "At the water hole on the south end of the town. Water hole at sunset. Until then, all I know is that everyone else is out there somewhere."

Gunshots rattled in the distance. Titianus clasped his hands behind his back and paced. "Two of your number are pinned down in a hut on the edge of town. Davis and Charles, I believe. Where are the rest? I believe Zsezsnky would have led the rest of you here, to the principium. Any scholar of the Romans would know the treasures are most likely to be held here. No matter." He turned his head to the riflemen and said something in Mongolian.

Two of the bandits lowered rifles and started for Ace. The third never wavered, his rifle pointed at the pilot's heart. The other two grabbed Ace's arms and gripped them tight. Titianus extended an arm, one finger pointed at Ace. His movement was slow, gentle. He brushed a finger against Ace's chest.

Pain bloomed across Ace's body; his muscles spasmed, wracking his body with agony. He suffered like never before, then the world went black.

Ace found himself slumping, held up by the bandits. A cold smile played across Titianus's features. "You see, Mr. Barrett? At the merest touch, I can bring you great agony. An ancient technique. Now, where is your team? Where is the mask?"

Ace closed his eyes and took a deep breath. "They're all gone. We found the mask yesterday; everyone else is running for Daroot-Korgon right now. I was wiring the tower with dynamite, then I'll go, too."

Titianus slapped him—just an ordinary slap across the face. "No. If you possessed the mask, you would all run. And there would be no reason to damage the tower. I doubt Ms. Atherton would ever approve of dynamiting any ruins. Where are they?" He extended his finger again, eyes filled with menace.

# Chapter thirteen

Verity took a deep breath. "Ready as I'll ever be. Pull out the slack from the rope so the knot is just above my head." She gripped the rope with both hands just above the grapefruit-sized knot.

Doc took in slack, so Verity's arms extended over her head. He stretched his hands up and gripped the rope above his own head. "You count off—one, two, three, then you jump while I pull."

Verity took another breath. "Okay, Doc." She closed her eyes. "One. Two. Three." She leaped up and away from the pedestal; the rope went tight, and she lurched higher than she could have jumped. Fiery pain shot through her left leg. She swung forward, released the line, landed at the entrance. She collapsed, her leg burning with pain.

Doc saw a flash of bronze as she swung—blades embedded in the pedestal that would have skewered Verity had she tried to walk away from the trap. He also saw something fall from the beam and land on the floor with a thump.

He knelt at Verity's side. "Are you hurt? Did the blades get you?"

Verity moaned and gripped her leg. "Something got my calf. Oh, it stings."

He shined his flashlight at her leg; blood oozed from a deep gash in her calf from the blades. "We've got to get you up to Alicia. Can you walk?"

She rose, putting most of her weight on her good leg. "A little. Let's go."

"One second." He turned back to the chamber, shined his flashlight around. There. A small rectangular object, perhaps a foot square and two inches thick, sat on the floor. He used the pole to drag it toward himself; it was a flat bundle, wrapped in leather. He picked it up, turned back to Verity.

Gunshots rang out again from above. "Doctor Zsezsnky? Miss Hester?"

Doc shouted back, "Coming, Margaret. Verity's hurt—have Alicia get ready. We've got the mask." He turned back to Verity. "How can I help? The tunnel is too narrow for us to walk together."

She smiled, weakly. "I can lean against the wall for support, I think. Follow behind me and help me up when I fall."

He tucked the bundle under his arm; they retrieved the jade mask and started up the tunnel.

—

Mickey looked up the stone tunnel; a faint trickling echoed down the walls. Ankle-deep mud sucked at his boots. He strained his eyes, trying to pierce the darkness. Distant gunfire rang out.

Davis prodded his back. "C'mon, Mick. Waiting does us no good."

Mickey shook his head to clear the cobwebs. He started forward, trailing one hand on the stone wall. Thirty yards down the tunnel, his hand groped air. A second tunnel intersected at a right angle to the first.

He spoke softly. "Intersection, Davis. The cross tunnel is the same size and shape as this one—man-made, I'm sure. I don't see anything notable in the cross tunnel. We should go straight, I think. If we start turning...."

Davis breathed softly for a moment. "You're right. Straight is best. Say, how's your ammo? If there's enough, we could drop a bullet here to mark our passage."

Mickey fumbled in his pack. "I started with fifty rounds—I'm down four or five now. We can spare a couple of bullets, I think. Drop two, next to the right-hand wall, bullets pointing the way we are going. A pair gives us a marker for where we came in, plus we will know which way we came from."

"Right. Marking now." He heard the fixer stoop, then the rattle of cartridges against the stone. "Okay, Mick. Carry on."

They covered another thirty yards; they found another tunnel intersection.

Mickey looked left and right. "Another intersection, D. I think maybe I see some light off to the left. Maybe."

Davis grumbled as he thought. "Should we try to find it?"

Mickey stared to the left. "I think no. We're not far from where we went in—the bandits may see us if we come up here. Also, this tunnel is pretty regular. I think it's a sewer system. We're uphill from the tower, and this might be the main channel. I think we can get a lot closer to the tower before we come up."

"What if you're wrong?"

"Worst case? We spend the night down here and try to slip out in the morning, when the bandits are gone."

Davis drew in a deep breath through his nose, released it slowly. "Lead on, but try to not get us killed."

Mickey marked the intersection with a single bullet pointing in the direction of travel. The pair stumbled ahead into the darkness. A dozen more cross tunnels appeared regularly, one every thirty yards. Faint light gleamed down a few of the tunnels—shafts of sunlight through breaks in the roof—yet they continued, deeper toward the heart of the city. Drips of water echoed through the tunnel; other than that, the only sound they heard was their own breath, marching deeper.

Mickey paused. "Hold up, Davis. We haven't seen a cross tunnel in, what, a hundred yards? More, maybe?"

"Yes, a hundred or hundred and fifty. What do you think?"

"Hmmmm. Back there the tunnels were regular, like rows of houses. That was probably the residential section of the town. Now, we're crossing under something else. Marketplace, maybe, or an army drill square. Think we'll find another way up?"

Davis breathed softly in the dark. "Surely the tower had a latrine, or water closet, or something. But if we miss it…." His voice trailed off.

"Yeah, we can't afford to miss a way up. What if we go a little further, just to see? Maybe we count out two hundred paces, then we stop and look. If nothing presents, we go back and try to find a way up one of the cross shafts that were lit up."

Davis inhaled, exhaled slowly. "Sounds good. Two hundred paces—you count 'em. Go when you're ready."

Mickey walked on, feet squelching in the mud. He counted under his breath each time his right foot hit the ground. At last, he stopped. "Two hundred paces, right here."

Davis responded without delay. "Two hundred paces, and not a single cross-tunnel. I think we've missed the town completely."

Mickey remained silent for a moment. "We can't have missed the town— we haven't come far enough. We should be close to the tower, maybe even short of it."

"Unless we missed it entirely. This tunnel could have bent a little, or even a lot. We could be as far off the tower now as when we started."

Mickey paused again. "I don't think we missed. We would have noticed some curve to the tunnel, I think. If it was enough to throw us far off, at any rate. Wait—do you hear something? Listen." The geologist fell silent.

Water dripped; the men breathed. There was no other sound. Then— something. A low murmur. A voice?

"Come on, D. Just a little further—just to see what the sound is."

Mickey counted another hundred paces, then stopped again. The sound was more distinct—a woman's voice. He shouted. "Margaret! Margaret Atherton—is that you?"

His shouts echoed through the tunnel. Then a response—faint, muffled. "Mister Charles? Mister Davis?"

"Down here! We're in a sewer or something. Keep talking so we can find you."

"I can't—it's not safe." She went silent.

—

Margaret and Alicia hauled Doc, Verity, and Zaldron out of the tunnel. Working in silence, Alicia examined Verity's leg right away. Muffled voices could be heard through the thick door; Zaldron scoured the inside of the room, looking for anything that could be used to make a barrier at the entrance.

Margaret turned to Doc as he emerged from the hole. "Did you find it, Doctor Zsezsnky? Do you have the mask?"

Doc nodded, held out the mask. It was dark, almost black in the dim light of her flashlight. The face was grotesque: wild eyes, flaring nostrils, tongue lolling grotesquely from an open mouth. The eyes were outlined red; gold strips like war paint streaked the cheeks and nose. When she shone her light against the back of the mask, it glowed a brilliant emerald green.

Margaret shook her head. "We have gone to a great deal of trouble for this old thing. I hope we have not been fools."

Zaldron reached out a trembling hand but stopped short of touching the mask. "That's it? That is really the jade mask?" His voice was almost a whisper, husky with reverence.

—

Mickey and Davis walked up the tunnel, uncertain about what to try next. Mickey squinted against the darkness. He thought he saw a faint glow coming from the ceiling ahead.

Davis tapped his shoulder. "Hey, listen. Do you hear that, Mick?"

Mickey stopped, closed his eyes. Did he hear someone talking ahead?

"Maybe. I'm not sure about the sound, but I think I see a light."

Fifty paces later, a yellow glow outlined a hole in the ceiling. The ceiling of the tunnel had partially collapsed. Whispers drifted down the hole.

Mickey whistled softly, once. The voices stopped. He called out, "Margaret? Ace? Who's up there?"

Margaret whispered an answer. "We are here, most of us. Where are you?"

"Down here—there's a hole in the floor. We can barely see your lights."

"Understood. Give us a moment to find you. Please keep quiet—Titianus is just outside the door."

The lights flickered, changed in quality as the beams roved the room.

A flashlight beam shined down from the ceiling. Mickey and Davis emerged into the light; Mickey held a hand over his eyes. After so long in the dark, even the dim beam of a flashlight seemed strong.

"Oh, thank God. It's good to see you." Alicia's voice was a whisper.

"We're locked in, and Titianus is in the entry chamber with Ace. He doesn't know we're here." Alicia explained their predicament as she lowered a rope.

~

Titianus stared at Ace, his red-bearded face expressionless. "I tire of this charade, and I tire of you facing me as an equal." He said something in Mongolian.

One of the bandits kicked Ace in the knee. Pain blazed through his leg; the pilot buckled but remained upright, arms gripped tight by the bandits. The bandits kept him on his knees, now looking up at Titianus.

The man smiled. "Better. You should know your place, Mr. Barrett. Few Americans do."

Ace spat on the ground. "I kneel to no man. You want to talk? We talk face to face, or not at all."

Titianus laughed. "As defiant as I expected. Yet you will remain on your knees, and you will tell me what I wish to know. You appear somewhat worse for the wear—your trip here seems to have been a hard one. Let me help you relive those difficulties."

Titianus extended a hand, caressed Ace's cheek. He felt all of his recent injuries—the black eyes and bruises from fights, the leg sliced by a leopard's claws, even the fresh pain in his knee. All flamed as though brand-new. Worse, even; Titianus managed to raise the stakes for each one.

Ace clenched his eyes shut and gritted his teeth; an involuntary groan escaped his throat. He twisted in the bandits' grip, writhing in pain.

It all stopped. Not entirely—Ace was still aware of his wounds, but the agony faded into the background of his awareness.

Titianus gloated. "You see? I can make you feel such exquisite agony. If I wished, I could break your mind with pain. I will, if you defy me too much.

Perhaps I will even if you do assist me. To break you might prove amusing."

"Go to hell."

Again the hand caressed his cheek; again he felt agony. This time electricity coursed through his body. His muscles clenched; the bandits holding his arms staggered as the pilot wrenched them.

The pain stopped; Ace panted.

"Tell me where the mask is."

Ace opened his mouth to speak. A muffled voice behind the door interrupted.

Titianus spun on his heel and went to the door. "Who is there? What did you say? Speak at once!"

The voice came through the door again, muffled by the thick wood. "Don't hurt him. We'll give you the mask."

Margaret grabbed Alicia, slapped a hand over her mouth. "Stop at once, Doctor," Margaret whispered. "You have given us away—we cannot permit that man—"

A voice boomed through the door. "Give me the mask at once, or I swear you will starve behind that door."

Alicia struggled free. "I won't let him be tortured. I can't. The mask has value, but it's nothing compared to a human life. I'd give all this and more to save a stranger. For Ace? He's risked so much to save us—we must do the same for him."

Margaret hesitated. "I suppose you are correct. Still, I hate to lose anything to that—that—beast Titianus."

Mickey nodded. "It's a damned shame to come this far, achieve this much, only to lose it at the last minute. But it's Ace. He'd do the same for us."

Davis chuckled. "Would he? Making a trade is the smart play. Ace isn't one for the smart play—he'd get himself killed trying to save us. The mask is a small price to pay for him."

"You are all such dopes." Verity's voice dripped with scorn. "We've got the mask. We've got a way out, and we know Titianus will spend the rest of the day trying to chop through the door, then all night on the trap door. We've got options here—there's probably an angle we can work to get Ace and the mask both."

Margaret's mouth was a tight line. She exhaled sharply through her nostrils. "Perhaps. Perhaps we could manage to lose both, as well. We cannot risk it—we must negotiate with Titianus."

# Chapter fourteen

Margaret called out to Titianus. "Sir, my name is Margaret Atherton. I am the leader of this expedition. I am quite certain we can
reach a mutual understanding. You will return Mr. Barrett to us
and allow us to depart. We will depart and leave the mask in a designated
place for your men to retrieve once we are gone."

Titianus barked a laugh. "No. I have, what is your expression, all the
cards, yes? You are trapped, outnumbered, and your pilot Barrett is my
prisoner. I can torture him until you decide to come out. I can guard the
door until you die of thirst. I can force the door and kill you all. What can
you do? Nothing—you can only wait for me to act. Let us try thirst a la
premiere. Please, enjoy your cell."

The principium grew hot with the afternoon sun. The team sweltered in
the heat; Titianus refused to engage with the cartographers.

Only Doc passed the time in comfort; he examined the bundle of parchment from the mask room. He was oblivious to the sweltering heat and tension suffusing the room. He turned page after page, muttering to himself.

At last, Titianus called out again. "Are you ready to open the door,
friends? It's time to deliver my mask. My men grow impatient. They have
brought a little toy they wish to use." He said something in Mongolian.

A sound tore through the afternoon, a ripping noise like thunder. A ragged hole appeared in the door; splinters and bullets rained into the room.
A single beam of light shined into the room.

"Did you enjoy that? It is the latest from Germany. I am told it can fire
one thousand, five hundred rounds in a minute. Perhaps now you will give
to me the mask and any other valuables you have found? I will swear to
you by my oaths to the glory of Rome that, if you give me the mask and
anything else you have found, I will let you leave here alive, with your pilot
friend Keep them from me and I will let my men use the little toy to take
you apart."

The explorers looked at one another in disbelief. Davis shook his head.

179

"I've faced machine guns before. We're sitting ducks in here. Zaldron—you know this man. Can we trust him not to kill us if we surrender?"

Zaldron nodded. "He swore by his oaths; he will keep his promise. He will let us live if we give him the mask. Once we have left this valley...." He shrugged. "He swore no oath to let us return to Dushanbe or even Daroot-Korgon."

Verity groaned. "We've got the mask, and we've got a way out. We can just climb down the hole and run. There will be some way to get Ace back once we're out of this trap."

"No." Davis' voice was hard. "Not with that machine gun, we won't. The gunner pick us apart from a thousand yards or more, even in cover. Trying to run from that thing is suicide. We deal or we won't make it out of this valley."

Margaret grumbled in the back of her throat. She shouted through the door. "Swear to us you will allow us to reach Dushanbe unharmed. Swear it, or we will smash every single item we have found here."

Titianus laughed. "You cannot smash the jade mask. It is unlikely you could even bend or mar it. You will give me—"

Margaret cut him off. "Then we will hide what we have found again and dynamite the tower on top of it. If we are to die either way, we will give our lives to keep you from finding anything here."

Titianus stood in silence for a moment.

"I swear by mighty Mithras that I will allow you to reach Daroot-Korgon unharmed, should you meet the following conditions. First, you must give me the jade mask and everything else you have found here. Second, that you will allow me to search your packs before you depart."

Doc Z shook his head furiously. He whispered to Margaret, "we can't let him search the packs—if nothing else, we must get out with these documents. We can re-write the history books—these are the find of the century."

Margaret shrugged. "It's hand them over or die, Doctor Zsezsnky. We have no choice."

Verity waved her fingers toward herself, the universal gesture for give it to me. "I can get the documents out, Doc. Let me have them, and bring me my pack. Don't worry; they will be safe with me."

Doc shrugged. He re-wrapped the packet and gave it to the research assistant. She opened her backpack and shuffled some items around to make space. She slipped the documents into her pack with care, then sealed it up again.

Margaret shouted to Titianus. "We accept your terms, sir. We will come out with our hands up."

They marched out of the principium, eyes downcast. Titianus met them, flanked by a trio of bandits with rifles. He plucked the mask from Zaldron's fingers, then smiled. "At last. Thank you, Zaldron, for leading me to this treasure. New Rome will not forget your...service, no matter how reluctant."

He tucked the mask into a pouch at his waist. He addressed the entire team now. "Open your backpacks. Prove to me you are not stealing more items from me."

The villain searched the packs, one at a time. He started with Zaldron; he removed everything from the sage's bag, examined each  pocket. He searched Ace's backpack next, then Margaret's. He clucked his tongue. "Tsk, tsk. So little food to get you back to Daroot-Korgon. It seems my oath may not be necessary—you may well die on your own."

He got to Verity's pack. Each of the cartographers held their breath, knowing she possessed the documents. He sifted through her pack, then dropped it. He moved on to Mickey, then Davis. He came to Alicia and Doc Z. He merely glared at his former captives, then laughed. "I suppose you two have no packs. Your exit from Daroot-Korgon was rather hasty, yes? Well, it seems you have taken nothing that belongs to me. You may go now. I pledge to leave you alone for five days; that is enough time to reach Daroot-Korgon. After that, I make no promises to your safety if you remain in the mountains. Go."

# Epilogue

The cartographers pushed as hard as they could to reach the base camp. They arrived late at night, in driving rain; each one collapsed into bed and slept like a stone.

The next day, they gathered in the cook tent. No one spoke; they were too tired, too dejected at the loss of the mask. They stared into mugs of coffee and tea. Only Doc Z was active, examining the bundle of documents Verity had secreted out of Emal Mora.

He muttered under his breath. "Fascinating, simply fascinating." His pen scratched on the pages of his journal.

Ace snapped. "Dammit Doc, keep it down. It doesn't matter how exciting the papers are—Titianus has the mask. We're all in trouble."

Doc smiled and shook his head. "No, Ace, we're not. According to these documents, the mask by itself doesn't do anything; it's a key to unlocking other items. Titianus needs to find those items and perform some rituals before he can do anything dangerous."

Ace shrugged. "So? Doesn't the mask have enough magic to lead him to those things?"

Doc nodded. "Yes, that's one way to find them."

Verity raised an eyebrow. "One way? Are there others?"

Doc smiled. "Yes. There is a map here, and a waybill. We have the key to reaching the other items Titianus needs. We also have descriptions of the rituals; there may be ways to disrupt them as well."

Margaret looked up. "Where? Do you think we can move faster than Titianus?"

Doc nodded again. "Perhaps. I need to examine the papers in detail and compare them against modern maps. My Roman geography is rusty, and I haven't heard of some of the locations. The ones I can place seem to be in the eastern empire—from Istanbul to the Caspian sea, south to the Persian Gulf, west to Alexandria. I suspect the others lie either along the silk road, between here and the Caspian, or south into Persia.

"Titianus can use the mask to locate the next item—but he's got to hike straight there. A direct path may be impossible; he will have to detour around obstacles, then start again. I suspect he will have to go over or through the more than one mountain range to get a fix on the next treasure. We know where we need to end up—we can take river and rail networks to get close. Perhaps even use the plane to locate things from the air. If we can make good enough time, we can head Titianus off and beat him to the punch."

Margaret smiled. "I can arrange for fast transport, if needed. Let's go find another lost city."

Read more of the adventures of the Cartographers Guild in:
*The Cartographer's Guild and the Mercury Crow*

For updates, check my website:
WWW.AACUMMINS.COM